Babe in Toyland

Babe in Toyland

Eugénie Seifer Olson

AVON TRADE

An Imprint of HarperCollins*Publishers*

HarperCollins books may be purchased for education, business, or sales promotional use. For information please write: Special Markets Department, HarperCollins Publishers Inc., 10 East 53rd Street, New York, NY 10022.

FIRST EDITION

Designed by Elizabeth M. Glover

Library of Congress Cataloging-in-Publication Data

Olson, Eugénie Seifer.
  Babe in Toyland / by Eugénie Seifer Olson.—1st ed.
    p. cm.
  ISBN 0-06-057056-3 (acid-free paper)
  1. Toy industry—Fiction. 2. Toy industry—Employees—Fiction. 3. Philadelphia (Pa.)—Fiction. I. Title.
  PS3615.L74B33 2004
  813'.6—dc22   2003021469

04 05 06 07 08 JTC/RRD 10 9 8 7 6 5 4 3 2 1

A big thank-you to my agent Stacey Glick, who always knows the right thing to say, and super-sized smooches to Lucia Macro and Kelly Harms, who always know the right thing for me to do.

Thanks to Natalie Makar for letting me in, and to Ritchie Weintraub for letting me out. This book would not have been possible without you both.

A Hamburger Special-sized thanks to my cheering section at Charlie's Kitchen in Harvard Square, and another one to my pals at Dana-Farber Cancer Institute. Elyse Park and Amy Einhorn get gold stars for selflessly lending a hand when I needed it. For inquiring about my book every Wednesday afternoon without fail, a thank-you to Andy Richards at the Ronald McDonald House. Sometimes motivation comes from the people and situations you least expect.

I will be forever indebted to Ed Mason for his insight and assistance, and I offer heaps of gratitude to Maryjane Carlin, Debbie Robinson, and Carolyn Komerska for their support. Amy King and Renée Gontarski, thanks for the toy memories. Neil Bindelglass and David Colp lent much-needed music expertise. Kerri Bennett spun on her bar stool and decreed, "You should write this book."

Most of all, I would like to thank my family—Les and Amy Seifer, Ben Seifer, and Julie Cargill—for their love and fabulous sense of humor. And to my love, David, who taught me about patience and all the wonderful things it can bring.

Chapter 1

"What do you think of this?" Kerrin says suddenly, turning away from the counter to face me. Her face is a patchwork quilt of overpriced cosmetics, with stripes of green and blue on her eyelids and blotchy pinks on her cheeks.

"Hmm?" I look up dewy eyed from my reverie. I've strayed from the circus of colors at the makeup counter to the bath and body products, where I've been fingering the beautiful bottles and inhaling the citrusy smells of the lotion of the moment. My obsession with bath products borders on the perverse, and my bathroom, a clutter of austere packaging and empty marketing promises, proves it.

We are in John Wanamaker's in Center City, with its hushed department-store atmosphere, high vaulted ceilings, and delicate railings. Wanamaker's has taken quite a hit in recent years, with Philadelphians instead preferring to go to the colorless local malls in the suburban spread. The sales help stands listlessly on the floors, seemingly unaware of the few patrons who still shop here. I do not own many elegant things, but I have a breathtaking box of lace hankies given to me by my great-grandmother when I was about four years old. They were purchased here, and I like to imagine the hustle and bustle of the place back then, before people felt it was their divine right to shop in flip-flops and torn sweatpants. To this day, the hankies sit in their signature Wanamaker's box in my bureau drawer, a reminder of a time when shopping was glamorous.

It's nearing the end of our lunch break—or Kerrin's lunch break, to be more accurate. As a result of a new touchy-feely employee program at the toy company where I work, we've been given half-days on Fridays during the summer months. With as much excitement as the CEO could muster, he told us the new policy would allow us to have summertime fun and develop outside interests. So far, it has afforded me more time to pursue lofty and mind-broadening goals, such as renting movies that feature the vapid beauty of Keanu Reeves, and conducting a personal taste test of Philadelphia's best cheesesteaks with my roommate Michael. If today's makeup shopping goes well for Kerrin, I will add this to my list of potential Friday afternoon outings. Kerrin, on the other hand, must get back to work by one-thirty, to her windowless, suffocating office at University of Pennsylvania Hospital.

"Well?" asks the saleswoman, arching her over-plucked eyebrows at Kerrin. Her lab coat and discreet enamel pin on its collar contrast vividly with her red talons, heavy foundation, and shimmery lipstick. "This new summer collection seems perfectly suited to your needs," she says with conviction, and I make a mental note to ask Kerrin exactly what are the cosmetics needs of a person who writes grants for cancer research.

"Ummm . . . that one," Kerrin says, jabbing a fingertip at an eyeliner pencil. She juts her chin out and tilts her head to one side, Kerrin-speak for "I've made up my mind." For just a moment, a hint of stress breaks through the makeup mask of the saleswoman. "Are you sure that's all you'll be needing? Maybe you'd like me to show you how to blend the eyeshadow colors again?"

She is playing a losing game. Kerrin hasn't come here to abuse her or waste her time; she genuinely wants to sample everything but won't be strong-armed into buying anything more than she needs. Try to swindle Kerrin, and you'll wish you had stayed home exfoliating today, I silently say to the hapless saleswoman.

"Can you believe that, Toby?" Kerrin says moments later as we walk toward her car on 12th Street. She takes a long drag on her cigarette and lets the smoke out through clenched teeth. "Thinking I'm going to buy all that crap. I told her I only needed one thing."

"Yes, but it's her job to try and get you to buy more stuff. Plus, you looked like you were really going for it, letting her keep putting different colors on you. You looked like Ziggy Stardust or something," I say, tightly clutching my bag of matching orange-scented bath gel and shampoo in my left hand.

"What did you buy?" she asks, rooting in her bag for her keys. I've always been amazed at friends who can walk and hunt for things in their purses at the same time. My one such experiment ended up with my checkbook falling down an open manhole, and I've been fearful ever since.

"Oh, just some orange bath gel and shampoo. I really can't even afford it, I don't know what I was thinking," I rationalize.

"You're weird with that stuff. You need some sensuality in your life. Remember pleasures of the flesh, Toby?" she grins. "It's going to be a long, hot summer. I think you should have some fun. And not the kind of fun that comes from"—she yanks the bag from my hand and squints at the label on the shampoo—"some cosmetic company on Long Island. I'll call you this weekend."

And with that, she gets into her car and lurches into traffic, nearly colliding with a temporary barrier routing cars around City Hall. How like Kerrin to fight City Hall on her lunch hour.

"Hello?" I call out as I open the front door. "Michael, are you here?"

I plop down on the sofa, thoroughly deflated from the bus ride from Center City. Surely that's not what the CEO of Toyland had in mind when he told us to enjoy our Friday afternoons, I had been thinking only five minutes earlier while watching the bus driver argue with a passenger about the live eel he was attempting to transport in a flimsy supermarket shopping bag. I wondered, was he going to eat it? Keep it as a pet? Let it loose on the bus so he could secure the seat of his choice? Visit the sights with it in tow? I knew better than to ask the question of my toothless seatmate, and instead entertained myself by thinking about this guy and his eel traveling around the city, taking pictures at Independence Hall, at the Liberty Bell with the eel snaking its way into the giant crack. And now I can't even pose the question to Michael or share my demented *Fodor's Guide to Traveling with Eels* fantasy.

Michael is my friend of almost four years and roommate of two. We met when I was an undergraduate at Philadelphia College of the Arts and he was a graduate student at the conservatory on Broad Street. His cousin, my junior year roommate, was a flighty fashion design student who liked to design using soft fabrics and pastel colors and whose command of language was so poor that I nearly fainted the day she said, "Toby, I knew you like plants, so I brang this fica from home." Still, Sheila was sweet and even-tempered, and most importantly, she held still when my figure drawing portfolios were due at semester's end and I needed to draw someone quickly. After graduation, Sheila moved to Illinois to take a job at a uniform company, where she designs surgical scrubs and the saccharine designs that grace pediatric nurses' tops. She still sends Michael and me catalogs that showcase her work, and our current favorites are "Thermometer on Thorazine" (our name, not the manufacturer's)—a pattern featuring a deranged-looking oral thermometer with dull, heavy-lidded eyes and its tongue flopping out—and "Junkie Bear" (again, our name), a sprightly, freckled cub clutching a syringe.

Because Michael is a few years older than we are, he would periodically check in on Sheila and take her out for a quick bite or lend her money for sewing supplies. At first, I found Michael unbelievably mysterious and enigmatic, owing mainly to the fact that he was studying music and had sweetly unkempt hair and therefore, in my mind, must have been dark and brooding. But as I tagged along with him and Sheila for pizza or a movie, I learned that my initial impression, as it is with most things, wasn't quite right. He was serene and introspective, but with only a hint of the bleakness that so thoroughly infected so many of the art and music students I knew. Make no mistake, at times he could brood with the best of them, snapping at Sheila and taking a haughty tone that I imagine he must have cultivated at a young age while his clarinet case was being swiftly kicked around the schoolyard. But for the most part, unlike his peers who scowled constantly and hunched under the weight of their instrument cases and their affectation, he was creative without being crazy, artistic without being angst-ridden.

I rouse for a minute, swearing I can hear the bleat of a clarinet upstairs. "Toby?" Michael shouts from the second floor of our house. "Is that you?"

Michael walks slowly down the tiny staircase, which is pitched at such a severe angle that it seems like I see his legs for a full five seconds before seeing his waist. After Sheila and I graduated, Michael and I both needed a place to live. He was finishing his master's degree and I was about to begin a search for a real job. His requirements were minimal: He needed someone who wouldn't mind him practicing his clarinet and would cheerily put up with kids of all ages traipsing through the house for private music lessons. I didn't really have too many demands, other than the house not having a wino-in-residence on the front stoop (like the place I shared with Kerrin for one semester). The search for a place to live was so painless that I took it as a very good sign, and we ended up on a tree-lined street close to the art museum. Our house is a trinity, so called because it is made of three tiny floors, each stacked directly on top of the last and connected by a labyrinth of narrow, steep staircases.

Michael grimaces when he sees the Wanamaker's bag, the end of which is now rolled under and damp from sweat. "Another bath thing?" he asks, crinkling his nose. He picks up the newspaper from the couch, sits down, and flips through it absently. "Well, anyway," he adds, "please don't be throwing that stuff around the bathroom. I think I might be allergic."

Michael is as allergic to my array of bath products as he is to the air in our apartment or the sheet music he reads every day. Raised by two prominent, brilliant Johns Hopkins surgeons in a tony suburb of Baltimore, Michael was left with a triple threat: lots of time alone, access to gruesome medical texts, and an active, creative mind. He developed such a case of hypochondria that he's convinced that he's suffered from diabetes, a brain tumor, allergies of every type, bipolar disorder, lupus, and leukemia, just to name some highlights. I try to explain to him on a regular basis that hypochondria isn't a very manly trait, but to no avail.

"OK. I'll watch it," I say, opting to take the high road about the allergies. "Oh, listen to this! There was this guy on the fifty-two bus with an eel. A real one. And the bus driver was giving him a hard time."

"What do you think he was going to do with it?" Michael asks, glancing up as he refolds the paper.

"My question *exactly*. I'm thinking maybe this city-wide tour where . . ."

"Do you want to go shopping tonight? We need a lot of stuff," he says, cutting me off, uninterested in the eel mystery.

"Too depressing to go grocery shopping on a Friday night, no," I shake my head vehemently.

"Yes, but Toby," he reasons, "I'm the one with the car and I'm going away for the weekend. What's more depressing than you going shopping alone and having to use that fold-out cart that you say makes you feel like a little old lady?" He raises one eyebrow for emphasis as he pushes his crooked, oversized wire-rimmed glasses back up his nose. Reluctantly, I agree.

"I'm going to get ready for my lesson with Linda," he says, standing up and smoothing his shirt. "Then when she leaves, we'll go." He pulls a tiny plastic case from his pocket and removes a clarinet reed, which he slides into his mouth like a veteran smoker languidly bringing a cigarette to his lips.

"Is she the one with the adopted brother from Bolivia? Or the one who still wets the bed?"

"Neither," he answers, removing the slender piece of wood, feeling it gently with his thumb, then frowning and popping it back in. "She's the one with the three pigtails."

"Oh, yeah," I say, immediately picturing the student. As if on cue, the doorbell rings, and Michael greets Linda. Three pigtails, two beginner music books, and one flute case covered with rainbow stickers.

"OK, Linda, off we go. Did you practice like we talked about?" She nods in a studied yet noncommittal way, as only kids can when they lie, while looking at Michael's shoes. "Oh, and by the way, Toby, Jenna called," he shouts over his shoulder. "Something about her new job. Call her."

Jenna. Preternaturally perky Jenna, with her white teeth and perfect figure and shiny hair. We graduated from college three years back and she had the most stunning portfolio our teachers had ever seen. They clamored to get her jobs, while the rest of us had to send out resumé upon resumé, pound the pavement, cry, and swear. The problem with Jenna wasn't that she was just a born designer—she could have been a born *anything*. She worked hard and never complained. She made deadlines and even had time to help her classmates. Don't know how long to put your photo in the fixer for? Ask Jenna. Not sure if that typeface looks good when italicized? Ask Jenna. Dropped and smashed your lithography stone into nine thousand pieces? Ask Jenna. We hated her.

Surprisingly, though, Jenna and I stayed in touch after graduating. She went to New York for a short time and worked for a company that designs and produces elaborate film title sequences for those blockbuster action-adventure movies. But she didn't like being away from her family in Pennsylvania, and she wasn't happy with the fast pace of Manhattan. When she returned, some people found a bit of glee in her failure, but I sympathized. I had done a summer working for a design firm in Greenwich Village and had felt as though I'd needed tranquilizers just to face the subway ride each day.

So every time that Jenna called, it was a mixture of happiness and envy that washed over me. We didn't speak or hang out that often, but when we did, I usually felt a sense of jealousy and regret for days after—jealous of her life and regretful that I hadn't been able to catch up yet. For awhile, Michael even forbade me to spend time with her, because I would be in such a weird mood afterward.

I sit in my room and carefully line up my new orange bath gel and shampoo bottles on the dresser, then catch a glimpse of myself in the mirror. I compulsively mash down my hair, an auburn frizz with a mind of its own. Summer in Philadelphia is unkind to my wild mane and skin and always makes me feel greasy and shiny. I'm thinking about lying down for a quick nap when I hear the languid *thunk-thunk-thunk* of a metronome, the first strains of Linda's lesson, and her shrill whining as Michael tries to gently correct her. A month earlier, in a fit of inspiration while tanked up on cheap beer, Michael and I painted the walls of my room a soft pale yellow. Now I feel like it's melting all around me, like I'm encased in a hot piece of buttered white toast. Kerrin was right; it's going to be a long, hot summer.

I take a deep breath, pick up my Snoopy phone, and dial Jenna's number.

Michael is placidly peeling open the husks of an ear of corn and peering inside. He grimaces and tosses it back on the pile.

"We don't need corn, anyway," I say impatiently. "Hurry up, this produce aisle is yucky." We are in the Super Fresh on Pine Street, and like all true urban supermarkets, it's small, dirty, cramped, and quick to ignite my temper. Michael slowly pulls up to me with the shopping cart, leans forward, and puts his elbows on the handle. His face is level with mine, and I watch him as his eyes dart back and forth over the apple display. Michael is all angles, with sharp cheekbones that you could grate a tough block of Parmesan on, and a big, square forehead. His bright blue eyes are his one pride point, although they are hidden to the point of obstruction by the glare on his thick glasses, and I've toyed with the idea of suggesting that he choose another feature to be vain about. His lips are slightly curled down at the edges, so it looks as though he's always ready to frown, even when he's quite contented. He claims this is actually ideal for a clarinet player, that his genes must have known to align just the right way so he could get the lips he did, but I have my doubts about that one.

We're turning the corner into the cereal and candy aisle when Michael asks, "So what did Jenna have to say?" He reaches over and hurls a family-size pack of Tootsie Rolls into the cart.

I sigh and wait for the announcement over the supermarket's PA system to finish, grateful for once in my life that there needs to be a cleanup in aisle three, as it gives me time to figure out how to share Jenna's news without sounding too bitter.

"She's got a job at WPHX. News graphics. Designing them and then producing them. Apparently it's quite gratifying, and I'm sure there's lots of money in it," I say as evenly as I can.

"Is that the station with the seventies theme or the newscaster with the bad acne?"

"Seventies theme," I answer blithely. "Well, I told her I'd watch this weekend. She's only doing the weekend news segments for now, then they'll move her to the week if it works out."

"Don't sound so thrilled for her, Toby."

"Sorry, Michael," I answer in staccato tones. "I *am* happy for her. It's just hard . . . you know how I feel; she always seems to get what she wants. I guess you can't really understand, living your dream and all that."

"Oh, yeah, living my dream," he says, sniffing. He breaks into a wide-eyed, spooky smile. "Do you think that working wedding gigs like I do is living my dream? Or that bribing my school-age saxophone students with Tootsie Rolls is living my dream?" He roots around in the cart for the bag of candy to make the point, but he can't find it and instead pulls a bag of chips into the air. He tosses them back. "Or composing these dumb commercials is my dream?" he asks, referring to a recent job he just landed, consulting for an area ad agency and composing music for local radio spots. It was lucrative, but even I had to admit that it was a huge waste of Michael's talents.

"I'm sorry, I don't know what I meant," I say, suddenly feeling contrite and embarrassed.

"Besides, you can 'live your dream,' whatever that is. You don't have to stay at the toy company, you know," he says, steering the cart into the pharmacy section of the supermarket. A little boy clutching a jar of Ovaltine darts in front of us.

"I know. I don't know if my dream is only career-related. I'm not really sure what it is exactly."

"Oh, I need these," Michael says slowly, rolling the cart to a stop in front of the condom display. "I mean, let's hope I will," he adds, looking away from me and glancing conspiratorially at the condoms. He quickly scans the seemingly endless selection and chooses a kind in an orange box. I look at the floor and try to remember who he is visiting this weekend. Was it the cellist he met at the gig at Bryn Mawr? Or his ex-girlfriend, the one who dropped him when she realized that a clarinetist wouldn't be able to provide her with lavish dinners, expensive jewelry, and a Volvo?

Everyone, from Kerrin on down to the owner of the All-In-One convenience store on the corner, wants to know what the real score is between Michael and me—and I'm always happy to tell them that the only score between us is the framed and autographed one that hangs in the hall outside his bedroom door, entitled "Suburban Speakeasy 2.0." It was written by his composer friend Anthony, full of angry oboes, grouchy bassoons, and digital bleeps and bips, and was featured briefly in a movie made by a local filmmaker. And even though I appreciate Kerrin's comment about pleasures of the flesh, having "Suburban Speakeasy 2.0" as the only score between us, between our rooms that mirror one another across a three-foot hallway in our tiny trinity, suits me just fine.

"Let's move away from this aisle," I say as the little boy drops his jar of Ovaltine to begin fingering the boxes of diaphragm jelly that line the shelves beneath the pegged condom display. "It's creeping me out. He's too little to be so interested in this kind of stuff."

❧ Chapter ❧
2

It's raining today, that humid kind of summer rain where even though it comes down in sheets, you know that it's not really washing anything away. It's just sort of moving the dirt around. Even the little kids who normally play unsupervised for hours on our street must be indoors with their Saturday morning cartoons. Although Philadelphia is a far cry from New York, our neighborhood shares something uniquely common with it: You only have to walk from one block to the next and you can go from fancy, gentrified apartments to run-down, sad-looking buildings and entirely questionable watering holes. It goes: seedy block-gentrified block-seedy block-seedy block-gentrified block-gentrified block-seedy block, ending down by the river. It's not hard to guess which type of block the clarinetist, the entry-level designer, and the kids who play unsupervised for hours live on.

With nothing but the newspaper and my thoughts to entertain me this morning, I begin to ruminate about what Michael said in the supermarket last night. It's true, I don't have to stay at my job.

I took it right after finishing college, partially because I was so grateful that someone would hire me, and partially because I thought it would be somewhat exciting or glamorous to work at a toy company. But as I soon found out, it was not so much like *Big*—more like *Big Joke*, and the employees were the recipients of the punch line. It was right over the river in New Jersey, and its hulking size cut an imposing figure over the local suburban landscape. But inside was total pandemonium: upper-management people who seemed less mature than the focal group kids rushed around, hollered, argued all the time. Over dolly underwear. Over whether or not a die-cast car should have .012 cent's worth of glow-in-the-dark paint on it. Over the shade of green of a blister-card package or the salience of a slick TV commercial showing a toy doing something it could never, ever do.

I was promptly given a job in the packaging and graphics department, where I spend my days toiling over instruction sheets for toys. After I got the job, Kerrin made me a little sticker that reads, "Toby 'Some Assembly Required' Morris"; it's still tacked to my cubicle wall. That's a pretty accurate description: When you see those three fateful words on a toy box and you pull out those drawings and instructions, I'm the one who has done them. Stickers, too.

It's not an unpleasant job and I admit to getting a thrill when a new toy lands on my desk and I get to play with it, disassemble it, and draw its parts. I am also probably the only one in my group of friends who can open her file desk at work and see folders labeled "Scrubbin' Scruffy," "Play and Clay Petunia," "Dinosaur Delicatessen," and "Tressie Trolls," to name a few. It's also a good icebreaker at parties, because as I said, everyone finds the notion of working at a toy company enchanting and thinks I must be a happy little elf. Well, *most* parties, that is. When I visited my older sister Julie out in Tucson last spring, she introduced me to a bunch of her thirty-something friends who all have kids. When one found out what I did, she snarled, "My husband and I hate people like you. We curse those instruction sheets every Christmas Eve." The rest of them snickered and sneered and nodded their heads in agreement as Julie shrugged apologetically.

So it's not bad overall, I reason. People do jobs that are a lot harder, or more demeaning, or where they don't get to use their skills at all. But sometimes when I'm illustrating how Axle A snaps into Rod C or how Sticker 7 fits over the entryway to the playhouse, I get the creepy feeling that I shouldn't be devoting my life to processed plastics. Processed plastics that will be played with for a few months and then relegated to a toy box and sold in a garage sale.

I'm about to stop thinking about work and begin thinking about my love life when the phone rings. It's

Kerrin, her voice swathed in Saturday-morning raspiness.

"Hey, Toby. How's it going?"

"OK, I guess. Michael's out of town, so it's just me today."

"Oh, boo hoo." Kerrin and Michael don't get along so well—they can tolerate each other but that's about it. Michael finds her a bit brash and scary. Kerrin finds him too given to introspection and has a zero-tolerance policy for his classical music.

"Well, anyway, how come I didn't see you last night at First Friday?" This is Philadelphia's answer to the gallery scene. On the first Friday evening of every month, all the galleries in Kerrin's neighborhood open their doors and serve wine and cheese, and people flock to ooh and aah over modern art. It's not a bad way to spend an evening, although I suspect that I don't own enough black clothing to make it a regular thing.

"I don't remember saying I was going to go. Besides, I had to go grocery shopping last night with Michael," I answer lamely. I hear the *tsssst* of a match striking a matchbook as Kerrin lights a cigarette.

"That sounds boring. Anyway, Will was there, that's why I thought you might come." Will is a tiny, bespectacled Amerasian guy who works in the art gallery below Kerrin's apartment. He is cute and sweet and smiley and has a waist that's smaller than mine. This last part could be a problem.

"Yeah, he was asking for you," she continues. " 'Where's Toby? Toby the Toy Girl?' That's what he calls you now, 'Toby the Toy Girl.' But you know what's weird? No matter what angle I look at him from, he doesn't look like John Lennon to me."

"No, *Sean. Sean* Lennon. Don't you know my taste better than that, Kerrin?" I ask with mock irritation in my voice. "Why would I even entertain thoughts of a guy who looked like John Lennon? You know how I dislike unwashed hippies."

"Oh, yeah, right. I thought you were going to incinerate your clothes after that stint in Cambridge," she laughs, referring to a month-long visit to my cousin up in Massachusetts after I graduated from college. My bath product consumption reached a fever pitch up there— probably because I felt as though I was bathing for a whole city. I found Boston pleasant enough, almost benign with its shiny-eyed, apple-cheeked college student culture, although coming from racially mixed Philadelphia, I kept wondering where they were hiding all the black people. But Cambridge was another story altogether—teeming with brilliant people who couldn't find the soap.

"Anyway, I don't know, I thought maybe you meant from their 'Twist and Shout' period," she sniffs. This brings a smile to my face as I think of Michael saying that he can tell a lot about a girl by the type of Beatles songs she references in a conversation. He says if he meets a girl who mentions "Twist and Shout" or "Octopus's Garden" or "Michelle," forget it. He's more "Glass Onion" or "Tomorrow Never Knows," idiosyncratic songs that suit his idiosyncratic self. My favorite is a nutty, meandering tune called "You Know My Name, Look Up the Number," in which John Lennon alternately mutters incoherently and shrieks over several tempo changes. Michael says I'm musically hopeless and that it's no wonder my love life is a nonexistent wasteland.

"Well, tell Will to hold on. Maybe I'll come to the next First Friday."

"That's a long way off! A bunch of us are going out tonight to see Knockout Mouse. Come with us and I'll run down to the gallery and invite Will right now."

"Is that a band or a movie?"

"Toby, don't be a loser. It's a band! That mambo one I was telling you about. You'll love them. Meet me at my apartment at nine o'clock, OK?"

"OK," I say reluctantly. Truth be told, I'm more in a hurry to wrap up with Kerrin than I am to see Knockout Mouse, because the news is coming on in three minutes. WPHX news, featuring Jenna's news graphics. I'm terrified not to watch, because I know Michael will ask me if I did. And if I don't, he'll accuse me of being jealous and petty. Which of course I am, whether I watch the news or not.

Da da da da da da da, da-da-da-da, da da da daaa daaa! The news starts with WPHX's signature cheesy music, the same one that they've been using since I was about three years old. I can distinctly remember sitting on my green beanbag chair in my parents' ochre den with the burnt umber shag rug and hearing these exact same notes. I haven't watched the weekend news in ages, and I crack open a bottle of nail polish as the first story begins, about a fatal fire in South Philadelphia. Sure enough, to the right of the overly coiffed newscaster's head is a small, rectangular graphic with a montage of a burning building and a fireman. So far, so good.

Next is a story about a product recall, and that same rectangular space is now sporting a baby walker and a rattle. Now a bit of international news, and Italy appears in the rectangle in all its boot-shaped glory. It's funny, I think as I look away from the TV and splay my fingers to admire the Purple Passion on my nails, I never paid attention to these graphics. I never really thought that someone had to sit down and make them. Which, coincidentally, is what people say all the time about my job and instruction sheets. Like they thought toy assembly instructions were developed at the North Pole, I presume.

Suddenly, a little glitch: a story about Gorbachev. His picture appears in the rectangle, but mixed in with his red head splotch is a bit of green. Uh-oh. I recap Purple Passion and lean in closer to the TV. Yes, there's no doubt about it: green. Jenna is probably shrieking, I think. No, wait—she won't be shrieking because it looks fine to her. Her bosses are probably shrieking, because they don't yet know Jenna's deepest and darkest—and probably only—secret.

Jenna's one imperfection is that she is severely color-blind. Not just a little, like in that cute way where guys sometimes wear one blue sock and one black one because they can't see the difference. A lot.

Like a stutterer avoiding certain words or a hard-of-hearing person saying "yup" to everything, Jenna had developed some keen coping mechanisms by the time she got to art school. She elaborately labeled her paint mixtures in painting class and created her own mysterious color palettes on the computer. Naturally, we all thought this was just her way of keeping things organized and methodical. But then one fateful day, her paints went missing and she was forced to use someone else's. When it came time to critique our grayscale paintings of a still life, she was ornery and red in the face. Our teacher, a man who would have been a brilliant artist and teacher if he hadn't been so consistently drunk, pointed to Jenna's painting and said amusedly, "Interesting use of color here. It seems like most of the class sees this as a warm color and used reds to warm up their grays. But this has *green*." Jenna said nothing, and he quickly moved on to another painting, but when I found her sitting sullenly in the bathroom after class, she clued me in. I was also sworn to secrecy, even though I kept telling her that color blindness isn't some kind of stigma, like having an addiction or liking Rush. But she kept sputtering,

"Toby, a *color-blind designer.* Think about it. Who would take me seriously?"

Well, our teachers and lots of employers, for one. As long as she had her palettes and fancy color systems, she could keep it a secret and wow them all. But I did feel for her then as I do even now: It must be difficult to keep it all together on the outside yet have this constant worry hanging over you that you'll be found out as a fraud and a fake. Lucky for me, I feel pretty confident that the world sees me as a falling-apart wreck, so there's nothing to fear in that department. Well, maybe no one caught Gorby. I mean, it's the Saturday noontime news, for crying out loud, how many people could be watching? Maybe she can blame it on some engineering intern there. I make a note on the front page of the newspaper to call tomorrow and tell her how nice I thought all the graphics looked.

I guess her portion of the news is done now; they're doing sports and there's some footage of Darren Daulton. Then it's time for the weather. I'm about to turn the TV off when I see him.

J.P. Cody.
The weekend weatherman.

I slowly sit back down and look intently at the screen. He's sweeping his hand across the Midwest and talking about drought, but I couldn't care less about the crops of Kansan farmers right now. I'm transfixed by his brilliant blue eyes and wavy black hair. He's got swollen, pouty lips that wouldn't look entirely out of place on a female supermodel, but they don't compromise his masculinity in the remotest way. He's wearing a suit like all weathermen do, but this one isn't the standard issue, boring blue number—it's dark gray and has groovy lapels that set him apart but don't make him look freakishly trendy. He turns sideways ever so slightly to explain the incoming cloud cover over Pennsylvania and I'm damning whoever decided that you should never show your back to the camera, because I wouldn't mind a rear view. I decide that he's thirty, tops. My mouth is actually hanging open, and I'm riveted to the screen.

Then it's "Back to you, Jill," and the weather report is over. No more J.P. Cody until next weekend. No more J.P. Cody until next weekend? Who is this guy and why did I wait so long to watch the weekend news? I blow on my fingernails and try to convince myself that it's really dumb to become infatuated with a TV celebrity. Not even a celebrity, a *weatherman!* (Or maybe he prefers to be called a meteorologist.) I think about how to ask Jenna if she knows anything about him. And then I shudder when I think about how I'd ever explain a crush like this to Kerrin. I'm squeezing my eyes shut and trying to visualize whether or not he was wearing a wedding ring (I don't think so, but perhaps this is wishful thinking) when the doorbell jolts me off the couch. I peer out the front window and see Hector, a runny-nosed student of Michael's from a seedy block two streets over.

Because Hector's interest in learning music is ridiculously out of proportion to his mother's ability to pay for it, Michael generously gives him a weekly lesson for roughly the price of a few purchases from the ice cream truck that winds its way down our street in summertime. (And I know to stick around when Hector's in the house, because the petty cash in Michael's wallet often results in a Bomb Pop for me.) Hector is wearing a tattered T-shirt and is gripping his clarinet in one hand—no case, just the clarinet.

"Hi, Hector," I say briskly as I open the door. "Michael's away, did he cancel his lesson with you?" I hate when Michael goes away and forgets to cancel his lessons; it leaves me to deal with the confused kids and angry parents. The kids can be calmed easily enough with a toy from my giant stash, but the parents are often inconsolable. "And why isn't your clarinet in its case?" I ask disapprovingly. "I'm sure Michael tells you to always carry it in the case, and especially when it's raining like this."

"No, I don't have a lesson today. And I just ran over, that's why I didn't put it in the case. I wanted to play something for Michael, something we were working on. I thought he would be here so he could hear me play." He looks so completely defeated that I suddenly feel terrible about scolding him.

"How about you play it for me, then? I'd love to hear it," I say, opening up the squeaky screen door wider so he can come in. "And when you get done, you can pick out a toy. I've got some of that molding clay that you like."

"Oh, good! OK, here goes."

As I'm serenaded by a slightly off-key version of "When the Saints Go Marching In," I think about what J.P. could stand for. John Paul? John Peter? I'm not too well-versed in name abbreviations, so it could be anything, really. Hector finishes his tune and I applaud a little too wildly and go fetch him some blueberry-scented clay.

Chapter
3

"Oh, Toby, you must come see this. Look at this face. Couldn't you just eat it up?"

I grit my teeth and poke my head over my cubicle. Sarah, my boss, is waving a 5x7 of her little angel, her little sweetie, her little starbaby, Tommy. He is about six months old now, but he still has the pushed-in face of a newborn, red and angry looking. My coworkers must be ovulating around the clock, because there has been a rash of pregnancies and new births in the last year. I'm all for little babies, but not when their mothers force you to look at their pictures, listen to feeding and diapering schedules, and generally act as though you can drop anything at any minute to hear about some hilarious episode that usually involves laughing or drooling. I swear that every time a woman announces a pregnancy here, I feel nauseated right along with her, imagining how I'm going to fake my way through another set of photos. Luckily, I'm saved by the bell.

"Sorry, Sarah, I'm expecting a call from a vendor." A vendor named Kerrin, I say silently as I pounce on the phone. Sarah puts on a big fake frown and promises to come back later.

"Hi, Toy Girl. How's it going? I was just thinking about you because I got a call from Will."

"Oh?"

"Yeah, he is wild for you. He was so happy you came out last weekend."

"Will doesn't seem like the type to be wild about anything, does he?" I ask. "I don't know—he might not be my kind of guy. A little too sweet, know what I mean?"

"Uch, Toby—you're not one of those women who wants a guy to treat her like garbage, are you? Will might be a nice change after The Head Wound." This was our code name for a cute, curly-haired guy at my company whom I dated for a little while, only to find out that he was mentally unstable, fiercely paranoid, and had to be coaxed into doing anything outside his own apartment.

"The Head Wound was never mean to me. He was just crazy."

"Just. Well, is there anyone else around there?"

I look around at all of the gay designer boys and pregnant or lactating women and almost laugh out loud.

"No, definitely not."

"OK, I'll get it to you in a few minutes. . . . Sorry,

Toby, just some freak who needs something finished soon. What about that guy from the model shop, the sculptor?"

"He lives in the basement of his parents' house. I don't need that. Besides, I think I like someone. I mean, someone besides Will." I look at my desk calendar and gulp when I realize that it's been four days since I promised myself to call Jenna and compliment her on her news graphics. And ask her about J.P. Cody, of course.

"Really? Who is it?"

"I can't say right here. But I'll tell you soon, I promise."

"You better. All right, I have to leave for a lunch meeting. I'll be sure to get the tofu quotient for you," she says, snorting as she hangs up.

Kerrin works as a grant writer in the cancer prevention research branch of University of Pennsylvania Hospital's oncology department. She is one of those people who have the unfortunate combination of being good at something that offers them no discernable pleasure. It isn't the research or the writing that she dislikes; it's the altogether peculiar environment of her workplace that she finds so irksome. Because she is in the cancer prevention area, all her coworkers embrace a healthy lifestyle. I mean, *really* embrace a healthy lifestyle. They shun red meat and alcohol. Smoking is out, obviously. They ride their bikes to work, braving the downtown traffic in the name of cardiovascular health and taut muscles. They gift each other with gym memberships at Christmas. Everyone drones about how much they exercise, I never miss a day, even when I'm on vacation or on a trip, I shouldn't have that piece of cake, oh my, that isn't real butter is it, blah blah blah. I've visited Kerrin on numerous occasions and was struck dumb by the icy feel of the place, where cookies go untouched and no one admits to having any vices or body fat.

Kerrin, on the other hand, eats what she likes and has the big, curvaceous body to prove it. She smokes like a chimney and drinks her boyfriends under the table. She rolls joints with her little brother in the backyard when she goes home for a visit and snorts cocaine on holidays and special occasions. Naturally, these "lifestyle habits" (as she says they are called in her line of work) don't sit too well with her superiors and coworkers, who for all their scrawny beauty and clear, healthy skin between them don't have one-quarter of the sex Kerrin has. Naturally, Kerrin rebels by taking every smoke break that she can ("even if I don't really feel like smoking," she once confided to me), swigs Coke from a can on her desk, and affixes her Vinnie's Cheesesteaks VIP Club Card to a prominent place on her bulletin board. When she eats nine cheesesteaks, she'll get the tenth one for free, and those tiny holes punched into that card truly represent an achievement for her.

Sometimes I think this rebellion must be a lot of effort for Kerrin to expend energy on, but after a visit to her office, I always remind myself that this stuff probably keeps her from going crazy. Always the one to try and get a rise out of people, she recently took her bad "lifestyle habits" to a big meeting, where she sat and solemnly ate a Pop-Tart with a knife and fork and daintily drank Mountain Dew. No one was too pleased, but I'd bet that at least some of the people at that table would have secretly traded their melon and grapes for a bite of that strawberry-and-goo confection. In any case, all that sugar, red meat, and tobacco did yield them a great researcher and writer, so Kerrin does get a sort of grudging respect from people. In the beginning, she tried to understand their views. "It's all about control, Kerrin," my mom said once when she was visiting and we were out to dinner. "They all think if they control these things to within an inch of their life, they won't get cancer. Or they'll live forever. But living your life the way you want to is your prerogative."

"I'll drink to that," said Kerrin, hoisting her shot of Jack Daniels into the air.

I am late as I run down the street to meet Will for lunch at the Twin City Diner. It is a true diner, not one of these prefab restaurants that feels like a '50s diner but is really part of a giant chain that trades on the NASDAQ. It was moved here lock, stock, and barrel from St. Paul, and they were too lazy to change the name. The diner sits solidly on a gritty corner in a dicey part of the city, its metal exterior crying out for a serious cleaning. Inside is just the same, with years of grease permeating all surfaces, from the red vinyl on the stool tops at the counter to the slick cream-colored circles of the old-fashioned cash register keys. Over the door hangs a picture of St. Paul, whom they've renamed the Patron Saint of the $4.99 Meatloaf Special.

My hair is matted down in front and sticks to my forehead. The heat is unbearable this week, and the air-conditioning is broken in Rich's car. Rich is the wiry, balding, middle-aged electrical engineer who gives me a lift to and from work and whose life is defined by his bitter and protracted divorce. He insists on detailing the divorce proceedings each and every day, and I have wondered on more than one occasion if his anger has ever spilled into his work and been responsible for, say, a radio-controlled car that began to smolder as a little boy played with it on Christmas Day, or a doll whose voice chip made her spew forth with sentiments full of bile and rage. He can usually keep it together and hold out until we reach the base of the Ben Franklin Bridge, talking politely about work and current events, but by the time we're over the river, it's all over. My ride always ends with some type of uplifting advice, such as "Never truly fall in love, Toby" (I think I've got that one covered) and "You think you know someone, you really do. . . ." Kerrin says that I should stop paying for gas and tolls and instead present him with a bill, since he treats me like his therapist.

Will is lazily tracing the boomerang shapes on the tabletop with his index finger and looks up suddenly as I appear. He smiles and then looks down at my chest, perplexed.

"Oh, yeah, this," I say, ripping the fluorescent orange sticker from my left boob and blushing. It says, SHAKE, THEN SQUEEZE. I put it there earlier to get a laugh out of Caroline, a friend of mine from the preschool department. The stickers are meant for tiny tubes of paint that come with Spin Art Sonia, a doll whose feature is her dress that can be decorated by the kid. It relies on that boardwalk classic where the white chipboard spins maniacally and you squeeze paints to create a hallucinogenic twist of colors. Who would let their child create such a massive mess in the house for the privilege of paying $34.99 (paint refills sold separately), I don't know.

I order my favorite Twin City Diner lunch (pb and j, chocolate milk, side of chips) and Will leans across the table so his head is disconcertingly close to mine.

"So how's toys?"

"OK, I guess, if you like that kind of thing," I say noncommittally, biting into my sandwich. Someone puts Frank Sinatra on the jukebox, and the diner fills with his smooth voice.

"Say, Toby, how about this? Tomorrow night there's going to be an opening at the gallery. It's totally postmodern, right up your alley. Want to go?"

How Will would know what kind of art is "right up my alley" is a mystery to me, mainly because even after six solid semesters of art history, *I* have no idea what kind of art is right up my alley. "Oh, I can't, Will. I'm going out with my friend Jenna." I shrug and frown, but

I'm so grateful that I have plans; it prevents me from having to lie on the spot and avert my eyes and appear shifty.

"Oh. Well, they're setting it up later this afternoon, and I'm going to be helping out. Maybe you could stop by. You know, it's just downstairs from Kerrin's," he says hopefully.

"Maybe," I say slowly, studying a potato chip and trying intently not to avert my eyes and appear shifty. The waitress plunks down Will's root beer float, and he wraps his tiny lips around the straw, never taking his eyes off me. "The thing is," I continue, "I sort of said I would do something with Michael later today."

"Ohhh, Michael. Kerrin told me about him. You spend a lot of time with him, I guess. Lucky guy." I grin, not because of Will's flattery, but because I can imagine Michael bursting out laughing at this pronouncement of his so-called good fortune. "I'm sure you're doing something exciting," he adds.

"Oh, yeah. You bet," I say, biting the inside of my cheek to try and hold back a smile. Michael and I have agreed to help four nine-year-old girls from down the block to choreograph an original dance. It seems that Mondays have been dubbed "Do Your Own Thing Day" at their summer music program and this Monday is their turn to entertain the group however they choose. Inexplicably, they've chosen "Legs" by ZZ Top as the song they'll dance to. The magic begins on our stoop in an hour.

Will refolds his napkin and sighs. "I have to get back to the gallery. Can I give you a lift home?"

"Um, you can give me a lift to Center City, if that's OK." I feel bad accepting a ride from someone whose love I've spurned twice in less than five minutes, but he did offer.

"What's in Center City?"

"Oh, I just need to pick something up from a store on Chestnut Street." I've been carrying around a torn piece of paper featuring a new bath oil that's purported to smell just like a mint julep. My sister had ripped the page from a magazine in her acupuncturist's office and mailed it to me with a Post-it that said, "Hey, sicko! Thought you'd like this." I located it at a tiny boutique, after making many calls.

We drive across town in Will's tidy Volkswagen, and I try to imagine what it would be like to hug a boy whose waist is smaller than mine. I just can't picture it.

When I finally arrive home, the dance practice is in full swing, with the twins Camille and Lea in matching halter tops and their friends Maria and Evie in glittery half-shirts. They are shimmying and laughing as Michael sits on the stoop, slowly shaking his head at them. A lank piece of dirty-blond hair flops over one of his eyes and he leans over and teases, "Thank God Toby's here. I'm going to need reinforcements for these girls." They giggle again, fluttering their eyelashes at him, practicing flirting without even knowing it yet. Lea comes over and hits the Play button on our paint-spattered boom box as I plop down on the stoop next to Michael. The four of them dash into the street to start their Rockette-style kicks and immediately begin knocking into one another.

"No, no, no," I say, irritated that Camille doesn't yet know her right from her left. What are they teaching these kids in school today, anyway?

"Let me get in front of you guys. Watch what I do, then follow it." More giggling. I rewind the song to the beginning and stand in front of them. I start kicking and spinning around, and surprisingly, they become serious and quiet enough to follow what I'm doing. Camille ceases to blink because she's concentrating so hard, and even Evie, the boisterous ringleader of the crowd, pops her retainer back in her mouth and falls in line. "Very good!" I yell. "Let's rewind it again and start over."

While we're waiting for the tape to rewind, Maria says to no one in particular, "Toby's got nice legs." I'm wearing my black-and-green polka-dotted bubble miniskirt today, and she points to my calves.

"And she knows how to use them!" exclaims Evie helpfully.

"No, she doesn't," says Michael, yawning. "Have nice legs, I mean." I narrow my eyes at him and surreptitiously try to give him the finger. Naturally, the girls notice and explode into another fit of giggles.

"Let's just drive," I say, sinking into the front seat of Michael's beat-up Honda Civic.

"Where?"

"Oh, anywhere. It doesn't matter." Michael and I have wrapped up the dance practice and eaten a little spaghetti for an early dinner. Now I'm itching to get out of the city and go for a drive. Or have someone drive me, as the case may be.

I have a deep adoration and respect for cars, much more so than any other girl I've ever known. This is a learned trait from my father, who is a hopeless car fanatic. When I was young, we used to take our family vacation to the Auto Show in Detroit every winter. (My poor mother.) So instead of becoming familiar with dollies and play kitchens and plastic-beaded jewelry, I learned about engine blocks and rear-wheel drive and rack-and-pinion steering. Instead of climbing on the jungle gym, I was sticking my head into concept cars. My dad swears that my first word was *chassis*, although I think it may have been *Cassie*, who was our dog at the time. No matter. In any case, I got the bug, and I live in a place where I can't even keep a car because I can't afford the insurance. My dad thinks it's a travesty. It's like going to Penn and ending up selling soft pretzels from a cart on the street, he says—nowhere to use that whole head full of knowledge.

"Oh, there's one place we shouldn't go," I say suddenly. "Kerrin's neighborhood."

"How come?" asks Michael, fiddling with the radio.

"Some guy asked me to go down to some gallery opening or something, and I don't want him to see me. You know."

Michael grimaces, spins the radio dial some more, and the car fills with a droning voice. ". . . rebel leaders claim that there were no mass murders, but peacekeeping forces discovered bodies in a ditch, covered with maggots and . . ."

"No NPR tonight, Michael. I can't deal. I know I'm as shallow as a birdbath, but please," I plead. He turns off the radio and pops in some Prokofiev instead.

He drives wordlessly for a little while, and I prop my knees up on the dashboard. The city lights are disappearing behind us like someone pulling the little pegs out of a LiteBrite screen one by one.

"My parents are visiting tomorrow," he says finally, absentmindedly scratching one of his sideburns.

"Is this good or bad?" I ask, but I know the answer already. Although he was awarded extra points for pursuing a career in the arts, Michael's parents never truly forgave him for turning his back on the medical profession.

"It's all right; whatever. It's just . . ." His voice trails off. "It was so weird last weekend. I drive all the way out there for Marisa to tell me that she wants to be just friends." He takes his hands off the steering wheel for a split second to put the word *friends* in finger quotes, then clutches the wheel again, suddenly angry. "What is that about?"

This is the way Michael always operates, bringing up one thing as the warm-up and then segueing into what's really on his mind. It's like his first gripe is the opening act and his next one is the featured artist. It's infuriating to me, because I hate wasting mental energy on the opening act, in conversations *and* at real-life concerts.

He slows down as a sweet family of deer cross the road, dopey and sleepy in the Honda's headlights. "Sorry. Toby. It's only that women are confusing. *Very* confusing."

"Maybe just this one Marisa person was confusing," I offer helpfully. "Plus, she's a musician too, and you said it's really dumb to date another musician."

"Yeah, probably," he says, frowning. "So who is the guy in Kerrin's neighborhood?"

"Oh, some boy named Will. He is too small for me."

Michael turns to me, puzzled. "Too small, like small-minded?" he asks.

"No, small. Like I could break him in half."

Michael furrows his eyebrows and gives me a quick, critical once-over, a look that reminds me of the time my senior-year sculpture professor took just thirty seconds to decide that my full-scale clay model of a cow skull was lacking a certain bovine beauty and only deserved a depressing C+. He stares back at the road and says, "He must be pretty small for you to break him in half, Toby. Are you sure you're not mixing him up with one of my students?"

I sigh and look out the window. Being looked over by any guy, even Michael, is unnerving. "I think it's time to go back."

I've just had a bath with my new mint julep bath oil and am sitting in my room, smelling for all the world

like a delicious mixed drink. Michael is downstairs puttering around, trying to straighten out our living room
in anticipation of his parents' visit. It is a pointless exercise; they won't stay long enough to even appreciate
that he put away all the *TV Guide*s and empty soda cans
and little handmade papier-mâché gifts from his music
students.

I sit on my bed and study my legs poking out from the
bottom of my bathrobe. So what if Michael says I don't
have nice legs? I'm not one of those girls with food issues, whose lives are ruled by calorie charts and minutes
on the treadmill and number of bags of M&Ms eaten
versus number of times puked. I'm five feet four inches,
one hundred and twenty-five pounds, with size seven
shoes and a B-cup bra. I'm completely average with OK
proportions, in other words. I guess that's the problem.

I decide to get a view of my legs from another angle
and stand upright on the bed. My only mirror is a big,
oval-shaped bit of glass that hangs over my dresser,
making for a fantastically awkward situation if I need to
see the lower half of my body. Basically, it means I have
to jump up and down on the bed and hope to catch a
glimpse of myself from the waist down. It has made for
some irredeemably horrible shoe choices and bad skirt-
length selections, according to Kerrin, who never uses a
mirror herself and always looks fine.

Michael hears the bedsprings squeaking as I jump up
and down and shouts, "Buy a new mirror! You're going
to fall and break your neck!" I silently reply that *I* never

complain when I hear his bedsprings squeaking for whatever reason. I'm satisfied that my legs look fine and slide under the covers.

Who cares what he says, I think as I drift off to sleep. He says he's not a leg man anyway, so what would he know? I wonder if J.P. Cody is a leg man.

J.P. Cody!

My eyes fly open as I suddenly remember that tomorrow is another weekend weather day. Less than twelve hours until I see my wonderful weatherman, I think as I look over at the toucan-shaped clock on my nightstand. I fall asleep smiling, dreaming of Doppler radar.

Chapter
4

"Hi, hon." Dot is standing at the door of the North Star Bar, and, amazingly, is inhaling on a cigarette and cracking her gum at the same time. "Shouldn't run like that in those crazy shoes you girls wear nowadays; you'll break your ankle. Here, I'll take you back." She casts a sour glance at my brown suede platform shoes, stomps out her cigarette, and leads me to the bar. Jenna is perched on a tiny barstool, smiling politely at the bartender as he chats her up.

"No need for that, Steve, her friend is here. Now you can leave her alone," teases Dot. He scowls at her and turns back to the baseball game on TV.

"Hey, Toby! You look great!" says Jenna.

Only twenty minutes earlier, I had been furiously scrubbing the remains of Purple Passion off my nails, creating a soggy heap of bruise-colored cotton balls on the living room floor. Michael had coughed from the acrid smell of the nail polish remover and declared that the lack of ventilation would surely kill a gazillion brain cells for us both. I was glad to be out of the house.

"And you smell nice, too," she says after hugging me. "Minty—like toothpaste or something?"

Well, toothpaste wasn't quite the smell that I was going for, but Jenna is the first to notice my new mint julep bath oil, so I can't be choosy. I drop my bag on the floor beneath the barstool and sit down next to her. My bag contains a list I drew up that morning while watching J.P. Cody on the noontime news. Mercifully, Michael went out with his parents for brunch, and I was left deliciously alone with our ten-inch TV set. This time I lay on the floor, my arms bent and my face propped up in my hands, so I could get a closer look. Seeing J.P. again was wonderful; he talked about a storm system so intensely that it made me go all shivery. I decided that I had to get more information about him, but in the meantime I made a list of everything I thought I knew. It read:

black hair
blue eyes
long eyelashes
about six feet tall
crooked incisor
struggles with phrase low-pressure system
accent I can't quite put my finger on (not *Philly*)

It wasn't a lot, but it was a start.

"So tell me about WPHX," I say, spinning on my barstool. "What's it like? Probably pretty cool, right?"

"It is," says Jenna, sipping her beer. "The work is OK. I had a bit of a problem in the beginning with . . . well, you know." She looks furtively around the bar, as if color blindness might get her thrown out, like being underage. "I had some little glitches the first few weeks."

I suddenly remember the green Gorbachev head and feel sorry for her. "It all looked good to me," I say into my beer glass, drinking quickly.

"Oh, and some of the crazies that work there, you wouldn't believe it!" she continues, shaking her head. "You know that sportscaster, Tom Griffin? Well, let's just say his nickname is Toupee Tom. And Edie, this woman who oversees production? Someone told me that when she has PMS, she comes to meetings with a *baseball bat*." Jenna widens her eyes so I can see her delicately applied and color-coordinated eye shadow and eyeliner. "Supposedly, she lays it on the table and says, 'I hope I don't have to use this today.' Can you imagine?"

Actually, I can imagine; the staff at WPHX probably doesn't hold a candle to the colorful cast of characters at Toyland. But instead of thinking about them, I calmly say to Jenna, "What about J.P. Cody?"

"J.P. Cody," she repeats, rooting intently around in the dish of mixed nuts like she's searching for bus fare. She pulls out a pecan and repeats his name once again. "Oh, right, J.P. Cody," she says, nodding. "Meteorologist, right? Really cute."

"Yes, really cute," I answer, steeling myself for the pronouncement that she's already dating him.

"Hmmm. Well, I know he lives in Delaware," she begins.

"Really?" I scrunch up my nose in displeasure. Everyone I ever knew who hailed from Delaware was either dead-eyed or crazy-eyed. Dead-eyed resulted from too little mental stimulation and too many trips to Home Depot and chain restaurants. Crazy-eyed was usually the result of some kind of weird religious fervor and meant that you could see a person's entire iris all the way around.

"Not the gross part of Delaware," she says, flashing a smile at the bartender as he puts down another beer in front of her. "He lives in Newcastle, down by the river. In one of those really pretty houses. You know, where the sweet restaurants and antique shops are?"

This cheers me momentarily. But then I think about the combination of words *pretty*, *sweet*, and *antiques*, and I'm sure my face registers anguish once again. It wouldn't be the first time I've developed a crush on a gay guy. Hell, it's practically required for graduation from art school. But I'll be damned if J.P. Cody is queer. "But he isn't gay, is he?" I ask slowly, dreading the answer.

"Oh, no!" Jenna laughs. "I overheard him talking about how he just got out of a relationship with some woman."

Excellent. A single, straight weatherman. What more could a girl want?

"I don't get the feeling he knows a lot of people out this way," she says. "He's pretty new. He moved here from Minnesota."

Oh my God, a Midwesterner. This undoubtedly meant good manners *and* a love of cheese. It just kept getting better and better.

". . . yeah, I guess he's from Minneapolis originally, I read it in his bio in the *PHX People* newsletter . . ."

I am deep in fantasy now, imagining myself and J.P. Cody frolicking around the giant Claes Oldenburg maraschino-cherry-and-spoon sculpture in front of the Walker Art Center in Minneapolis. I'm thinking about finding that revolving door so I can throw my hat up in the air like Mary Tyler Moore did. I'm gon-na make it after alllll . . .

"Hello, Toby?" Jenna is lightly rapping her knuckles on my head and grinning. "Do you want one?"

"Another beer? Yes, that would be good."

"No, not a beer, silly. An autographed picture of J.P. Cody. I can get you one if you want."

"Oh, yes," I say, trying to sound nonchalant. I guess I'll put it next to my bed like my mom said she did with a picture of Elvis when she was a teenager. A picture of J.P. Cody! I'll never get any sleep.

"So speaking of cute guys, didn't you say there was someone interested in you? Some guy from an art gallery?"

"Oh, yeah. Will." I roll my eyes, and this makes Jenna giggle. Thinking of Will makes me sigh, but not the type of sigh that the sight of J.P. Cody elicits. "Jenna, I don't get it. It's just so hard to find a boy who I like and who likes me." I suddenly feel angry. "It shouldn't be so hard—I like cars and sports and sex. I would even have sex in a car while listening to sports on the radio, if it were the right guy!"

"Oh, Toby!" Jenna laughs, her shiny brown curls bobbing up and down. "You're so quirky, only a real nut could love you."

The days are getting shorter and shorter now, and the air in the house has changed from stifling to merely stuffy. The neighborhood kids are all back in school, which means that Michael's students no longer come at all hours of the day but after school and in the early evening. Usually the sight of them cheers me, especially after my long workdays and grueling rides home with Rich (they're now trying to determine who gets the sailboat, God help us all).

But lately I haven't felt up to the kids' goofy antics and the new fall selection, "Go Tell Aunt Rhody." I've managed to warm to one kid, a twelve-year-old albino named Jared with the biggest buck teeth I've ever seen. Michael swears that when he bites down on his saxophone mouthpiece and closes his translucent eyelids, he looks just like a bunny. I like him because he once paused in front of my room on the way back from the bathroom and was able to correctly identify a young Bob Dylan grinning out from the poster above my bed. This kid will go far, I told a skeptical Michael that night over a dinner of cheese and crackers. These kinds of things are important.

I am now watching J.P. Cody with a regularity bordering on the compulsive: No matter what my weekend plans, I always catch the noontime news. I think I've become a bit of a connoisseur of his style and moods. He favors ties with swirly blue patterns (they make him think of a cool front, perhaps?) and abstract tan and green checks. I've gotten the hang of when he raises his arm, when he moves slightly to one side to sweep his hand over western Pennsylvania, when he smiles, when he says, "Back to you, Jill." I think I can tell what type of weather he likes (he waxes lyrical about hurricanes) and what he doesn't like (discussing the dew point always seems to make him cranky). I think he may grow wistful when looking at Minnesota on the map, but I can't be sure.

"Rachmaninoff, Schmachmaninoff, whatever," says Kerrin huffily as she flops down into her seat and throws her plush jacket over the chair in front of us. We are at Michael's fall recital, and she is less than pleased. I begged her a few days ago to come and help fill the seats; she grudgingly agreed, but not before citing ten thousand reasons why classical music stinks. Now she is frantically searching around in her bag for her headphones, swearing that "it's Led Zep all the way if I get bored, you know." She waggles the Walkman in my face to show she means business.

"So where is the great musician, anyway?" Kerrin asks, not waiting for my answer. "Oh, get this, Toby. There's this kid who is the daughter of some lady I work with. For her sixth birthday, she made her eat a *wheat-germ* cake and *tofu* ice cream. Scary, right?" She shudders at the thought of it. "So today she's off from school and hanging around the office, and I say, 'Darla, sweetie, how was your birthday cake and ice cream? Did you know that your mommy forcing you to eat that kind of stuff as a kid will turn you into a transsexual drug addict when you're a grown-up?'"

"Uh-huh," I answer absently, not really listening to her tale of torture. I scan the room for Michael, who naturally woke up today complaining of a sore throat, a headache, and, in his mind, seventeen symptoms of terminal illness. His hypochondria gets out of control right before a performance and usually results in him fretting for hours about whether or not he should perform. For some reason, I took pity on him this morning, and instead of bellowing at him to stop whining, I brought him a cup of tea. I came into his room with a clatter, tripping over a fallen music stand and nearly losing my grip on the tiny Wallace and Gromit cup and saucer. He eyed it and me suspiciously and pulled the covers up to his chin. When he turned his head to look out the window, the light hit his face in a way that made him look as fearful and vulnerable as the shyest of his music students, so I stayed for a few minutes and tried to talk him into rallying for the concert. But my efforts at being tender didn't help; he snarled at me, so I left. Maybe he really was sick.

"So," I begin coolly, turning to Kerrin, "I never told you about the guy I like."

"No, you never did. No one ever tells me anything," she says, pouting.

"That's not true. I tell you lots of things. Anyway, the guy I like is"—I take a deep breath—"on TV. He's a meteorologist." I thought calling him a meteorologist rather than a weatherman would give him some extra cachet.

"What!" she exclaims, blinking hard and letting her mouth fall open. "Say it again." At just that moment, Michael and the other three members of the quartet take the stage. In the bright light, Michael looks even more underfed, lanky, and pale than usual, tugging nervously at the collar of his tuxedo shirt with his free hand. The other three musicians are equally anemic-looking, sporting the skin of people who regularly bask in the glow of fluorescent-lit basement practice rooms. They make the discordant sounds of tuning up as the lights start to dim.

"What the *hell* are you talking about?" asks Kerrin amusedly. An older woman wearing a wool hat turns around and tells Kerrin that she's going to ruin the musicians' concentration. "Oh, that's not possible," Kerrin says cheerily to the old woman. "Ask this one here," she says, jerking her thumb at me. "She lives with one of 'the musicians,' and he could play that thing through a nuclear war." The woman shoots a disgusted look at both of us and turns back around, folding her arms across her chest.

While the quartet performs, my mind starts to wander. Why should Kerrin be upset? I close my eyes and imagine myself slow-dancing with J.P. Cody to the beautiful music, although I can't quite picture the scene without a giant topographical map of Pennsylvania behind us. When I open my eyes, Kerrin's eyes are slits and she's looking at me, half-smiling and half-smirking.

"Let's go congratulate Michael," I say quickly as they finish and take their bows. He is sweating and his skin is taking on a slightly greenish cast, but he doesn't look nearly as perturbed as Kerrin does. I take two steps at a time down to the stage to get away from her, but she's too fast for me. She collars me as we reach the bottom step.

"You like a *weatherman?* You're kidding, right? Is this someone that Jenna introduced you to?"

"Well, not really. I mean, not yet. I don't really know him, exactly." I stumble over my words as they rush from my mouth. My cheeks feel hot, like when I've had one too many vodka martinis at the Mars Bar.

"Oh, my God, you don't even know him?" she asks incredulously, her eyes widening. "You're *stalking* a weatherman? And I thought your roommate was a kook." By now Michael has made his way to the edge of the stage, and she gestures to him with a dramatic flourish as she finishes her sentence.

"Know who?" Michael asks, smiling as he absently watches the spit dribble from his clarinet and hit the floor. The fact that Kerrin has come suddenly registers and he looks up from the puddle to say in a slow and polite voice, "Kerrin, I didn't think you liked classical music. I'm glad you could come. Did you enjoy it?"

"I'm not sure," she answers, looking at me. "Let's just say it had some interesting surprises."

"Oh, well, that's Rachmaninoff for you!" says Michael excitedly, his brain full of music and completely oblivious to the nuances of the world around him.

When I wake up the next day, it's blustery and windy and all I can think is, I wish Shamzammy Jammers would just go away. These little cars that light up and play music have been the bane of my existence for a solid two weeks, and I can't bear to look at them another day. I'm told they need red Mylar holographic stickers to really sell the commercial, but red Mylar holographic stickers just won't adhere to their slick, shamzammy surface. I want to climb under the covers when I realize that not only am I worrying about the fate of a sixty-cent plastic car, it's also going to be a full four days until I see J.P. Cody on the weekend weather again.

A few hours later, I'm sitting at my desk feeling despondent, wondering if Kerrin has written me off for a saner friend, when Sarah ambles over with new pictures of her baby. She fans them out, and I immediately grab my prototype Shamzammy Jammer and yelp, "I have to go to Engineering! I have a deadline!" I stand up as straight as I can and clutch the car to my chest.

"No, silly, you can stay a minute! Engineering's not going anywhere; sit and look at my starbaby," she says, all gooey-eyed.

"No, there's only one man for this job, Sarah, and I need to talk to him right now. It's Rod. You know. The Ty Cobb of the toy industry."

"The *who* of the *what?*" Sarah asks, cocking her head like a sweet but stupid puppy. "I swear, Toby, little starbaby is going to be four years old before you see these pictures!" She scoops up the photos with her fat hand and goes off in search of another victim. I start to leave but suddenly remember my offering, a one-piece dental floss container. I slip it in my pocket and make my trek to the cold and sterile engineering department to see Rod.

Rod Winters is a Southern-born, middle-aged, brilliant manufacturing engineer who reportedly was lured away from one of Toyland's competitors about two years ago with the promise of giant stock options and fantastic bonuses. He has a quick, agile mind and can close his flinty eyes and imagine in an instant how anything can be designed and manufactured. His engineering drawings are immaculate and his calculations beyond reproach. Unfortunately, even though he is unlike anything the toy industry has ever seen, this doesn't always render him kind or compassionate. He has a volatile, unpredictable temper that can go from zero to sixty in seconds. He holds his staff in contempt, checking and rechecking their drawings until long after the sun has set. His face flushes a fiery red when he is forced to interact with any person from packaging, product development, or, heaven forbid, marketing. Rod is also fiercely competitive; a young, nervous engineer named Joe whispered to me at our company picnic that when our main competitor came out with Potty Penny last year, Rod smashed her little plastic toilet clear through the wall of the testing room. It appeared that he had designed even better potty technology for us, but they happened to get it to market first.

So it is with trembling hands that I carry my Shamzammy Jammer, red holographic Mylar sticker sheet, and dental floss container over the threshold of Rod's office. He is focused on an engineering drawing that covers the expanse of his desk and doesn't deign to look up as I enter the room. I stand there for a full thirty seconds, half in and half out of the doorway before he coldly beckons me in. He still doesn't glance up from his drawing; he holds his mechanical pencil poised over the desk and I'm staring at him, thinking I'd like to stab him with it. Instead I offer the dental floss container, setting it down on the drawing like it's a soap bubble. He picks it up, turns it over slowly, grunts, looks at me through narrowed eyes, and gives the slightest hint of a smile. This trick was something that Joe clued me in to about a month after my arrival at Toyland: offerings of unusually manufactured plastic products are like very valuable wampum to Rod. You give him plastics, he grants you requests. Apparently I have struck gold with the dental floss container—he leans over and explains in a low voice that this is a real beauty, see how it's all made in one piece, no weird parting line, look at these living hinges. I feign interest and he places it in The Box, his polystyrene collection of toys, housewares, and pet products. Excited over my find, he rubs his hands together and folds up the engineering drawing into a neat rectangle.

This process is arduous, as it must be folded just so, and to make conversation, I look out the window and say lamely, "Well, I guess it didn't clear up like they said it would."

He scowls and casts a glance at the rain-spattered pane of glass. "Last time I listen to J.P. Cody," he mutters.

"What?" I ask, sitting on the edge of my seat. "Do you watch J.P. Cody?"

"What do you mean, 'Do I watch J.P. Cody?'" He mimics my voice, and I can feel my face start to sting with anger. I want to throw The Box out the window, but the windows don't open in this climate-controlled building. Probably for just that reason: I bet defenestration is a major problem at toy companies, with their impetuous employees and turn-on-a-dime timelines. "I watch the morning news, if that's what you mean," he says a little less snippily, leaning back in his lumpy chair.

"Oh, I didn't know he did the morning weather, I mean," I say quietly. When did J.P. Cody get moved to the morning news? Was this a temporary thing? Or something permanent? I am so excited that Rod's spare, unadorned office seems to be spinning.

"I don't care who does the weather. What do you have there?" He nods in the direction of the Shamzammy Jammer. I put it on his desk and pull out the red holographic Mylar sticker sheet, causing his nostrils to flare with anger. He grabs it away from me and starts to growl about how the hell he is supposed to make this stick, why are marketing people so stupid, who is your boss, and why do they have me wasting his time like this? But even Rod Winters's rant can't hurt me today; it bounces off me like the Glitter Glow Balls that Caroline is working on over in the preschool department. My mornings will have new meaning now.

Chapter 5

Winds have been gusting lately, making it feel a lot colder than what your thermometer says. The old wind-chill factor will get you every time.

I am sitting on the floor in front of the TV on Monday morning, quickly eating Apple Jacks to quiet the rumbling in my stomach and eyeing the clock while J.P. Cody does the morning weather. This has been my routine for about three weeks now, since that serendipitous day in Rod Winters's office. I indulge in my two pleasures before work: eating sugary cereal and watching J.P. Cody with cocker-spaniel eyes. Each morning I eagerly await his report with a racing heart.

. . . so you might want to take a heavier jacket today, because that cool front will be moving in.

"Why are you suddenly so into the news?" Michael asks, leaning against the banister. "I thought you said my making you listen to NPR was enough."

"Noocacamushels," I say, shoving a huge spoonful of cereal into my mouth. Why did he have to ask me this now, during the weather report?

Strong winds and heavy rain later in the week that might cause some flooding in . . .

"Huh?" asks Michael. I wish he would keep quiet; there are only about thirty seconds left of the weather report, and J.P. is wearing my favorite tie, the one with the blue and silver checks.

"New car commercials," I say, clearing my throat. "This is the time of year they come out." This is a blatant lie, of course, but one I feel pretty sure that I could keep under wraps. Michael doesn't give one whit about cars, as long as his yucky Honda gets him and his clarinet from place to place.

"Well, I have to admit, I don't know what the big deal is," he says, waving his hand dismissively. "They all have four wheels and an engine."

So predictable. "It's not my fault something went wrong with your Y chromosomes and you ended up liking fairy music instead of cars," I snap back at him. "You should be glad that at least one of us wears the pants in this house." I look at Michael angrily just in time to catch his confused expression, then he just shakes his head and goes out the door. In one smooth, stupid motion, I've missed the rest of the weather report *and* pissed Michael off. Nice work, Toby.

When I'm sitting in Rich's car twenty minutes later and successfully ignoring his story about his ex-wife's slashing his tires, I try to figure out the best way to tell Michael the real reason I'm glued to the weekday morning news. Without having him commit me, I mean. By the time Rich has finished his story about the tires and moved onto the tale about the family iguana, I've decided that I just don't want Michael to know quite yet.

I am hungry the rest of the day, dunking my hand repeatedly into Sarah's ugly, snowman-shaped candy jar on her desk. Going back for seconds of slimy, electric orange macaroni and cheese at lunch. Stuffing my face with a powdery donut as I keep Joe company while he smokes outside and curses Rod Winters between angry puffs. Making Rich actually stop at the intersection where the greasy vendors sell soft pretzels and warm, runny mustard. I eat mine with gusto and suggest we go for a cheesesteak, my treat. Rich declines, mumbling something about calling his divorce lawyer this evening.

It isn't until later that night, after pizza and French fries and ice cream and some Flavor Ice, that I realize what is going on. It starts with a little twinge right above my belly button, and all of a sudden, I know I'm a goner.

Every time I am about to get a stomach flu, I become ravenous, eating everything in sight. My voracious appetite has even impressed Kerrin on a few occasions, and that is saying something. It's a bit like what our dog Cassie used to do: When she was sick, she would mill around the backyard and eat lots of grass. This is something dogs do when they don't feel good, my mom assured me as I watched Cassie in horror. Sure enough, the grass would make her sick, she'd feel better, and we'd be left with rags and club soda, swabbing the new cream-colored carpet with the technicolor stains.

So my body is no more advanced than a dog's, in other words. At least Cassie knew to eat just enough to make her sick. I eat much more food than I need to, so there's plenty to throw up later. I've been had by my body again.

After a terrible night, I climb into bed, shaky, teary, and aching. My stomach feels like a paint shaker and I fall into a fitful, feverish sleep, where Shamzammy Jammers collide and a gigantic iguana races through my REM stage.

The next morning, I wobbily make my way down the stairs to see Michael peering up at me with inquisitive eyes. "Are you OK?" he asks, biting into a piece of toast and spraying the tabletop with charred crumbs. "You sounded pretty bad last night. I think at one point I heard you yell that you were like a sick dog and that I should put you down. Do you want some toast?"

"Ooh, no," I say, my dry tongue like sandpaper. "I mean, no thank you." I still feel bad for snapping at Michael yesterday morning, and I may be able to lessen my guilt by at least being polite. I shiver and close my eyes, which feel like two fiery holes in my head. I sit down across from him at the kitchen table and hold my clammy face in my hands. He reaches out and puts his palm on my forehead.

"You're hot."

"Ha, ha, that's what all the boys say," I croak, trying to smile.

"You need some aspirin," Michael says as he walks to the sink, where he lathers up his hands in an effort to destroy any energetic germs that may have leaped from my bangs to his fingernails during that split second. He dries them on a towel, goes upstairs, and returns with a fistful of aspirin and a spare metronome from his studio, one of my favorite toys. It's old-fashioned, this chunky wooden pyramid with a big swinging pendulum—nothing like the new tiny digital timekeepers that all of Michael's musician friends favor. It can go from a sluggish 40 to a zippily insane 208 beats a minute, and I think it appeals to me because it's so regimented, so unaffected by outside forces, so methodical, so unlike me. He sets it down on the table and I eagerly snatch it up and start playing with it, sliding the weight up and down the pendulum and listening to the *thunk-thunk* as it speeds and slows according to my whim. Michael smiles and shakes his head as I stare fascinated at it, like a cat or a preschooler. Then he fills up a glass with water and hands it to me, and I take greedy swallows.

"Not too fast, Toby, or you'll get sick—and you know if you throw up and I see it, I'll throw up too."

"Is that so?" I ask, holding an aspirin between my

teeth. "Oh, yeah, I remember that baby-sitting story you told me," I say, grinning weakly. "Those poor parents. What time is it?"

"Nine-twenty," he answers, glancing at his watch and getting up and tossing the paper towel he was using as a plate into the trash.

"Oh, good, The Monkees are on soon. Micky Dolenz will make me feel better, for sure," I say, pushing my hair off my forehead.

"Oh yeah. Sheila always used to make me watch them when we were younger, even though their 'music' made my skin crawl even then." He pauses a minute to consider what I said. "Micky Dolenz is your favorite? You always go for the weirdo," he laughs.

"I do not!" I say stubbornly. "Besides, everyone knows that Peter Tork was the weirdo."

Michael rolls his eyes and smirks, putting on his coat and muttering to himself. "Micky Dolenz," is the last thing I can hear him cluck before he heads out the door, clarinet case in one hand and a tidy pile of sheet music in the other, and then I'm all alone with my up-tempo metronome beat and my pile of aspirin.

"So how's my little girl?"

"Oh, much, much better today, Dad. I probably could have even gone to work this morning, I guess." Yesterday, in between sips of water and tea, I managed to call my sister, whose newfound interest in herbal remedies assured me that she would have some funky way to combat nausea. I was right: gingerroot was the prescription, and I persuaded Kerrin to visit a health-food store and buy some for me. The gingerroot she brought over on her lunch hour was helpful, but I like to think that the hysterical image of Kerrin in a health-food store—with her leather jacket and tatty, black, smoke-infused hair, talking to some hippie guy wearing Birkenstocks—aided in my recovery process quite a bit. In any case, after giving me her advice, my sister promptly hung up the phone and called my father.

"Well, you shouldn't go back until you're one hundred percent, Toby. Remember what happened when you had lice in the fourth grade."

"Thanks, Dad."

"So, have you seen? The new two-door Audis are out," he says excitedly.

"Oh, yeah, wait a minute," I say, rooting under my bed for my *Auto Week.* "Here it is: 'On twisting roads, the new Audi maintains itself with Teutonic composure. And when it's time to stop, the pedal effort is linear. The brakes grab quickly, with no fade or pulsation.' Sounds nice. When are you getting me one?" I tease.

"Why doesn't that guy you live with get you one?" he asks in all seriousness. I burst out laughing. "Dad, Michael wouldn't know an Audi from a Buick. And he's not my boyfriend, anyway. Even if he could afford a car, he would never buy me a gift like that. No one I know would, come to think of it," I add wistfully, pouting and momentarily wishing for more posh friends. We settle into a quick discussion of the new Mazdas, my sister's husband, and a few of the top-secret developments at Toyland. Before hanging up, I promise to drink lots of fluids and pay attention to the weather report so I can dress properly. As if I paid attention to anything *but* the weather report these days.

By three o'clock I'm antsy and anxious and thoroughly sick of daytime TV, with its shiny soap operas and sad-sack ads for people at home during the day. Do you want to get your degree in dog grooming? How about becoming an airplane technician? When I decide that it's too frightening to think about flying when you consider who is watching these ads (or getting your dog groomed, too, I guess, if you're a real dog lover), I turn off the TV. I put on my slippers with the giraffe faces on the toes and scuff around for awhile, pacing the floor in the living room. I don't feel like drawing; that's too much like being at work (and thinking about Sarah's starbaby might bring on another wave of nausea). Too bad I can't play music to unwind like Michael or binge drink for fun like Kerrin.

I grab a piece of Michael's sheet music from our scrap paper pile and flip it over. I start doodling clouds, lightning, the sun, the moon—the mishmash of weather that I've been watching for weeks has made it into my subconscious and is coming out of the pencil point. I make a list of all the types of clouds I remember from my weather unit in high school: nimbus, stratus, altostratus, and cumulus. Inspired by this list of words, I write a little poem. I have experience in poetry—of sorts—from my job at Toyland; all the girls' toys always come with an inane little poem on the back of the package. The problem is that no one can bear to pen them, and by the time the package design had to be sent overseas for production, everyone had passed the buck on being the bard, and the strange responsibility always seemed to fall into my lap. It was usually no more complex than:

I'm little Lottie
With my eyes so blue
I can't wait for you to take me home
So I can play with you!

or

Pretty kitty
To keep in your pocket
She's got her own magic leash
And keepsake locket

or

I'm Fuzzy Bear
With my sweet purple hair
You can comb it, brush it, and dye it, too
What fun things will you do?

Today, though, fueled by gingerroot, soup, and lots of sleep, I feel truly inspired:

Altostratus, cumulus
Clouds I observe once in awhile
But the thing I adore most
Is seeing J.P. Cody's smile.

Nimbus? Stratus?
They all seem light as a feather
But nothing is more sublime
Than watching the morning weather.

I giggle at the ridiculous love poem and fold it up into a tiny little square as I flop onto the couch to watch Oprah. There's some guy on who is talking about how women can get "empowered" and get what they want from relationships. How a man would know this is beyond me. But he's pretty engaging nonetheless, and as he talks, I keep folding and unfolding the piece of sheet music and looking at the poem, reading and rereading until I'm convinced that it's the cleverest and sweetest thing ever.

My poem. Empowerment. How women can get what they want from relationships.

I go upstairs and into Michael's room, tiptoeing over the piles of books and CDs and clothes that litter the floor. I open his closet door and push my way through his tuxedo shirts and weird T-shirts until I get to a tiny shelf all the way in the back. It's so dark that I can't see, so I must feel for the smooth, pebbly surface.

My hand finally lands on it, and I pull it out from the cluttered closet—Michael's old manual typewriter case. It's heavier than I remembered, and when I yank it out, it suddenly gives me the posture of the roadie who was hitting on Kerrin at the Knockout Mouse show. I regain my balance and get a better hold on the handle, shuffling out of his room sideways to avoid smacking into anything.

Downstairs, I open the lid, and the hinges give a little groan. Mr. Clackety Clack sits on the kitchen table in all his plastic, inky glory, the ribbon taut and at attention. This is the name I gave this noisy, beautiful relic when Michael first showed it to me a month after we moved in together. At the time, he insisted he would never refer to his typewriter with such a cutesy name, but I have heard him use it lovingly in unguarded moments. I pull a sheet of typing paper from a yellowing envelope in the lid and marvel at how papery thin and nearly translucent it is. While Oprah grills her guest, I type up my poem—just the eight lines, no more, no less. I finish with a flourish by yanking the page from the roller, and I flop back on the couch to admire my handiwork. The *e* key on Mr. Clackety Clack was acting up, giving the poem a slightly deranged feel. But other than that, it's not so bad, I'm thinking, when I peer outside and see the mailman driving up the street. He is very overweight, and he huffs and puffs as he walks from his mail truck to each doorway to deliver the mail.

I'm looking from the empowerment guy to my ratty bathrobe to Michael's marble collection to my dying ivy plant, when I lunge for the phone book. Just to see if it's there, of course. In between Wollman's Piano Refinishing and WQRY is

WPHX-TV 525 Market Street Phila. 555-2414

Before I can decide to change my mind, I'm running upstairs for an envelope, shoving it into Mr. Clackety Clack, and typing the address and J.P. Cody's name. One hurried folding, licking, and stamping job later, my letter is ready to go. The mailman waddles up our front steps, using his beefy arms to pull himself up the banister. When he reaches the top, I swing open the door.

"Hi. Can you take this?" I ask, waving the letter at him.

"Sure." Perspiration is dripping off his face, even though it's only about fifty degrees outside. He looks me over derisively, starting at my giraffe slippers and ending at my unwashed hair. "Got a stamp on it? 'Cause I can't sell you none."

"Yup, stamped right here." I hand him the letter, but I don't let go of my corner as he tries to take it from me. It becomes a three-second battle of wills, and he finally says exasperatedly, "Lady, you want to send this thing or not?"

"Yes," I say, releasing the letter from my grip. "I do."

*   *   *

When Michael comes home an hour later, I am shaking and sweating and ashen-faced. He looks up from the piece of mail he's reading as he walks in the door and says, "Are you going to . . . whoa! Didn't you feel better? You look terrible."

"I'm a little . . ." I gulp. Since handing over my poem, I have been gripped by an anxiety that is rivaled only by the time I accidentally leaned against our answering machine in college and recorded a mean-spirited conversation my roommates and I were having about another roommate. When she came home to listen to her messages and pressed the Play button in front of us, I finally understood what people meant when they said they wished the floor would open up beneath them.

"You look very anxious," he says, glancing away and spotting the typewriter on the kitchen table. "What's Mr. Clackety Clack doing down here? You know the *e* key has been funny."

"Oh, I had to type something up for work; I thought I'd get a jump on it." This clearly makes no sense, since Michael knows I have a state-of-the-art computer at work, but luckily he has a lesson soon and the clock distracts him.

"Well, I was going to ask you if you minded making yourself scarce during my lesson with Shana," he says. "Her mom might not want her to stay if she sees you all bagged out in your robe and *those*"—he points to my

70

giraffe-face slippers—"and I really need the money. One of my big gigs fell through for this weekend."

"Yeah, sure," I say, dazed. I go upstairs into my room, chewing my nails and wondering what I've done. And wondering what I would have to do with the fat mailman to get my letter back.

Chapter
6

"Hi, Toby!" Will says warmly, holding the door of the gallery open for me. "You look great. Not at all like you were so sick earlier this week. Kerrin told me. I'm so glad you're better, " he finishes earnestly.

He's right; I look better than usual in my black First Friday ensemble because I've lost about four pounds being sick. And I'm wearing lots of makeup, because before I left the house I had the sudden and strange idea that maybe J.P. Cody might go to First Friday sometime. Although ostensibly, I was there to meet Will and Kerrin.

"Yeah, right, modern art. It's just a pile of sticks!" laughs Kerrin, leaving a group of artists and gallery goers laughing, as well. If I said that in front of people like this, I would be burned at the stake. She walks over to where Will and I are standing awkwardly and says, "Well, come on, let's make with the smooch smooch!"

She leans over and kisses Will on the cheek and insists I do the same. When it's my turn, he blushes and turns away, and I can't decide if this is endearing or just plain fey when his cell phone rings, a quick little chirp from his pocket that allows me to exhale again.

Kerrin swoops into the center of the gallery to pick up a generous pile of cheese cubes and beckons me into the far corner. We are standing in front of an incredibly ugly piece of sculpture, something that looks like a cow from Three Mile Island. It has seven legs and three horns, and its udders are almost pornographic. Kerrin is munching on her cheese cubes and staring at the cow and snickering. She then turns to me and smiles that Kerrin kind of smile where you're about to find out something monumental. The eyebrows and corners of the mouth go up, but the teeth don't show.

"I have a date," she announces triumphantly.

"Really? With who? Or is it *whom?*" I live in perpetual fear of Kerrin's keen grammatical ear and editorial eye.

"A second-year resident at CHOP. His name is Len. I met him outside one day at work."

"Len? That sounds like the name of a roofer, not a doctor. What kind of medicine is he studying?" Will is talking animatedly on the phone on the other side of the gallery, and he catches my eye and waves. I timidly wave back.

"You're right—it does sound like a roofer! I think he said urology. I'm quite sure that's pee," she says, chewing noisily. "Anyway, I was on my smoke break at work

73

and he stopped to smoke there, too. I think he is from Maryland or Virginia, way down south."

We've been drifting around the gallery as she's been speaking, and we are in front of a large, abstract painting that appears to have been painted with coffee grounds. "Kerrin, Maryland and Virginia aren't 'way down south.' We're two states away from Maryland right now."

She ignores the geography lesson. "Also he has that tooth thing that I like, you know where a person has a big space between his two front teeth? When he smiled, I didn't know whether to smile back or try to kick a ball in for a goal. I told him so, too."

I'm picturing Kerrin and this white-coated cutie grinning at each other, the cigarette smoke streaming from their nostrils. I have always thought it somehow reassuring that some doctors smoke; it's a testament to the strange language of addiction and how a person can be intelligent in one way and thick as a board in another. Although she isn't a doctor, Kerrin speaks the language of addiction quite fluently, albeit with an English accent—she insists on smoking Dunhills.

"Anyway, so he seems cool, for now," she says, pouring herself a glass of cheap wine. We've ended up in the center of the room again, where people are standing in small groups and murmuring in hushed tones about the art. "This place is dead," she declares, throwing back her wine in one swallow. "There's some Doors cover band performing down the street at Ozone Gallery. Let's go there."

"What about Will?" I ask. "He's still on the phone over there." I point to the corner where Will is standing.

"What *about* Will? I thought you were holding out for a local TV personality," she teases, with the tiniest hint of malice in the edges of her voice.

"I just think it might be rude to leave without him, if he's supposed to be part of our evening's plan. And I don't like the Doors, remember?" I ignore her comment about J.P. Cody, although it stings. Will strides over to us, claps his hands together, and begins talking about the new artist they are planning to show who paints exclusively while riding around in cabs.

"Will," I interrupt him while trying to look demure, "can I borrow your phone for a minute?" He and Kerrin both look surprised, but he hands the phone over and I walk about two feet away to call Michael.

"Who are you calling?" Kerrin asks.

"Michael. He'll know about the pee thing for sure." I was calling partly to satisfy my own curiosity but also to get back at Kerrin for making that comment about J.P. Cody. There was no network show on Thursday nights with adorable doctors called *Urology*, was there? Urology, indeed. "I'm not sure if he's there," I say as the phone rings for the third time.

"Of course he's there. He's probably by himself, jerking off, like every other night," she snorts, making Will blush again. It's so unsettling to see a boy blush, I decide, just as Michael picks up.

"Michael! I'm on a cell phone!" I shout into the phone.

I'm unfamiliar with cell phone etiquette, and it shows; a group of well-heeled people turn and stare as I yell.

"Toby, this isn't like two cans and a piece of string. You don't have to yell. Are you OK? Where are you?"

"I'm at First Friday. Kerrin has a date with a urology resident. Is that pee?" I ask urgently.

"Yes. Where is he doing his residency?"

"CHOP, I think."

"Ugh, that's worse than pee. CHOP is *Children's* Hospital of Philadelphia. That's kiddie pee!"

"Ewww," I say, realizing I got more than I bargained for.

"Well, tell her not to let him get away until she gets you those pharmaceutical giveaways you love," he says, referring to the little pads and Post-its and pens and highlighters and mouse pads and toys that are imprinted with scary-sounding names like Zivocor 200mg or Metaron 500 or Claratex QT. I love it when Michael's parents go to surgical conferences and send me their stashes of tiny, weird drug company trinkets. One of my most memorable Christmas gifts was a stocking filled to bursting with these items, from the ulcer medicine flashlight at the top to the tiny wind-up elephant whose trunk was emblazoned with the name of a new mood drug stuffed in the toe. Elevar, I think it was.

By the time we get done talking, Kerrin and Will are already outside, and I've been outvoted on the Doors show. I hope my stomach holds up. Who knows, maybe J.P. Cody is a Doors fan. I hope not, though.

*   *   *

"Toby? I know you're not there, but I don't have your number at work. I don't know what happened to it. Perhaps it's here in my other file? *(pause, sound of shuffling papers)* Sorry . . . anyway, if you get this message, I won tickets to see the Flyers tonight. In the WPHX skybox, of all places. I didn't do anything to *win*, it was more of a raffle. But I can't think of anyone who would want to go more than you, so please, please if you get this, come to the *(beeeeeep)* . . . Sorry, me again, I'm talking too long. So please come to the Spectrum right after work and I'll meet you at the Will Call window. I hope you can make it. One of the sound engineers here told me that some Flyer just got over his groin injury and that the 'legion of doom' is back in full force, whatever that means. I'm sure you'll tell me. So I'll see you later, I hope. Oh, and I can give you that picture of you-know-who!"

When I hear Jenna's message, a slow smile spreads across my face, although hearing her say "Will Call" reminds me that I'm supposed to call Will, who wants to get us tickets for the Nutcracker. But a hockey game is just what I need these days. It is perfect for my mood, to help me vicariously vent some anguish about what I silently call The Lisa Carlton Conundrum.

After an uneventful day at work last week, I leaped up the front steps of our house, looking forward to regaling Michael with tales of the meeting I had attended that morning. Rod Winters wanted to make a point to Patty from marketing about a playset's plastic roof that he felt was too sharp. She contended it wasn't. He snarled, "You're four years old. You're running after your brother. You trip over the dog and fall on this, breaking the fall with your hand." With that, he grabbed her arm and pressed the flesh of her palm into the piece in question. She yelped and looked at her palm, which bore the imprint of the roof. I was giggling to myself, reliving the scene, when I opened the door and saw it from the back, seated at the kitchen table.

The bun with the scrunchie. The high turtleneck. It could only be Lisa Carlton.

Lisa Carlton was Michael's girlfriend when he and I moved in together; a girl with small, catlike features and eyes that seemed permanently narrowed in suspicion. She had thin lips that she liked to press together when I talked to her, making her look meaner than usual. Her hair was honey-colored and possibly very pretty, but every time I had seen her, it was pulled back in a severe, tight bun with a color-coordinated scrunchie that matched her turtleneck.

Michael met Lisa while shopping downtown for some pants. At the time, she was a salesgirl at a men's clothing store chain, cooing over customers and making commissions by exploiting the fact that most guys are pretty clueless when it comes to matching clothes. She complimented Michael on a shirt he was wearing at the time, and because he is insecure about his musician's rags that barely pass for clothes, he found this enchanting. They dated for almost a year, but she and I took an instant disliking to each other from the moment we met. It wasn't that I disapproved of Michael having a girlfriend; Marisa, the cellist who came after Lisa, seemed really nice to me, and the other objects of his affections never troubled me all that much.

But Lisa was something different because she brought out the worst in Michael. She encouraged his hypochondria by willingly sticking a thermometer in his mouth. She infuriated him by acting sweet and vulnerable one day, then coy the next. She insisted on listening to Top 40 radio and singing in her grating, nasal voice, even though she knew that with *very* few exceptions, Michael hates any piece of music written after the 1890s. They would spend entire weekends together and she'd make him hyper and irritable, then send him home to me, where I would have to listen to him drone on about her. Once during one of their fights, she smacked his knuckles with a book, knowing full well that Michael is so sensitive about protecting his clarinetist's hands that he developed a nervous habit of holding them under his armpits when he's in big crowds. The day he came home with bruised knuckles was the day I decided I could never, ever like Lisa Carlton.

When they finally broke up, it took four tries to make it stick, because he kept crawling back to her. "Just this last time," he would say to me, zipping up his coat and heading out in the dead of winter to try and reconcile with her once again. I told him he sounded like an alcoholic.

So it was an unpleasant surprise to see the back of Lisa Carlton's head as I entered the house that day. As I got closer, I heard the unmistakable sound of squeaky springs and brittle plastic and knew that she and Michael were playing with my vintage Rock 'Em Sock 'Em Robots. It had been a gift from a gentle, avuncular VP at Toyland who once said I reminded him of his daughter, "before she got in with that cult, God bless her." I kept it in my room and played with it gingerly, allowing Michael to play with it sometimes, but only after receiving permission. I came into the room just in time to see Lisa knocking Michael's block off. Just like old times, I thought. Michael looked sheepish; he knew he'd been caught on two fronts. One, he wasn't supposed to play with my toys without asking, especially when his playmate was a bitch I hated. And two, well, there was the issue of the bitch I hated. I sighed and stomped from the room.

I check the newspaper on the secretary's desk and see that we're hosting the Rangers tonight. Even better! Jenna's invite couldn't have come at a better time. I want to see some blood.

Jenna is bundled into a tan, puffy, quilted coat that makes her look a bit like a pineapple, peering around as she stands beneath the Will Call window. She does a little jig when she sees me.

"Toby! I'm so glad you got my message. I knew you'd want to come," she says gaily.

"Of course! I've never been in a skybox before. Also, I never turn down the chance to see guys beat the stuffing out of one another, skybox or no skybox," I say, watching all the beery Flyers fans streaming by in their jerseys.

Up in the skybox, I size up the sumptuous spread of hors d'oeuvres in front of us, while Jenna opens up a square leather case. "Binoculars," she says, seeing my strange expression while she's fumbling with the tricky locks on the case. "They were my grandfather's; I figured this would be a good place to use them."

We settle down in the front row, Jenna's plate piled high with fresh vegetables and dip; mine with buffalo wings and a beer between my feet. Except for three teen boys who are meandering around the box, it's just the two of us. Jenna groans when I tell her about seeing Lisa Carlton in my house a week earlier. "Was she the salesgirl? Or the musician?"

"Salesgirl. Well, now she's been promoted to store manager, or so Michael tells me." Over these last few nights, he's been filling me in on what is happening with Lisa. Each time he talks about her, I get a headache right in the center of my forehead, the same kind I get when I enter the paint booth at Toyland's model shop. "I don't even like to think about it, to tell you the truth. That's why your invite really came at the right time, Jenna—thinking about them getting back together puts me in the right mood for some needless violence."

"Then I think you should take these," she says, handing me the binoculars. A big fight is breaking out, and I put the binoculars up to my eyes just in time to see Brian Leetch touching his gloved fingertip to his nose, pulling it away, and looking at it with the wonderment of a baby studying a flower. The blood shines red and glimmery on his beat-up blue and white glove, and in a split second, he is pummeling Eric Lindros and the crowd is on its feet.

When the game ends, the Flyers have lost 3-2 and Jenna is very apologetic. "I'm so sorry, I'm sure this isn't good for your mood," she says sadly, shaking her head and looking down at the Zamboni on the vast expanse of empty ice. I assure her that I enjoyed myself immensely and ate much better than I would have in my own kitchen, had I eaten in my kitchen at all—I think Michael is having Lisa over tonight to have dinner and "talk." This would have undoubtedly meant I would have been holed up in my room with a bowl of Apple Jacks and back issues of shiny car magazines.

"Oh, and here," she says lovingly as I get in line for the bus. "I promised you this," she smiles as she hands me a manila envelope.

Chapter
7

"Not one question, Michael. Got that? *Not a one.*"

Kerrin is standing in the center of my room with her hands on her hips and her feet splayed. She has had three dates with Len and has decided that it's time for him to Meet the Friends. Well, me, especially, which is flattering. Michael is coming along because another one of his gigs was cancelled and Lisa Carlton is at a marketing seminar at her company's headquarters in Columbus, Ohio, and he's got nothing to do. Kerrin also thinks it might be good to observe Len interacting with other men. I personally don't think that art boys should mix with science boys, because the art boys get intimidated by the science boys' arrogance, and the science boys get creeped out (but I think may also be secretly fascinated) by the art boys' creativity. But Kerrin has made up her mind, so I know to keep quiet. She's taking this moment to make sure Michael doesn't ask Len health-related questions. When she came in, I told her in a whisper that Michael's getting back with Lisa could only mean a marked increase in hypochondria for him, so she should cover her bases.

"So, strange swellings, weird coughs, a rash that looks like Australia—he doesn't want to hear about or see *any* of it. Got that?" Michael nods yes and sits down on the floor next to my bed.

"OK, then. Now for some party shoes." She flings open my closet door and studies my shoes. Although I don't share many physical attributes with Kerrin, we do have the same shoe size. Unfortunately, she always gets the better end of the deal. My tastes don't ever seem to run to her Doc Martens and weird boots, whereas she is a shoe chameleon and loves shedding her normal footwear on a night out for a pair of my groovy platforms or sparkly sandals.

She stares into the depths of my closet as I suddenly remember what's in there. "Kerrin," I say hurriedly, "I want to find shoes first. Can I look?"

"Yeah, sure," she shrugs, stepping back and turning around to face my CD player. She sifts through my CDs and puts on David Bowie, smiling evilly at Michael.

I practically dive into the closet, where I unearth the cardboard box that contains the smaller cardboard box that contains the brown envelope that contains the manila envelope that contains the picture of J.P. Cody. Whew. I just wanted to make sure I had remembered to put it away after looking at it the other day. I keep it hidden—partly because I'm still not ready for Michael to know about it, and partly because I don't want to wear it out. I thought if it was up on the wall in my room or at work, I'd get too used to it, like wallpaper or a longtime spouse. It is a fantastic picture, a close-up shot, all smiley with his beautiful eyes dancing. The only thing I objected to and nearly laughed out loud about when I first looked at it on the bus was his hair. It looks like a helmet and had obviously been shellacked with quarts of hairspray. Poor guy, I thought; I wouldn't mind washing his hair to get it all out.

Satisfied that my picture is well hidden and that I won't out myself as a weatherman fan to Michael, I lie on my stomach and settle on a pair of shoes. Kerrin is fast-forwarding her way through the CD, stopping at her favorite songs and making Michael wince at the synthesizer and electric guitars. When I hear David Bowie growl in "Ashes to Ashes" about Major Tom having become a junkie, it reminds me of something my mother said when I told her that Kerrin is dating a med student. "Hey, Kerrin," I say, my voice muffled from the bottom of my closet, "my mom said that her friend's daughter was going out with a med student, and he pricked her full of holes. To practice drawing blood, I mean. He was so bad at it that he had to practice for months and left her looking like a junkie, all bruised and icky."

"Well, I think it might be a little late in the game for that; I would think he's done that already," she answers airily. "But," she adds, brightening, "then they would *really* think I'm on drugs at work. That would be *great* if they thought I was a dope fiend! Even better than now, where they think I'm just a fat-ass alcoholic. Oh, I can see your underwear."

It's true; my skirt hitched up a bit and you could just see my underwear, the ones with the little Volkswagen Beetles all over them. "Kerrin, please," I say with mock modesty, "we're in mixed company here."

"Yeah, right, you know Michael's more like a girl than we are," she sneers. "Look at him now, he's playing with stuffed animals."

I sit up on my knees to get a better look and she's right; Michael moved to my bed and is holding my Secret Wish Horse, a pink, fluffy, four-legged confection that Toyland released two years ago to tepid sales. I liked it because of its doleful eyes—like the toy itself almost knew it was destined to be a loser on the shelves. Michael throws the horse back onto my bed when he sees me and Kerrin staring at him, and busies himself by pretending to select an art book from the shelf next to my window. He chooses a slim photography book and flips through it.

"Should I wear these jeans?" I ask Kerrin, pulling them off my bed. "They're a bit wrinkly," I add. "Maybe I should iron them."

"Of course not. You want to be seen as the kind of person who worries about whether or not she's got wrinkly jeans?"

I'm puzzled by this logic but don't have the time to

discuss it, so I settle on my black, fuzzy jumper with the pink T-shirt underneath. Kerrin, who is always unconcerned about her looks, freshens up by donning a pair of my black boots and putting on lipstick without a mirror.

About twenty minutes later, we're walking to meet Len at The Guilty Bystander, a neighborhood bar that has one of its sides on a gentrified block and another of its sides on a seedy block. This assures a mixed and often confused clientele, which I like. Kerrin likes this bar because you can smoke and no one will give you dirty looks or make choking noises. Len is standing outside with his fists jammed in his pockets, pacing and looking at the ground. He looks very serious. "I wonder what he's thinking about," I whisper to Michael as Kerrin sashays three feet in front of us. "I *told* you before, Toby, kiddie pee," is what he hisses back.

When we get closer, Len looks up and gives us a gap-toothed smile. He has inky black hair and inky black spots for eyes, and he is very pale and tall and exactly Kerrin's type. He is skinny, not to the point where he looks unmanly, but just enough that you want to sit him down and cook him an omelet. When we reach the door, he bends down to kiss Kerrin on the head, but a poster in the window catches her attention; she turns her head at exactly the wrong moment and he winds up with a mouthful of her knotted hair. He laughs it off, which I take as a good sign.

Inside is dark and smoky, with locals from Philly's

more depressed streets bellying up to the bar alongside their better-off neighbors. There is a TV on with the sound turned down, and even though it's hours since J.P. Cody's been on, I can't help but turn my eyes toward it. A beer materializes from somewhere and I take a long swig, wondering where J.P. is right now and what he might be doing. Maybe out looking for a meteor shower? Playing host to an old girlfriend from the Midwest (I hope not)? Or at home in Delaware, wondering where, oh where, is the person who is sending him love poems? I think for a minute about J.P. Cody lying on his back, one arm bent with his hand behind his head, puzzling over the pieces of typing paper in his other hand. Kerrin interrupts my thoughts with a loud voice. "Isn't that right, Toby? This trough here is so men wouldn't have to get up to the bathroom. Len doesn't believe me." She reaches around Len and points to the metal trough that runs the length of the bar, level with our feet.

"That's what I've been told," I say politely. "This bar only used to be for men, so they had this feature. Now there are bathrooms, of course," I add as an afterthought.

"Well, he knows that, duh. He wasn't going to go *here*, Toby," Kerrin says, cocking her head at me and smiling.

"See, it's all about pee," Michael whispers to me on the other side.

"What is he saying to you now?" Kerrin asks sharply. Len looks positively mystified but also amused at the volley of conversation on either side of him, turning his head to and fro like he's courtside at Wimbledon. When he suggests we all get a table, Kerrin vetoes his idea, preferring instead to switch places with Michael, so she can talk to me. Michael reluctantly agrees, and he and Kerrin hop down off their stools. Kerrin buys everyone another round of drinks, settles onto her new barstool, and asks me how I'm doing with my Christmas shopping. Surprising question, I think before answering. Kerrin rarely questions me about anything as mundane as holiday shopping.

"Well, it's only the beginning of December, so I guess I have—" Kerrin cuts me off before I can finish, leaning into me with a funny smile.

"So check *this* out. Here's an idea for ya'," she says, warming up. "I'm walking out to meet Len for a smoke"—as she says his name, she waves over to him, and he smiles back, that funny snaggle-toothed smile— "and I'm waiting for the elevator with this guy I work with. He tells me that I should do what he did for Christmas gifts this year and donate money for renewable resources. Do you know what this means, Toby?" she asks, wide-eyed and open mouthed. I shake my head no, draining my beer bottle.

"It means you donate money to this organization where they send an animal to some poor people in a horrible Third World country. Oh wait, what did Carl call it? 'A developing nation,' that's it. Not a 'Third World country,' like a normal person would say. So a family learns how to pluck and eat a chicken or scale a fish or become beekeepers or something, and he says that's why it's a 'renewable resource'—so these people can show their neighbors and family members how to do this shit." She reaches across me to light Len's cigarette, the match warming my already glowing face.

"Have you ever heard of anything so ridiculous in your life?" She lights her own cigarette, inhales deeply, and shakes her head at the thought of it. "He's like, 'I got my dad shares in a goat for Christmas—it's too expensive to buy a goat all by yourself, so you buy shares.' And I said, 'And to think I was only going to get my dad a sweater from the Gap!' " She throws her head back, laughing, and wipes tears from her eyes. "Those tree-hugging losers. When will they learn? And I can bet you that the money isn't going to poor people in Guatemala or wherever. Whoever is running this business is getting rich as hell, and these poor people are standing around, wondering where their bees or goats or whatever-the-fuck animal is supposed to be."

I'm giggling now too, embarrassed at laughing at such holiday altruism, but I can't help it. The warmth from the beer is rapidly spreading from my face to the rest of my body, and all of a sudden, everything seems funny. I turn to see Michael and Len talking animatedly; Len's back is to me so I can't see his expression, but Michael's face is lit up and he's almost smiling. So I guess art and science do mix, I'm thinking when Kerrin announces she's going to the bathroom. "But not in this trough," she adds before sliding off her barstool and trotting up a comically steep and narrow flight of stairs to the bath-room. I've seen more than one drunken person fly down these stairs in Saturday-morning-cartoon style, with their heads hitting each and every step on the way and their limbs flailing in every direction. I hope that none of us will be a casualty tonight, although I do feel a tiny bit safer with Len here.

I prop my head in my hands and eavesdrop on Len and Michael's conversation. It appears that they both have the same all-time favorite car-chase movie scene, the one in the end of the original swinging '60s version of *The Italian Job*. I see this all the time when I sit in on kids' focus groups at Toyland: two kids like the same thing, and it's the beginning of a friendship. One girl will remark casually to another that she used to wear pony-tails but now she likes braids and the second girl will say, "Ooh, I love braids, too!" Or two little boys will both discover that the blue die-cast car with the neon-orange racing stripe and the magnet action is their favorite, and before you know it, their mothers are setting up a play-date after the focus group is over. I grow wistful when I watch this happen—if only your favorite flavor of Pixy Stix or your love of ponies was enough to help you find your soul mate, adults would have a much easier time of it in this world.

Luckily for Len and Michael, they haven't lost this boyhood quality, and they are eagerly making future plans to drive their cars down the front steps of the art museum just like in the movie's final loopy scene. I lean over and remind them that it won't be quite the same with a scrappy, battered Honda Civic and a, a— what kind of car do you have, Len? Oh, your sister's Neon; I'm sorry, that's a terrible car—a Dodge Neon. Len, who is still in that being-polite-to-the-best-friend-of-the-girlfriend phase says, "Perhaps you're right." But Michael reaches across Len to punch me in the arm and tells me to shut up. Blasphemy, I think. A purist would figure out how to find vintage Minis and do it properly.

Kerrin comes back from the bathroom and decides she's had enough of the beer and that we should take the leap to hard liquor. Len orders us the first round and from there, it's a blur.

My Snoopy phone is ringing over and over, and although I am trying to will myself to answer it, I just can't do it. Five rings, six rings, seven. I am lying facedown on the floor of my bedroom, still wearing my black jumper and pink T-shirt. My door is open and so is Michael's; if I prop myself up on my elbow, I can see him in his bed, with his tousled hair sticking out from the covers and his skinny arm trailing on the ground.

Nine rings, ten rings, eleven. "OK!" I yell, my voice hoarse from shouting and secondhand smoke. I sit up too quickly and the room starts to spin a bit, so I squeeze my eyes shut and slowly and carefully drag myself over to the phone.

"Hello?" I say quietly while looking at the clock. It's eleven o'clock.

"Good morning, starshine!" Kerrin says pleasantly. Her voice cuts through my head like a piece of sheet metal. "How are you today?" she continues in a singsong voice. I'm so shocked that she's calling me before noon that I don't know what to say. That, and I am suddenly so overcome by a wave of nausea that I'm afraid if I do open my mouth, I may throw up. I hear Michael groan from across the hall, and I crane my neck to see into his room; he's now got the covers pulled over his head and is whimpering pathetically.

"I . . . I'm all right," I croak into the phone while rolling my eyes at Michael's fragile constitution. "What's up? Are you all right?"

"Ooh, I'm great! We stayed out drinking even longer than you two. But this morning, Len gave me some IV fluids and my hangover is almost gone. It's amazing, Toby, honest."

"*What?* That sounds horrible. And probably illegal." I'm sitting up now, looking in my night table drawer for the bottle of aspirin that I know is in there somewhere. "And why didn't you ask me if I wanted to do it? I got just as drunk as you, I think."

"I don't know," she says distractedly. "We just got up this morning and it seemed like a good idea."

"Wait," I say. "So he stayed over?" I ask, looking in the hand mirror that I found in the drawer. My eyes are ringed with mascara.

"Uh-huh! Hard, hot, and a helluvalot!" she gloats.

"Blecch," I respond. "You don't have to tell me in that much detail, you know."

"Maybe you're just jealous because one of us is getting busy. Oh, hold on, dude, I'll come with you! Sorry, Toby, I was talking to Len. We have to go buy smokes."

"You mean he's *there?*" I ask incredulously. "Look, I have to go," I say, irritated. This was just too much, Kerrin getting to sleep with a cute guy who can also cure her hangover.

"Yeah, OK," she says dreamily, deaf to the snippiness in my voice. "Oh, one more thing! You were so funny last night! Do you remember talking about poetry?"

The last thing I remembered was the fruity sting of a vodka madras going down my throat.

"It was so funny! Something about you sending anonymous love poems to that weatherman you like. Cody, or something like that? Yeah, I remember now. You kept blaming Oprah Winfrey. You kill me, Toby!"

She hangs up and I feel a zing go through my chest, a feeling not unlike the electric shock I received earlier this week at work. Joe was working on Slobberin' Sam, the drooling dog for the preschool line, and he wanted someone to test the tongue mechanism. Apparently there were some kinks to be worked out with the drooling and its vicinity to the battery pack. He and Caroline brought it to me, and when I bravely grabbed the tongue, I promptly felt a hot zing travel at light speed from my pinky up to my wrist. I yelped and threw the dog down—more out of surprise than pain or fear—and Caroline's eyes grew round with terror, while Joe clamped his hand to his mouth to keep from howling with laughter. He felt so bad that he bought me an ice-cream sandwich the next day.

This zing is exactly the same, ripping through my front and leaving me breathless, scared, and surprised. By now, Michael has risen and put on a pair of sweat-pants and is standing in my doorway with his eyes closed, frowning and massaging his temples. His hair is matted on one side, and his face is lined with the wrin-kles of his pillowcase. He finally opens his eyes and croaks, "Nice eye makeup. Who was that?"

"Kerrin. Listen to this: Len put her on an IV this morn-ing, and her hangover is all gone already."

"That is repulsive. And it may be against the law, too. How come we weren't offered this service?" he asks in-dignantly, scratching the stubble on his chin.

"I dunno," I answer, fiddling with the ties on the shoulders of my jumper. I take a deep breath to ready myself. "Michael? Do you remember anything last night about poetry? Anything I said?" I try to sound noncom-mittal enough, but my voice is coming out pinched and squeaky.

He stands there for what seems like five years, think-ing and looking up at the ceiling. "Yes," he says slowly. "Yes, I do. What was it?" My stomach is in knots and I'm kneading my Secret Wish Horse, waiting for him to continue.

"Oh, yeah! That's it—you were saying that you sent a

love poem to some weatherman. Something Cody, was it? Oh, God, Toby, if you ever did anything like that, I would really think you had gone off the deep end," he says, crossing his arms in front of his chest. "I mean, a weatherman is bad enough. But sending a love poem— stalking him—that would really be something!"

"Well, you'd better sit down, then, I guess," I sigh, drawing my knees to my chest.

Chapter 8

I am practically pirouetting as I make my way down Walnut Street, singing to myself as the wind takes the end of my striped scarf and flips it into the face of an unsuspecting old man walking in the other direction. The business card of a delightful boy named Alec sits warm in my coat pocket, and I can't wait to get home so I can produce it as evidence—to prove to Michael that his recent accusation that I am living in a fantasy world is unfounded.

I had been standing in the classical music section at HMV, chewing on my bottom lip and poring over Michael's Christmas wish list. The December *Car & Driver* was poking out from under my left armpit, the one with the plucky, new Mitsubishis on the cover, and I clutched a Velvet Underground CD for Kerrin in my right hand. Just as I ungloved my left hand to reach for *Handel-Halvorsen's Passacaglia for Two Violins*, I heard someone behind me say, "Oh, a real Renaissance woman—classical music and car magazines." I whipped around to find myself face-to-face with a skinny, blond-haired guy with a ready smile and the lightest sprinkling of freckles across the bridge of his nose. He introduced himself and I told him my name, but not after making sure he knew that the CD was for my roommate, not for me. I didn't want to misrepresent myself as *that* much of a Renaissance woman.

Fortunately this didn't deter him one bit, and after talking for a few minutes, he asked if he could call me. I made a mess trying to pull out my business card, scattering my gloves, CDs, scarf, and magazine all over the tiled floor in the process, but when I finally did, it was worth it. "Ooh, toys," he said, his eyebrows jumping up so high they were in danger of grazing the Mozart display over our heads. One thing was for sure: Even though I often felt certain that Toyland would land me at the doctor's office with a bleeding ulcer before age thirty, I could put money on the fact that my career choice made any potential guy even more interested. Whether they thought they would have the chance to clamor onto the floor to play with race cars or miniature eighteen-wheelers by going out with me, I don't know. Unfortunately, I hadn't yet had the occasion to get to know anyone well enough to ask. In any case, in a bold move, I ended up asking for his card as well. You never know, I thought.

It isn't that I really have anything to prove, I think as

I sit on the bus, flipping through *Car & Driver* but not actually looking at any of the pictures or reading a single word. Instead, I'm thinking about when I told Michael about my poems to J.P. Cody, the morning after our night out with Kerrin and Len. At first he couldn't believe it, shaking his head violently as if doing so would somehow help him understand better. Then he changed tactics, looking at me carefully out of the corners of his eyes as if I were our former neighbor Leon, a gentle sort whom the health care system had failed in the early '90s. He was fine when he took his medication, but when he didn't he remained utterly convinced that the mayor of Philadelphia was poisoning the water supply. I hollered at Michael, asking him not to look at me like I was crazy, but he just sat there and looked at me curiously. Finally he said haltingly, "Doesn't your life have enough excitement? Don't you think stalking a weatherman is just a little . . . over the top, maybe?"

"I don't know," I stammered, staring at myself again in the hand mirror. My reflection surprised me that morning because I suddenly looked so forlorn.

"Michael, when I think of excitement, I think of how I got the cost down for the Fingernail Frenzy nail decal sheet or how the twins' guinea pig down the street had a new litter. Or . . ."—I looked around the room in a panic, seeking excitement within the butter-yellow walls—"I think of how I organized my sweaters in my closet. It's pretty sad. So yes, maybe that's it. A bit of excitement, and with any luck . . ." I trailed off and Michael looked at me then, his mouth twisting into a smile that he was doing his damnedest to hide.

"Well, leave it to you, Toby. Most people take up bread-baking or enroll in adult school when they're bored." But then he suddenly became serious and haughty, his tone taking me by surprise. "But I still don't think it's such a hot idea. I'm just not so sure that living in a fantasy world is all that good for you in the long run—it's a little silly, know what I mean?" he asked, looking at me with an expression that suggested the question was rhetorical. I shook my head then, just as I am shaking it now, marveling at once at the new Mitsubishi and how Michael can know me so well in some ways and so little in others. Fantasy world, no. A little excitement, yes. A little excitement is all a girl like me needs. And the new Mitsubishi, of course.

Wind chill
What a thrill
Record lows prevail

But J.P.'s weather
Leaves me light as a feather
And cheery without fail

I'm sitting on the floor before work with my legs tucked underneath me, watching the morning weather and penning my latest poem. J.P. looks a little tired lately, to tell the truth—he's mentioned more than once on the air that he just can't shake this winter cold that's been going around the station. I make a little mental note to ask Kerrin to ask Len if this could mean there is something really wrong with him. Perhaps I could use one of my poems to suggest some kind of treatment for the poor dear. Then I worry a bit, biting on my eraser as I wonder what rhymes with *bloodwork*, and I know I should really be focusing on the task at hand.

I'm vaguely dissatisfied with today's poem, and I'm sure I know why; it's hard to concentrate with Lisa Carlton cleaning the kitchen at seven forty-five in the morning. She has inexplicably decided that our kitchen countertops have to be cleaned *right now,* and she is furiously scrubbing with all her might, with the water rushing out of both taps and hissing into the sink. Michael is on the phone to a friend in New York who is supposed to get him tickets to a performance, but rather than ask his scrunchie-wearing sweetie to turn the water off, he has stretched the phone cord to its limit and is tucked behind the basement door. Between the water and Lisa's off-key caterwauling to the kitchen radio (she's moved the dial from Michael's beloved NPR, an offense punishable by death if anyone else were the guilty party) and J.P.'s hoarse voice, I can barely hear him as he does the weather.

I turn the poem over—I'm not ready for Lisa Carlton to know about my fan club of one, and although I didn't specifically ask Michael not to tell her, I'm sure he understood that I wanted to keep it under wraps—and walk around the table into the kitchen. Lisa is rubbing the countertop with what appears to be a white rag, but then I notice what looks like those little unmistakable black curvy lines that comic strip artists use to illustrate movement, like when a character is jumping or falling or has a brick bouncing off his head. Or dancing: These lines look remarkably like the ones that Charles Schulz used around Snoopy's feet when the irrepressible pooch danced on Schroeder's piano. I squint to get a better look, and when Lisa sees me she straightens up, tilts her head, puts one hand on her hip, and gives me the most nauseatingly fake smile I've ever seen, save the one from my fifth grade Brownie Troop leader who thought I was the kid stealing her makeup (it was really her own kid, we all found out later). Lisa reworks the rag into a different shape, searching for a clean spot, and then I see it for sure—Schroeder's blond hair and his stubby hand and a tiny slice of the piano and the edge of Snoopy's foot. Not a rag at all, in other words, but the T-shirt I gave Michael last year for his birthday.

I open my mouth, and at just that moment, Michael pops open the basement door and puts the phone back on the wall.

"Michael," I ask dejectedly, "why is she using the T-shirt I gave you as a rag?" Michael looks from the T-shirt to me to Lisa, who is standing as smug and sly as the day she first walked into this place. "I didn't know," she says curtly, throwing the balled-up shirt into a heap in the sink. I stare angrily at Michael, who is expressionless and looking at the floor, and stomp back to the TV set where I'm lucky to at least catch the few final seconds of the weather report and J.P. Cody's winning grin. And Michael questions why someone might find living in a fantasy world appealing.

The two of them begin talking in hushed voices at the table, and I snap off the TV and busy myself by getting my coat and boots on, all the while wishing Lisa would march out in a huff and never come back. I also decide to set the metronome in motion—Michael's old spare never made it back upstairs to the studio after I was sick, and a sprightly tempo at this early hour will surely drive Lisa up the wall, I decide evilly as I slide the weight down the pendulum. Yes, 175 beats per minute sounds just about right for this morning. Now Michael is telling Lisa that he is going into New York City this evening for a performance at Carnegie Hall and that he'd love her to come when she's done with her shift at the clothing store. She is getting audibly irritated at the idea of making her way into New York alone, without Michael to guide her through 30th Street Station, and they start to argue when I hear Rich's horn outside. I'm hoisting my bag onto my shoulder and opening the door when she sputters, "How do I get to Carnegie Hall?"

I can't resist, and I scream, *"Practice,"* grateful for the opportunity to vent some of my anger under the guise of Catskills-era comedy. To my utter surprise, Michael says the exact same thing at the exact same moment, albeit without the angry tone. I snap my head up and Michael looks over at me, the two of us grinning moronically at each other as Lisa fumes. I dash out the door and into Rich's car, breathing a sigh of relief that I was able to get the last word in with Lisa Carlton. And a funny one, too, which I'm sure must be worth extra points.

"Tsk, tsk," says Kerrin ruefully, shaking her head and bending over to press her face to the long glass case. "If she only knew she was going to end up here."

It is a windy Saturday afternoon and we are at the Mütter Museum, across the river near University of Pennsylvania. The museum is run by the College of Physicians of Philadelphia and houses a large, eclectic, gruesome, and fascinating collection of medical oddities. Dusty skulls from every corner of the globe. An elaborately curated history of Siamese twins, complete with exceedingly detailed photos. And the Soap Lady, who is the current object of Kerrin's fascination.

Kerrin's long hair is now trailing over the glass as she contorts her torso to get an even better look. For better or worse, I am already familiar with the Soap Lady, who was buried in Germany in the 1700s in soil so rich in lime that it actually turned her body into something quite like soap. The museum was one of the few places that The Head Wound would venture out of his apartment to visit, so I had already had the pleasure of wandering the dark halls and trying to determine when I should cover my eyes and when I should go ahead and look. I am comfortable in the Soap Lady's presence today; the last time we met, the room started to turn on end and I had to grab onto the nearby railing to steady myself.

"I wonder what kind of soap I would turn into," Kerrin muses. "I guess Ivory. Nothing too fancy for me." She pats the glass lovingly as she turns away from the case.

"Why are we here again?" I ask wearily. I've already glanced in one place that I know I shouldn't have—the pig fetuses at all the different stages, pink and squishy—and I'm starting to feel queasy.

"I told you. I'm trying to get involved in Len's interests. He said that we always do stuff that *I* want to do, and I asked him where he thinks is a cool place to go. He said here. So I thought I'd come here and check it out, hit the gift shop and pick him up something."

Well, I've got to hand it to Kerrin; I don't know any other girls who would do their boyfriend's Christmas shopping at the Mütter Museum. "I think you two make a good couple," I say as we make our way to the wall of skulls.

"So what about you? Did that guy from the record store ever call you?"

"No," I answer, my voice catching in my throat. "It's been a week now, so I don't think it's going to happen."

"It's not," Kerrin agrees bluntly. "Shit, what the hell is wrong with these guys? I hate that. How about Will?"

I was dreading this question, because I'd eventually begged off going to The Nutcracker with Will and prayed that it hadn't gotten back to Kerrin. I'd honestly wanted to see the show, it had just been the thought of all that tulle and Will in the same place that had repelled me.

"No, I just don't think it's meant to be with Will," I say carefully as we head down the winding, majestic dark oak staircase. I can feel a trickle of sweat on my face, and I stop to take off my coat. Kerrin follows suit, and after shimmying out of her grandfather's old pea coat, she hikes up the sleeve of her sweater to show me all the green-gray bruises on her arm.

"Check it out," she says proudly. "Len said he was never very good at getting blood, so he would be happy to practice on me. Remember, it was your idea?"

"It wasn't my idea," I say defensively. The sight of her arm is upsetting me more than the Soap Lady did, and a few other museumgoers cast anguished looks at her arm as they pass us on the landing. "I just told you what my mom said. You really shouldn't parade that around at work or whatever, they really will think something is up."

"Yeah, right! I'm too fat to be a junkie; everyone knows that. Oh, my God! That's gotta be one hell of a stomachache, huh?" We've stopped in front of the tall, imposing megacolon display, complete with photos of the unfortunate soul who had the gigantic colon and, to Kerrin's delight, the actual colon itself. She is marveling at it from all sides, slowly circling the case. "So what's the deal with Lisa?" she asks from the other side of the case, peering at me through the glass.

"Well, she's back and . . . Kerrin, I can't see you

through that colon. Come around to this side and I'll talk to you." She walks around and I continue, "She's back and nasty as ever. More than I remembered, even."

"What a stupid bitch. Hey, how about seeing the Siamese twins exhibit?"

"I think they like to be called 'conjoined twins' nowadays," I answer, stalling for time to ready myself for another revolting display.

"Who cares what they like to be called? I'm sure I'll never meet one. Or two, as the case may be," she shrugs. "Nah, forget it," she says, changing her mind as we enter the cavernous lobby. "I think I've had it with all this weird stuff. But talking about Siamese twins does remind me: I have your Christmas present! I couldn't wait," she smiles, pulling a small silver-wrapped package from her bag.

"Oh, you shouldn't have," I say. "No, I mean it, you really *shouldn't* have," I repeat guiltily, picturing her Velvet Underground CD under a pile of shopping bags and car magazines and poem drafts to J.P. Cody strewn on my bedroom floor. I rip open the paper, revealing two sleek bottles that fit together to create a beautiful wavy shape. One contains bath oil and the other moisturizer, both in a soothing shade of strawberry sherbet. "Neat," I say, unscrewing the top of the moisturizer and inhaling deeply. "I love it."

Kerrin gets an "aw, shucks" expression on her face and we head to the gift shop, which is actually just a glorified glass case with a few items haphazardly displayed. Kerrin chooses a calendar for Len that features a striking black-and-white photo of a different museum oddity each month. As the woman rings up the purchase, Kerrin fingers one of the skeleton key chains near the register. "Hey, is this cool, Toby? Do you think he'd like one of these?" she asks, flinging it my way.

I catch it and turn it over in my hands, studying the plastic parts. "The rib cage is molded in a pretty interesting way," I say, looking up to see Kerrin and the woman staring at me quizzically. "Yeah, you should get it; he'll love it," I say. "And one for me, too," I add, plunking mine down on the counter and reaching for my wallet. I'm thinking about how much Rod Winters would like the molding on this piece and how this skeleton could find a new, cozy home in The Box the next time I need engineering help from him.

We head outside into the crisp December air, and as we climb into Kerrin's car, I complain that I don't feel any Christmas spirit.

"Well, of course you don't, not with that jerk camped out in your house and that weirdo roommate of yours drooling all over her. And not really anyone else to divert your attention."

"Thanks, Kerrin," I say sarcastically. "Don't remind me, OK?"

"Look," she says, holding the car lighter to the end of her cigarette, "you want to come to this thing next week at CHOP? Len's roommate Mark is in pediatric oncology. These people with cancer, I can't get away from them!" She pauses to take a long drag and give the finger to a guy in a green Ford Escort who cuts us off. "Anyway, it's like a big Christmas party they have on the floor for the kids, with Santa and magicians and cookies and whatever. I'm going with Len. Kids and stuff, might be your thing."

"It sounds nice, maybe I will come," I say. I'm peering out of Kerrin's dirty car window at all the shoppers hurrying through the streets and dreading going home to Michael and Lisa Carlton. And no J.P. Cody until Monday morning.

Kerrin reads my mind as I'm counting the hours until the Monday morning weather report and says, "So any more poetry for that guy?" I guessed it would come up eventually; my original declaration of love for J.P. Cody got lost in the shuffle of Kerrin's new lust for Len. In the darkness of the car and the absence of adequate nighttime lighting in my neighborhood, I can't see her expression and I don't know if she's smiling or smirking. I take a deep breath and tell her that I am sending more poetry in fact, two more poems since the first one.

" 'Cause I was thinking about it," she says, turning onto my street. "You don't know if he's into it or not. Why don't you make it more—what's the word— interactive or something? Ask him to do something or say something on the air if he's getting the poems. That would be fun, I think."

"It would be fun," I agree, mystified and grateful that Kerrin is on my side. I don't know why she's had such a change of heart since that first fateful day at Michael's recital; perhaps it's love that's softening her. Or perhaps despite her penchant for brusque words and her distaste for all things even marginally touchy-feely, she is truly a good friend.

Michael has been in the bathroom for the better part of the evening, busily cleaning the humidifier and talking to Lisa Carlton, who is sitting on the toilet lid in sweatpants and her ugly pink turtleneck. I'm taking refuge in my room, studying some sketches for the PowerWheels garage, when the doorbell rings. When I emerge to answer the front door, I'm overpowered by the smell of the bleach-and-water solution that Michael has concocted in his crazed attempt to remove any trace of mold or bacteria from the humidifier. He's been convinced that his winter cough is the result of germs pouring into the air from the humidifier and obviously a frantic scrubbing is the only answer. I don't have the heart to tell him that not only is it unforgivably wussy to spend the evening cleaning the humidifier, but the fact that a guy would even *own* a humidifier is even more suspect.

It is one of our neighbors on Town Watch, and as I trudge back up the stairs, I hear Lisa Carlton roar, "*Toby Cody?* Toby Cody! Imagine if they got married. It's the funniest thing I've ever heard. Like a rodeo clown's name!" I slam the door to my room and throw myself facedown on the bed, counting backwards from ten to try to keep from crying. When I reach six, Michael knocks and comes in and I turn over and watch the water trickling down his arms and making little spots on my daisy throw rug.

"Toby."

"What?" I sputter, furious at him.

"The other day after you went to work, she . . . found your poem and was curious, I guess. So I was just telling her about it. I didn't know it was a secret," he says quietly, setting his mouth in a line that looks suspiciously like Lisa Carlton's.

"Well, it is! From her, anyway," I say bitterly, stifling a sob.

"I'm really sorry, Toby," he says a little too disingenuously for my liking, holding his hand to his chest and leaving a damp handprint over the silkscreened Speed Racer on his T-shirt. "I wasn't thinking, I guess."

"Yeah, I'll say you weren't thinking, Michael." I order him out of my room, miserable that he shared my secret with Lisa Carlton. Miserable that he betrayed me. Miserable that she knows what I am up to. And miserable that she is right: Toby Cody is a ridiculous name, indeed.

Chapter 9

"Toby. Toby. *Tobeeeee!*" Sarah says urgently, leaning over my desk and touching my shoulder. I snap my head up and look at her, bewildered. I've been so engrossed in my current project that I didn't hear her squeaky squawk until the third try.

I've got them spread all over my desk, and together they create a motley pile of card stock with ugly type, poor punctuation and spelling, and blaring, glaring graphic design:

END BEDWETTING FOREVER!

DO YOU WANT TO MAKE MORE MONEY!
DON'T WAIT—MAIL TODAY!

GET YOUR DEGREE AS A
PROFESSIONAL BRIDAL CONSULTANT.

SEND NO MONEY—THE WEIGHT-LOSS LOTION IS **FREE.**

YOU'RE FUTURE IN GUN REPAIR IS NOW!

I've been stealthily collecting these cards for some weeks now from the lobby of the Super Fresh, and now I am calmly writing in Lisa Carlton's name, work address, and work phone number on every single one. Kerrin thinks my idea is ingenious, the perfect victimless crime. It costs me nothing to send in the cards (NO POSTAGE NECESSARY IF MAILED IN THE UNITED STATES sits tantalizingly in the upper right corner of each one, of course), and it costs the companies very little to send out their information or free samples. But it means that Lisa Carlton will be plagued with mystery mailings that come from sea to shining sea—and hopefully some badly timed phone calls, as well. It's not that I want her to get a broken leg or some horrible disease, but I do want her to be mortified. And perplexed. And inconvenienced. And whatever else will make her as generally miserable as she's making me this holiday season.

"Anyway, Toby," Sarah continues, looking at the desktop full of postcards like it's a pile of dirty laundry, "you did it again. You need to fix this, OK?" She hands me the package proof for Talk 'n' Sing Tyrannosaurus and sighs heavily.

I take it from her and immediately spy the mistake, embarrassed that I forgot again. I push the pile of postcards to the side and fire up my Mac, cringing. We often have photographs of kids gracing the sides and back of the package, their angelic faces peering out and success-fully hiding any trace of the precocious brattiness that I've seen in every one of these child models. Beneath the photo would be a little snippet or quote about the toy, like "It's so much fun for me *and* my mom!" (the one from the toy blender, the perfect domestic drudgery product for the five-and-under set) or "I love you, Snug-gle Pup!" (the one with the kid model who cursed like a sailor as he squeezed the life out of the plush pup, un-doubtedly bringing home more money that day than I make in a week). Most times, we didn't get the quote from marketing until the eleventh hour, so I got used to typing DUMMY QUOTE GOES HERE as a placeholder. When the quote finally came in, I had to remember to take out the dummy line and put in the real, inspired text. This was the fourth time I forgot over the course of just a few months. I rifle through my inbox and there it is, the quote from marketing. I bang on the keyboard with anger, changing it to "I love to talk 'n' sing with my dino buddy!" all the while thinking that perhaps this J.P. Cody thing is taxing me more than I initially thought it would.

I decide to clear my head by taking a walk to visit Joe, who was recently dumped by his girlfriend and is de-cidedly glum. Every time I look out the window, he is there under Toyland's ugly green awning, pacing and smoking. The other day I considered telling him that if she ever decides to get back together with him, a guy in an iron lung's not much of a catch, but I thought better of it. He had been up most of the night, and the purple rings under his eyes had frightened me in that serial killer kind of way. I push my chair back and feel around in my purse for the cool, plastic skeleton I bought for Rod Winters, and I head off to engineering.

When I get to Rod's office, he is standing in front of the window with his back to me, gripping his hands behind his head with his fingers laced together against his yellowing hair. He is holding his hands so tightly that the blood has left his knuckles and they are white, the tendons in his hands straining against the skin. He turns around and is ashen-faced, a real switch from his regular scarlet hue.

"What do you want?" he asks quietly. I immediately wish I scrammed when I saw him in this eerily contemplative position, but now it's too late and I'm not quick enough to lie on the spot.

"Um . . . I brought you this." I clear my throat as he looks at me dully. "I thought it might have good molding." I throw the sorry specimen on his desk, and he immediately picks it up.

"What did you like about this?"

"Oh, um, the rib cage?" I ask, suddenly wishing the guys in the model shop would exhibit one of their patented displays of boobery and accidentally trip the fire alarm so I could rush outside, far, far away from Rod Winters.

He gives me a quick, fake smile. "This rib cage is just injection molded like all the other things we do here, nothing unusual. Do you want it back?"

"OK, yeah. Sure," I say, deflated. He throws it to me and turns back to the window. "Better luck next time," he says softly, staring off into the distance.

I trudge down the hall to Joe's cubicle, where he is sweating profusely over a drawing. Literally sweating. The heat at the end of this hallway is stifling, and little beads of perspiration have popped out all over his fore-head. He also stinks to high heaven, but then so do most of the engineers on even cool days, so I decide to let it slide.

"Hi, Toby. What's that?" I hold out the skeleton and tell him about my discussion with Rod Winters, and all he can do is shake his head. "Well, it's *not* unusual," he says, studying the rib cage and pursing his lips. "But what the fuck, how are you supposed to know that? The bastard could at least give you credit for trying." He looks back at his drawing. "Got to figure out the gear system for the Perfect Pony stable *dance floor*. No wonder Donna broke up with me."

"Don't talk that way, Joe. The dance floor will bring someone somewhere some happiness." I try to say it seriously, but he looks at me with such a dubious expression that I can't help burst out laughing. Luckily, he laughs with me, holding his head in his hands.

"Hey, at least you can do your job right, even if it is a pony stable," I add, wiping my eyes. "I forgot to change that stupid dummy copy on a package again. One more time, and Sarah's going to have my head."

"Don't worry about it. That's why she's there, to catch these things before they go to production. What would she be doing otherwise, besides making everyone look at her ugly baby?" I remember the time Sarah paraded through engineering with her starbaby and the engineers recoiling in horror—a baby, so squishy, no angles, no gears, not programmable.

"Yeah, you're right. OK, sorry to bother you. You want this?" I ask Joe, holding out the skeleton.

"Sure, if you don't." I hand it to him and he hangs it on his architect's lamp, the ulnas and tibias swinging as I walk away.

I am embracing J.P. Cody as he holds me, kissing my neck and nuzzling his face in my hair, which is miraculously coiffed and beautiful. I am wearing the periwinkle dress with the sweetheart neckline and the long zipper that I haven't fit into in three years, and it hugs me in all the right places. J.P. has grabbed hold of the zipper and is pulling it down, down, down, and the zipper starts with a tiny *zip* sound but gets louder and louder and louder, until . . .

baaaaaaaaaaaaaaaaaa.

The zipper makes a high, one-note sound, and I wake up to realize that it's fourteen-year-old Paul practicing blowing into his saxophone mouthpiece. I'm in a stupor, touching my torso and trying to figure out where the periwinkle dress has gone. "Maybe we should practice without the mouthpiece," I hear Michael say calmly as I become more conscious and try desperately to get back to my dream. "Here, hand me that, and let me see you put your lips in the right position."

I slide off my bed and onto the floor, where I grab my sketchbook. I'm yawning and rubbing the sleep from my eyes in the early evening light as I write:

Sending poems
Is like reporting snow trends
You may like it
But does the person on the other end?

So on this day so crisp and fine
I am asking for one little sign
If you like these poems and the feelings they speak
Wear your blue-checked tie on Thursday next week

"This seems like fun, don't you think? Here, Toby, let me take you to meet Mark." Len grabs my wrist and we make our way across the crowded hospital hallway and into a giant room, past Santa and an elaborate ginger-bread house display and a giant punch bowl and a collection of kids with shiny, bald heads and sunken eyes that still glitter with mischief and curiosity. I'm glad to finally meet Mark, even though Kerrin's fantasy of us double-dating was quickly quashed when Len told her early on that Mark has a voluptuous girlfriend who is doing her residency up in Cooperstown, New York. Well, of course I wouldn't stand a chance, I told Kerrin; this girl has a bigger bustline, better brains, and the Baseball Hall of Fame, and honestly, who can argue with that?

Mark is making his way across the room, ducking under crepe-paper streamers and dodging dancing elves until he reaches us. Len introduces us and I'm immediately relieved that I'll never have the chance to date him. He isn't unattractive—wavy chestnut hair and chocolate brown eyes—but he exudes a kind of nervous energy that sets my teeth on edge as he pumps my hand up and down. He's got a piercing, unblinking gaze, and he looks at me hard, with his eyebrows furrowed when I talk, like I'm speaking in another language. After he leaves, I remember that Len once told me that Mark is very interested in preventing the kind of gastrointestinal problems that kids have when they receive chemotherapy. I decide at that moment that if I were a kid, just meeting this guy would give me gastrointestinal problems, chemotherapy or no. I'm about to ask Len how Mark gets along with his wee patients when Kerrin appears. Her face is troubled, and her eyes dart around the room, looking for someplace to rest.

"Hey, there!" says Len. "What's wrong with you? Trouble in politically correct world?"

"Oh, always," she answers distractedly, giving an unnecessarily wide berth to a little blond girl rolling by in a wheelchair. "Ummm . . . oh yeah. I was helping someone in the patient materials department write something saying that a good wintertime activity is to build a snowman. They kicked it back with a sticky note that said it has to say 'snowman or snowwoman.' "

"Well, that doesn't make sense," I reason aloud. "Building a snowman would be better exercise, because a snowman is bigger than a snowwoman. Right?" I appeal to the two of them, but before I can gauge their response, I feel a tiny tug on my sleeve.

"Can you help me get a drink?" I look down to see a small, bright-red-haired boy with a crooked grin and a crazy zigzag scar on the top of his head that divides his hair like some kind of pinking shears through the Red Sea. One of his eyes is half-closed, but the other is bright and alert and an excellent indicator that he is singularly focused on having some Pepsi. I crouch down so we're face-to-face and ask him his name, and he solemnly replies, "Ben."

"Hey, that's her brother's name! What a coincidence, huh?" I say jubilantly, pointing to Kerrin. When he gives her a shy smile, she shifts her weight awkwardly and digs her fingers into Len's arm.

"Is it OK for you to have a drink? If we can find someone who says it's OK, I would be very happy to get you one," I say cheerily. He leads me across the room, past piles of toys and a noisy group of chattering parents, to a chubby nurse in a Santa hat who is smiling beatifically as she helps a little girl choose a butter cookie from a large silver tray. We get the go-ahead and I pour him some soda, which he drinks in noisy gulps. He lets out a loud burp and I try my hardest not to laugh, but he knows an adult who is trying to act adult when he sees one and grins from ear to ear.

"Do you know Megan?" he yells over the din of the Christmas music that's started playing, and when I shake my head, he can't quite believe it. I try to remember when my world was so small that I thought everyone knew every person that I knew, but it's hard. While I'm letting this idea swish around in my mind, I catch a glimpse of Kerrin and Len from across the room, and Kerrin is looking downright miserable. I'm trying to plot a course over to her when I feel a tug again.

"Want to meet her?"

"Who?"

"*Megan,*" he answers impatiently.

"Oh, sorry. Of course. Where is she?" Ben grabs my hand again and pulls me to a corner where a fat ten-year-old is holding court. She is surrounded by boys and girls of all ages and is wearing a glittery, pink tiara and matching pink ballerina outfit. Her arms strain at the seams of her leotard as she outstretches one of her hands and loudly asks a bald kindergarten-age boy wearing two hearing aids to bring her a cookie, pronto.

"Wow, she is something," I remark to Ben, who is staring at Megan. "Will you introduce me?"

"Maybe later," he says, suddenly losing interest. "Do you work here at the hospital?"

"No."

"What do you do, then?"

"I work over in New Jersey. At Toyland. I make toys." Bingo! Ben practically leaps in the air as soon as the words are out of my mouth. He races over to a small table, where he pulls a fluorescent orange XR7 racer from a pile of ribbons, bows, and torn paper festooned with illustrations of goofy-looking reindeer. His eye shining, he crows, "Look! I have the XR7 racer!" He pauses to catch his breath. " 'New from Toyland! Battery pack sold separately!' " he intones. I laugh mirthlessly at this one, on the one hand inwardly cursing our marketing department for encouraging such brand loyalty at such a tender age, and on the other hand, delighted to finally have evidence for Joe that his work *does* make someone somewhere very happy.

"Know what?" I ask. "Pretty soon, the XR7 is going to have a programmable sound feature you can add on. You're gonna love it. But don't tell anyone—it's top secret." Ben's mouth slowly turns into a giant *o*, and he places his hand over his lips, his one working eyelid narrowing as he considers the importance of being the keeper of this cutting-edge industry development.

"Look, I have to visit my friend over there for a minute. It looks like there's a"—I search the room for a diversion and I spot a cluster of kids—"an ornament-making art thing going on over there. How about I meet you there in a few minutes?" Luckily he agrees and dances off to the far corner that's littered with construction paper, and I make my way over to the punch bowl where Kerrin, Len, and Mark are standing. Mark is shouting something into Len's ear and Kerrin is looking into her paper cup, her lips pressed together. I arrive and start gushing about Ben and how cute he is and how when the new XR7 comes out in a year, two years, tops, it's going to change these kids' lives. Programmable sound! Maybe I could get one for every kid here.

I'm thinking about how I could get Toyland to donate some when Mark tilts his head and says quietly, "Toby, the way it's going for some of these kids, programmable sound in two years isn't going to matter." I'm stunned and blinking hard and Kerrin slams her drink down next to the punch bowl and shouts, "That's *it!* I'm outta here." She walks off with Len trailing behind her and Mark cringing.

"I'm sorry," Mark says, fixing his scary gaze on me. "I didn't mean to—"

He doesn't finish, because suddenly, one corner of the room is awash in light; bright, eye-wateringly searing light that causes the kids to screw up their faces and rub their eyes and makes the dust in its path dance in the air.

"It may be *cold* outside, but it's all sunshine and smiles at Children's Hospital Oncology Department's Christmas party. It may be cold outside, but it's *all* sunshine and smiles at Children's Hospital Oncology Department's Christmas party. It may be cold outside, but it's all *sunshine and smiles* at Children's Hospital Oncology Department's Christmas party."

I know this voice. He is here. It's J.P. Cody, broadcasting from the party, running his lines and deciding which word to stress. And here I am, in my ugly green overalls with the Woodstock patch on the butt that I wore because I thought the kids would like it. A little yellow bird on my rear end on a day like this. I'm suddenly short of breath, and I reach a hand out to the punch bowl table.

"Oh my God," I say. *"Oh my God."*

"Look, Toby, I didn't really mean—" Mark continues.

"No, it's fine," I say, his voice sounding far away, like the time I passed out during my school play and the voice of the girl playing Rizzo got smaller and smaller as I fell into a heap on the stage in my poodle skirt. My mouth is dry as I inch toward where the cameraman is setting up and the hair and makeup people are putting the finishing touches on J.P. Cody. Incredibly, he looks even better in real life than on TV, and when he turns to answer someone, I'm amazed and touched to see a tiny tuft of gray hair on the back of his head. He seems very comfortable here, winking at Megan when she runs in front of him and does a little dance. I'm within ten feet of him now, excitement buzzing in my ears. He is pointing to the punch bowl and saying something to the chubby nurse in the Santa hat, and she nearly leaps up to bring him a drink. *Damn,* I'm thinking, why didn't I wear a Santa hat?

Suddenly a person in a WPHX baseball cap claps his hands and asks the kids to gather round behind J.P. Cody, and there is a slow swoosh of little feet running, wheelchairs wheeling, and IV poles clattering over to the corner. Ben runs to the front of the crowd and when he spots me, he yells, "Hi again!" J.P. notices this and glances at me as I'm waving at Ben, smiles, and then looks away quickly, his attention grabbed by the cameraman. My legs feel like they are full of ginger ale, light and bubbly and fizzy and airy, and my mind starts racing. Should I try to talk to him? What would I say? Do I have "maniac poet" written on my face? Do I seem like a stalker psycho? Or should I play it cool, a phrase unheard of in my personal lexicon of love?

The cameras start whirring and they successfully tape the piece, with J.P. ultimately deciding to put the accent on the words *sunshine and smiles,* after all. As the crew wraps up, he leans against a table and runs his fingers through that beautiful black hair and looks around the room. Checking his watch, he stands up again and begins walking toward the door, chatting amiably with a grandfatherly type who tells him what a good job he's doing. J.P. blushes a bit, making me swoon, and thanks him graciously as I slowly walk toward them. I'm tongue-tied and I'm sure I smell like an engineer in the hot hallway at Toyland, but how could I forgive myself if I didn't say something?

"Hi, I'm Janet. You have quite a way with the kids." *What?* Out of nowhere a fifty-something hippie with chunky jewelry and a dress that looks like a throw rug has appeared in front of me. She smiles broadly and tosses her frizzy hair behind her neck as I crane mine to watch J.P. going out the door.

"Huh . . . yeah?" I say, vexed. My stomach is churning

now, all the butter cookies and chocolate treats and punch exacting their revenge during my high anxiety.

"I'm the Child Life coordinator here. Have you ever thought about volunteering?" Volunteering? What's that? All I can think of is my sweet meteorologist walking down that hall, away from the din of this room.

"Um, yeah, I guess," I say, confused and panic-stricken. My big chance to meet J.P. Cody is evaporating like morning dew. Janet gives a little yip of joy and starts telling me what is expected of volunteers and how many hours they must commit to. She presses a business card into my hand and warmly tells me that she can't wait to hear from me.

"Uh-huh, OK," I nod and gulp. "You'll be hearing from me." I run from the room and into the hallway, leap onto the dingy elevator, and race through the lobby. No J.P. anywhere down here. And a Child Life lady who thinks I'm going to volunteer up there.

The honeydew-scented aromatherapy candle smells lush and beautiful as I sit on the couch with the VCR remote and my holiday booty. It's the day after Christmas and I spent the day before in northern New Jersey with assorted family members celebrating what my mom affectionately calls Dysfunctionpalooza. It isn't all that bad, as long as you don't count the six cats that belong to my aunt that travel everywhere with her and my grandfather who can't hear a thing and my extremely masculine twenty-year-old cousin who still can't provide a satisfactory answer about why she doesn't go on dates with boys.

I'm the easy one to buy for, the top of everyone's list, and this morning I came back into Philadelphia with: one tube licorice exfoliating gel, one lemon and verbena bath oil set, one loofah and lavender face scrub set complete with travel case, one Calvin Klein talc and lotion kit that I will promptly return to Wanamaker's this week, two seaweed masks, a collection of tiny tubes of flower-scented shampoo, one honeydew-scented aromatherapy candle, and the Ken Burns baseball documentary boxed set. I threw off my coat as soon as I came in the door and popped the first video in the VCR, and I planned to spend the day sitting and soaking up baseball history and greedily sniffing my new presents.

The video is just starting when I hear movement upstairs and think, oh God, not Michael and Lisa Carlton. They were supposed to go to her family's house out in Lancaster and I pray that the sound is a burglar, such is my disgust with them these days. A moment later Michael comes loping down the stairs.

I must be wearing my dismay on my face like a seaweed mask because he says in a sarcastic tone, "Don't look so glad to see me, Toby." I peer around him to see if Lisa is in tow and he reads my mind, adding flatly, "Lisa had to work today. After-Christmas returns." Of course—how could I forget? The day after Thanksgiving, Lisa worked a double shift at the clothing store and Michael and I were forced to listen to her complain for over an hour about her sore feet and tired legs. Michael looked sympathetic, whimpering and frowning along with her, and I wanted to ask if her feet and legs were as sore as Michael's hands were the day she whacked them with a book.

"So how's it going? How was Christmas?" he asks after a long minute, sitting stiffly on the couch next to me and picking up the Calvin Klein toiletries.

I'm angry and still wanting to give him the cold shoulder after the humidifier debacle but also secretly wanting to talk to him about anything and everything. It's been a long time since we've been in the house together without Lisa Carlton, but I'm torn and tongue-tied, so I nod at the TV and say, "Hush, Daniel Okrent's talking."

"Who is Daniel Okrent?" he asks, squinting at the screen.

"A historian, can't you read?" He recoils a tiny bit, barely perceptible, but I immediately feel terrible for being so curt. *Nice Christmas spirit, Toby,* I can practically hear my dad saying. "I'm sorry. My Christmas was nice. How was yours with"—I swallow hard—"Lisa and her family?" The only thought more revolting than one Carlton was a whole house full of them. I liked to imagine them all in their turtlenecks, with even the family dog wearing a scrunchie around its tail.

"It was . . . fine," he answers. "We came back late last night. I didn't expect you back so soon."

"Well, here I am," I say, a bit too defiantly. Then I turn off the video and tell Michael about my experience at

Children's Hospital—relaying the story strategically so I can edit out the parts about J.P. Cody, of course. That definitely isn't something that I want Lisa to know about. But while I was in New Jersey, I decided that Michael's opinion about how I should handle the volunteering would be invaluable. As I explain my discussion with hippie Janet, I'm growing more animated, and my body language becomes less tense and I'm forgetting how angry I've been with him lately.

"So you want to know if you're obligated to go there and volunteer?" he asks, squeezing out a little bit of licorice exfoliating gel and turning up his nose. "This looks like a skin rash waiting to happen," he warns me sternly.

"I think my skin will be OK. Am I obligated?"

"I don't think so. But could it be that this person saw you in a way that you don't see yourself? If she felt so strongly that you would be able to help out, maybe you should trust that instinct in her. Believe me, volunteers aren't always so reliable. Or *normal*." Michael ought to know. When he was in middle school he had been forced by his parents to volunteer at the local hospital, and an older male volunteer kept wanting to know when he could take pictures of Michael, pestering the poor thirteen-year-old until he ran crying to his mother. That was the end of Michael's illustrious volunteering career, although strangely, not the end of the pervert's volunteering career.

"You're probably right," I say, impressed at the way

Michael can look at a situation upside down and backwards, shake it, flip it, and come up with an answer that never ceases to amaze me. "It's just the way . . . it's probably stupid . . . Len's roommate made it sound like it could get pretty depressing, if you know what I mean."

There's a long pause and he finally says, "That could be true. But sometimes something is still worth doing, even though it might have the potential to be depressing." His face clouds over and he stares into space for a minute, until the phone rings and shakes the music from inside his head, snapping him back to reality. It's Lisa Carlton and I can hear her loud voice coming through the receiver, even though Michael is the one holding the phone. She's done with her shift and I watch him pull his new fleecy Christmas jacket over his head and grab his car keys from the tiny Fred Flintstone ceramic dish by the phone. Then he is out the door, leaving me with Daniel Okrent and my candle.

Chapter 10

"It's a new year, my dear, a new you," Kerrin says thickly into the phone. "Come over and celebrate by getting high with us." I can hear Kerrin's little brother Ben laughing raucously in the background at something on TV that sounds suspiciously like a rerun of *The A-Team*. I could swear I just heard Mr. T pitying some poor fool.

"I thought that was Ben's car I saw parked at the end of your street the other night!" I exclaim. Rich was in such a hurry to get downtown to meet with his lawyer and soon-to-be ex-wife that he took a topsy-turvy circuitous route through town that may have actually added time to his trip, rather than shaved critical moments reserved for arguing. When he was barreling down Arch Street, I thought, when I looked down one of the side streets, that I saw Ben's green Volvo station wagon with the battered back end and the SATAN IS MY COPILOT bumper sticker. "How is it going for him, anyway?"

"Uch, NYU," she spits. "One semester down, seven to go. I told him he wouldn't like it up there. Those New Yorkers are eating him *alive*."

"Ooh, so awful, I know," I say, agreeing immediately. "With their, 'Oh, that's my cab, I was standing on this corner first,' right?"

"Yeah, what's that about?" she practically shouts into the phone, making me hold the receiver six inches from my ear. "Know what I did the last time that happened? This skinny bitch says, 'I was here first,' and I just said, 'I no speak the English!' Those people are the worst!"

"They are *barbaric*," I say enthusiastically. Philadelphians have a vitriol reserved for New Yorkers that they are generally able to keep under wraps, but get them drunk or high or in a foul mood and it's all over.

I catch my breath and Kerrin returns to her original question. "So are you coming or not?"

"I can't," I say. "I think I have to take a drug test." This is what Janet told me when I phoned Children's Hospital bright and early on the morning of January second. My New Year's resolution was to call her, and I was afraid if I waited, I would chicken out. I also don't entertain the idea of getting high with Kerrin and Ben for two other reasons: One, the last time Michael and I got stoned was about a year ago and it was bad pot, leaving both of us sweaty and convinced that someone was trying to break into the house via the mail slot. Two, there was something poignant and heart wrenching about witnessing Kerrin and Ben together when they were drunk or high. They invariably ended up strutting around mocking and imitating their father, who left their mother when Ben was six to take up with the first in a long series of personal secretaries.

"Oh, why's that? Is Toyland going fascist?"

"Remember how we went to Children's at Christmas? I think I'm going to volunteer there," I say carefully, recalling Kerrin's perplexing discomfort at the party.

"Oh, really? Huh. Well, hold on, Ben really wants to talk to you," she says, putting the phone down. It falls on the hardwood floor, first scratching its way across the table and finally hitting with a thud that makes me wince.

"Hey, get me some salsa, too, while you're in there, yeah, Kerrin? Hey, Toby, how's it going?" Ben asks slowly.

"All right, I guess," I lie. I hate my roommate's girlfriend, the sticker sheets I designed for the Berry Babies playhouse came in at forty-three cents over budget, and I'm in love with a weatherman who doesn't know I'm alive. Oh, and Michael was right: The licorice scrub has given me a rash and I am currently wearing a mask of white, gooey cream to soothe my skin. "What about you? You don't like New York?"

"Too early to say," he answers, crunching on a tortilla chip. "I don't have to go back until January seventeenth or something, so I'm trying not to think about it. But hey, Toby? That thing you're doing with the weatherman? It's so cool. Kerrin told me about it. With the poems? Like, did you ask him to do anything yet?"

I'm taken by surprise for what seems like five minutes—I don't know what takes my breath away more, the fact that Kerrin has told Ben about my J.P. Cody plan, or that Ben is responding to it so favorably. Then again, Ben was always a master of retreating into a fantasy world when he was younger, dealing with his father's philandering and his mother's depression through play and music. So perhaps he could identify with the situation better than anyone else I know.

"I have a poem that I wrote asking him to wear a certain tie if he likes getting the poems," I answer quietly.

"Well, send it then, man! What's the holdup?"

I hang up and think, what's the holdup, indeed? I guess I had been living in abject fear that if I sent it and J.P. Cody didn't wear the tie, that would be the end of it and I would be miserable.

But what if he did wear the tie? What then?

I find the poem that I'd drafted on the floor after my nap, type it up on Mr. Clackety Clack, and mark my calendar. Next Thursday morning. Today was Tuesday, so that meant that even if the letter took a week to get downtown, he still had a day to decide and wear the right tie. *Please wear the right tie*, I plead silently as I lick the envelope. *Please.*

"Well, I guess that went as well as can be expected," I say to my Secret Wish Horse as I flop facedown onto my bed.

I sailed in a few minutes earlier, eager to tell Michael about my evening and to thank him for encouraging me to trust hippie Janet's instincts. Instead I discovered him and Lisa curled up on the sofa together, giggling over the Victoria's Secret winter sale catalog and dog-earing pages. The two of them didn't so much as bat an eyelash, so I marched up here and promptly lit my honeydew-scented candle before even removing my coat and scarf.

The evening had been a combination of fear, euphoria, and funny odors—not a lot unlike my relationship with The Head Wound, I realize with a start as I stroke the mane on my horse. When I showed up at the playroom on the pediatric oncology floor after work, I immediately looked for Janet, who was nowhere to be found. Eventually she showed up, this time wearing a top with a swirly pattern that was reminiscent of a wall tapestry favored by the acid-dropping guy who lived across the hall from me during my freshman year of art school. Last I heard, he was now living in Hollywood and making a killing animating TV shows for adults. She quickly got me settled without much fanfare and ambled off, leaving me to my own devices.

First, I offended a teenage girl by telling her how I loved her hair color (a lush, dark red, deeper and sultrier than my Bozo frizz), only to have her tell me in a surly voice that it was a wig. I clumsily backed up into a little boy in a wheelchair, making us both yelp with surprise. I asked around for Ben and got nauseated with anxiety when I thought about what fate might have befallen him—until a nurse told me that he and his family had gone home for the week.

But I also read aloud to a little girl with luminous eyes and one leg, and she applauded when I did the voices of Ariel, the Little Mermaid, and her sister Arista. A few takers gathered around when I showed how to fold a piece of paper so it looked like a sailboat, although the origami session came to an abrupt finish when someone had to throw up in a blue basin. And I got to meet Tracie, a shy, frail five-year-old with alabaster skin and a shock of wavy black hair. She was strong enough to walk around on her own but spoke in a whisper, a quality that made everything she said that much more cute and engaging. She decided that Tracie and Toby sounded like they could be names of twins, and when I confided in her that I always wanted to be a twin, she broke out of her whisper and said in a loud voice, "Me, too!" I promised to wear my purple shoes next week to match her purple sneakers so we could really look like twins, and she gave me a crooked smile before timidly waving and walking away.

So I guess I will stick with this, then, I think as I blow out the candle and flip through the back pages of *Motor Trend*. I don't know when exactly I finally drift off to sleep, my mind a curious mix of wheelchairs, wigs, and ads for car detailing kits.

Less than eight hours later, I am poised at the top of the stairs, taking a deep breath. I've put on my checkered pants with my black V-neck sweater and a sparkly pair of silver earrings that were a gift from Kerrin two birthdays ago. In the name of glamour, I've brushed on extra blush and little chartreuse sweeps of liquid eyeliner that bring out the green in my eyes. I've spritzed myself with perfume, and the sweet smell envelops my face and hair. Checking my watch, I put my foot down the first stair.

It's seven forty-five.

It's Thursday morning.

It's time to see if J.P. Cody is wearing his tie with the blue checks.

Chapter 11

I walk down the stairs slowly, almost in a stately way, holding my head high and my back straight and tall, the way my grandmother always passionately implored me to. I breathe deeply as I position myself on the couch, my calm face masking the fact that my heart is beating a mile a minute. Lisa is plopped in our oversized red stuffed chair, eating a waffle with her hands and chewing with her mouth open, curiously eyeing me in my dressy clothes and elaborate makeup.

The news is already underway and it's a mere two minutes until J.P. Cody comes on. One hundred twenty seconds, one hundred nineteen seconds, one hundred eighteen seconds. Michael is puttering upstairs in his room, and when he runs down the stairs three at a time, it makes me jump slightly. Lisa Carlton shoots me a "What's your problem?" look, tossing her waffle plate aside to begin fingering her scrunchie, a yellow-green number that matches her bile-colored turtleneck. When Michael glances over at me from the foot of the stairs, he lets out a gasp.

"Toby, get up! You're sitting on my box of reeds!" He quickly crosses the room and plants himself one foot in front of me, just as the brassy intro music to the weather begins.

"No, I'm not!" I yell, panicked. "Move it!" At this, Lisa looks up and sees that the weather is coming on. She lets out a cold laugh that makes want to bash the bottle of maple syrup on her head, but I haven't time for cruelty with condiments. I can hear J.P.'s voice, the beautiful sound that makes dogs bark, traffic stop, waves in the ocean change direction.

"OK, OK," I say angrily. I shift my weight and find the tiny box nestled between two sofa cushions. I hand it to Michael, who says earnestly, "See? I'm trying to help you. You wouldn't want splinters in your behind, would you?"

The thought of me with splinters in my behind sends Lisa into loud peals of laughter, but I don't care. I'm staring at the TV with two single tears streaming down my face, my mascara and green eyeliner pooling into moss-colored shapes at the outer corners of my eyes. I lick a tear from the edge of my lip and look back at the TV again to be sure.

J.P. is wearing his tie with the blue checks.

He likes the poems. He likes the poems! I smile broadly, delicately wiping my tears and artfully trying to ignore Lisa and Michael's quizzical stares. Michael knows that I've always been one to cry when I'm happy—he was there when we found a home for a stray neighborhood cat with three legs and I needed to stop at the All-In-One for a travel-size pack of tissues, such was my joy. But there was no way I could justify my glee over possible snow flurries but probably rain and a little ice that would make for a rough morning commute.

I spend the remainder of the week in a blissful state. I willingly dally over Sarah's starbaby pictures and coo at exactly the right moments. I clip an article on holistic health and mail it to my sister without a trace of irony. I pat a beautiful BMW downtown and compliment its balding, middle-aged owner. Love can change the world, I decide on Saturday night as I'm on my way to meet Kerrin and Len at Kerrin's favorite Mexican restaurant on the corner of South and Fourth Streets. I left my good news for her on her answering machine, and she's decided we need to celebrate.

"Love can change the world!" I say excitedly as I sit down at their table. Kerrin is already well into her second margarita. She is glowing and grinning in stark juxtaposition to Len, who is paler than I ever remember and looks exhausted. He is throwing back a cup of coffee along with his burrito and I scrunch up my nose—not just at the strange culinary combination but at the thought of the gastric distress that would befall me if I had Mexican food and coffee at the same time.

"We were trying to figure out how many hours Len has been awake this week," Kerrin says, answering to the look on my face as I stare at the coffee cup. She holds up a napkin covered with a long string of numbers, many of them crossed out and rewritten in her unmistakable scrawl. "But then we realized it would be easier to tally how many hours he's been *asleep* instead. The answer is: not many."

"Wow," I cough as Kerrin blows smoke rings across the table. "Well, if it's any consolation, I like your hair," I say sweetly to him. It's gotten longer and is now flopping over his forehead a bit, the black strands lush and shiny and a bit wavy.

"I know; it's *so* early Jimmy Page, isn't it?" Kerrin gushes before Len has a chance to answer. She reaches out to tousle his hair and he smiles, excusing himself to go to the men's room.

"Look at that," Kerrin says. "What did I tell him? You eat a burrito and drink coffee at the same time, you're going to be shitting like crazy in five minutes."

"I kind of thought the same thing," I admit, and we both laugh. "So can I tell you about the tie?" I implore, itching to share my Thursday morning story.

She holds up her hand, stopping me as I'm about to launch into my vivid and wonderful description of how the visage of J.P. Cody in his tie moved me to tears. "Len has something to say about it. Wait until he comes back."

I pout and Kerrin takes a big bite of Len's burrito,

chewing slowly. Finally she says, "All right, I'll tell you a story instead, OK? Len and I got caught at work."

"Caught doing what?" I ask, sipping the margarita that's just appeared in front of me. The salt stings my lips and Kerrin is looking at me like I'm from outer space.

"Playing *Battleship*. What do you think? Fooling around!"

"Oh, what was it, then?" I ask tonelessly. Hearing about Kerrin's sexual escapades lost a lot of its luster when there was nothing on the horizon for me in that department, and she often seems obtuse about this. I'm suddenly not up to a lurid story about a supply closet or a huge medical tome shaking off a shelf and falling on her head or some other such nonsense.

Surprisingly, she hears the tone in my voice and says, "No, you'll like this one. We didn't get caught having sex. We got caught afterward, when I lit a cigarette. I forgot that they have that sprinkler system in there, and there is one right over my desk. I'll bet those fuckers I work with have it turned up on High so it's supersensitive to cigarette smoke."

I laugh and nearly spray margarita all over her. "You're not serious, Kerrin," I giggle, pulling in my chair as a guy with a thick stomach squeezes by our table. "So what happened?"

"So of course this woman I work with is there and the alarm goes off, then the sprinkler. She comes running and sees us there. Talk about being caught with your pants down, yeah? I'm sure she's going to tell my boss, then I'll get quite the talking to. And Len was really embarrassed."

"He ought to be!" I exclaim self-righteously. Before I can say another word, Len returns and catches both of us with our giggly-girl faces. He slowly pulls out his chair and sits down heavily, his long legs sticking out from under the table.

"Len," says Kerrin leaning across the table and smiling slowly, "tell Toby what you told me about the tie."

He looks up and to the left for a minute, studying a string of Christmas lights shaped like tiki heads as he searches for the words. "Science," he begins as he clinks his spoon on the edge of his coffee cup, "is something that's reproducible."

I bite my lip as I nod and feign comprehension. "Meaning you need to do something more than once to prove that it isn't a one-time thing, or coincidence. Otherwise there are too many variables," he finishes slowly, looking at his hands.

I sip my margarita, bluffing and murmuring, "Mmm hmm."

"He's saying you have to send another poem, stupid," blurts Kerrin quickly, turning to me. "It might have been a coincidence, get it?"

"No way!" I shout angrily, the liquor in the margarita making me flush. "He wore that tie for me!"

"Probably," says Len, pushing his hair off his forehead. "But not definitely."

"So you need to do another experiment," urges Kerrin. "Just one more. Right, Len?"

"I would do more than one, but that's me," he shrugs. "But yeah, you have to do it at least once more, to prove your hypothesis."

"You guys are taking all the fun out of this entirely," I complain. "It's not so scientific."

But even as the words are leaving my mouth in between gulps of margarita, I know Kerrin and Len are right. I have to call upon my muse and pen another poem to my sweet weatherman. Len is staring at the tiki lights again and Kerrin is absently picking at the pulls in her olive green sweater, and I decide to write my poem asking J.P. Cody to wear his olive green suit.

"Jessica! Jessica! Get back here right now!"

The little girl from two streets away comes flying down the stairs with her blond ponytail swinging behind her, and without so much as a backward glance, she dashes out the door and into the icy road. After a split second, Michael comes bounding down the stairs with a flute in his hand, flushed and sputtering with anger. I peek out the curtains and see him catch up with her as she runs down the street. A moment later they are back in the living room with me, sitting on the couch as I try to watch inning five of my video series.

"You can't run into the street like that," Michael admonishes.

"But I *hate* it," she wails plaintively. "I hate the flute. I hate the mouthpiece, I hate the fingerings, I hate the music."

"OK, I get it," he says, sighing deeply. "But you should still play something. You have talent, you know," he says, wagging a finger dangerously close to her pert, upturned nose. "What do you like?"

"I don't know . . . maybe violin?" she asks, shrugging.

"Oh, no, no, not that," he says quickly. "You're not right for a string instrument. I was thinking you might like clarinet or sax better. Everyone likes sax, how about that?" It's all I can do to hold back my laughter as Michael tries to sell this poor little girl on the wonderful world of woodwinds. Teaching violin would be as foreign to him as fixing a V6 engine, and since taking up with Lisa Carlton again, he has gotten lazy in pursuing weekend music gigs. Now he needs little Jessica to help pay the bills, and if he loses her to the Suzuki method, it would be a wallop in the wallet that he doesn't need.

"I dunno. All I know is I don't want to play the flute tonight," she says, folding her arms in front of her chest and settling down deeper into the couch.

"Well, that's OK, but you can't leave until seven-thirty. Your mom isn't home until then, and she expects you to be here. You don't have to play, but you have to stay. You can sit with Toby and watch this if you want," he says, getting up and rubbing his eyes from behind his glasses.

Jessica sits quietly with me all the way through the Gas House Gang with Leo Durocher and Dizzy Dean and stays riveted to the screen during Lou Gehrig's farewell speech. She asks me why he would say that he's the luckiest man on earth if he's so sick. I'm about to explain when Michael comes back downstairs and says sharply, "Seven-thirty, Jessica. Time for you to go."

He stands with the screen door ajar until he sees her go into her house and flops onto the couch next to me. "Violin? Where would she get that idea?" he asks angrily.

"Why did you have her leave, anyway? I was just getting around to talking about Lou Gehrig. I thought I had a protégé there for a minute," I say proudly. "Besides, you always say you can't force music on a kid—it only makes them hate it more." I shudder when I remember my ill-fated oboe lessons in the fourth grade. I thought my head was going to explode every time I tried to play scales.

Michael stares straight ahead and shrugs. "No big deal, I guess." I know he's lying; he hates it when he loses a student, and not just for fiscal reasons. "So what was up with you the other day, crying over the weather report?" he asks with calculated casualness.

"Me? Oh, I don't know," I reply, swinging my leg and scratching my face.

"Come on, Toby, you have to admit it was a little weird. Are you cracking up?"

"Why should I tell you?" I ask angrily. "You're only going to tell her anyway." I don't need to say who; he knows already.

"Not true. Come on, tell me," he whines.

"I don't feel comfortable discussing it," I say evenly, cribbing a line from a sexual harassment video that we'd been forced to watch this week at Toyland. The sample scenarios with the cheesy actors were painful to watch, so scripted and oozing with overt lasciviousness at every turn. "Hey baby, I'd love to get a piece of that; how about it?" the middle-management type said to the secretary with the frosted hair and the red dress that was at least twenty years out of date. She faced him and curtly said, "I don't feel comfortable discussing it," before turning on her heels and going to her boss to blow the whistle on the offender. It was so ridiculous and boring that Caroline fell asleep next to me, her head lolling on my shoulder as she snored quietly.

"What?" Michael asks, confused. I start laughing and tell him about the video and its pathetic specimens. Soon he is laughing too and begging me to tell him what happened the other morning.

"Only if you *swear* you won't tell Lisa," I say sternly. "Don't laugh. This is serious!"

"OK," he says, sitting closer to me on the couch.

Chapter 12

Scores upon scores of men are walking by, bumping into one another, stepping on each other's toes, and backing up into each other's wives and girlfriends without so much as an "Excuse me" or even a "Hey, buddy, get outta my way." Their eyes staring straight ahead in their sockets and their mouths open with something between reverence and lust, they are fixated on the candy apple reds and the brilliant cobalt blues of this year's cars. The twin cams, the double-wishbone suspensions, the eight-cylinders, the two hundred seventy horsepowers, the torque, the powertrain, the leatherlike interior, the valves, the induction, the B-series, the S-series, the in-dash CD changer, the alloy wheels, the power sunroofs. The air is thick with testosterone, mingling with the scent of new-car smell.

My dad, however, is fixated on my sweater at the moment, the silvery glittery one with the short cap sleeves.

I hand my coat to the cheery coat check lady, and he gives me a disapproving look. "Aren't short sleeves a little cold for the end of January?" he asks, stuffing a dollar in the coat check lady's tip jar.

"Oh, no, I don't think so," I answer with a dismissive wave of my hand. "Look, the new VW concept cars!" I squeal.

"Well, I don't pretend to know anything about what women wear," he harrumphs. "I just don't want you to catch a chill." He glances over at the Volkswagen area. "And you can forget about anyone in this family getting a VW, Toby. You know your sister would have our heads." He is actually talking about my sister's husband, who is Jewish and hell-bent on the idea that buying a German car is like endorsing the Holocaust. I could sort of see his point, but sometimes when I'm salivating over the BMW 3 Series, I think, how could these beautiful cars ever hurt anybody? Rear-wheel drive never sent anyone to his death, did it? Oh, wait, maybe it did.

"Yeah, yeah, I know. And don't worry about me; I won't catch a chill," I say as we plunge headlong into the fray of the Philadelphia Auto Show. The real truth is that I've worn my glitzy sweater in the hopes that perhaps J.P. Cody might be here, broadcasting once more. I conceived this far-fetched notion last night while taking a walk around the block in an effort to escape the noises of Michael and Lisa's amorous adventures. Just thinking about it now makes me feel sick, and no one would forgive me if I tossed my cookies in the plush backseat of the new Isuzu, so I shake off that disturbing mental image and focus on trying to look fantastic in case J.P. Cody does turn up.

I languidly drape my legs out of the new Lexus, looking for J.P. I preen in a Porsche, look alluring in an Acura, check my makeup in a Mazda, flip my hair in a Ford. I exude sexual energy in a Subaru and bend over just so to investigate the braking system in a Buick. I turn coy in a Toyota and make va-va-voom eyes in a Volkswagen. I stretch out nymph-like in a Nissan, make kissy faces in a Mercedes-Benz mirror, joke and smile in a Jeep. But alas, no J.P. to be found.

In desperate need of sustenance after ninety minutes of car hopping, my dad and I head across the street to Reading Terminal Market. It is a hustle and bustle of food vendors, with the wide-eyed Amish teenage girls with their pinafores and white caps and ruddy skin jostling for space in between the plucky Korean fish vendors and the big, sweaty cheesesteak guy holding fast over his sizzling griddle. My dad decides on pizza, and by the time we finally find a place to sit (perilously close to a giant pile of apples on the perimeter of Manny's Produce, in my opinion), I'm ravenous and headachy. My dad quickly shakes oregano on his slice and says, "Everything OK? You looked a little disappointed when we left there."

"Oh, no, Dad," I lie, swallowing a bite of life-giving cheese and dough. "Nothing, really—I'm sure I was just hungry."

"Because I'm sure we could work *some*thing out with Bruce if you really wanted a BMW, you know. The people who make those cars now have nothing to do with World War Two Germany!" he says emphatically, folding his pizza into a V and watching a blob of sauce drip in slow motion onto his shirt. "Crap! Would you look at that? Your mother's going to kill me!"

"I'll get you some napkins," I say as I jump up. I'm relieved to have the opportunity to get away for a moment; I suddenly feel a sting of emotional angst when I consciously realize that I was disappointed at not seeing a TV weatherman at the auto show. What was happening to me?

I walk briskly over to Vinnie's Cheesesteaks, the first place in my line of vision that has a dispenser bursting with tiny white paper napkins. I yank out many more than I need and head back via the fish vendors, breathing through my mouth to keep from being overwhelmed by the briny smell.

"Toby? Is that you?" I turn and see Jenna, who is wielding a tiny plastic shopping basket brimming with packages neatly wrapped in white paper. She looks utterly shocked to see me, and a little nervous. "*Are you OK?*" she asks, staring at me with her eyebrows furrowed.

I'm wondering if I'm looking crazy-eyed and answer cautiously, "Yes. Why shouldn't I be?"

"Because I've left two messages for you. And the second time I called, Michael's girlfriend said you were in the hospital! I've been worried sick!" she says breath-lessly, twisting one of her mittens into a tight wooly ball.

Lisa Carlton, you had to love her. I sigh so deeply that I wonder if Jenna can smell the oregano on my breath. "*At* the hospital, not *in* the hospital," I say, my eyes turning into slits. "I'm volunteering there. That stupid, stupid girlfriend of his—she doesn't give me phone messages *and* she has you worried sick. I'm ready to kill her."

"Oh boy," Jenna twitters nervously. "I'm so glad you're all right, though. Can you wait for a minute? I'm on a fish-buying binge right now, but I should be done soon."

"My dad's over there and he just spilled sauce on himself," I say, waving the pile of napkins to prove my point. Jenna nods, and I promise to call her this week to catch up. I'm fuming as I make my way back to my dad, thinking about the many ugly things I'd like to say to Lisa, when I feel a poke in my back. I'm in front of a butcher's counter and I'm ready to yell at whoever is so excited about buying pigs' feet that they can't control where they put their fingers, but when I whirl around, it's Jenna again.

"Sorry, Toby! I totally forgot to tell you," she says. "I saw J.P. Cody this morning at work—" She pauses for a second, cocks her head to the side, and asks tentatively, "You still like to watch him, right?"

Watch him? I think and very nearly begin to giggle hysterically. Watching isn't the half of it, my friend. But since Jenna doesn't have a clue about the workout that

Mr. Clackety Clack has been getting in the name of J.P. Cody lately, I just nod quickly and without emotion, as though she asked if I still had the same mailing address or if I owned a lint brush.

"OK, well I had to go in for a little while today, even though they don't have me doing the Saturday news anymore," she continues.

"And?" I ask, my pulse quickening.

"Well, not a lot; he was bringing in some clothes. Some of the TV people do that, I guess—they bring in things they are going to wear for the upcoming week. I was trying to see if there was anything unusual."

"What do you mean, 'unusual'? Like women's underwear or something?" I ask while waving to my dad, who is gesticulating wildly and pointing to the stain on his shirt. "So what did you see?"

She bites her lower lip and shrugs apologetically. "Well, just suits, I guess. There was one on top that I like—it's kind of a dark reddish one?"

"Huh, that's kind of weird," I say, rapidly combing through my mental archives of J.P.'s wardrobe and coming up blank. "Well, thanks for telling me, Jenna—I probably should get back to my dad now."

On my way back to help my dad with his pizza problem, though, I get stuck in a crowd of people next to the market's most popular hoagie vendor. With nothing else to do, I begin fretting over whether or not J.P. liked my last poem, the one I wrote to make sure the tie wasn't a fluke:

The blue-checked tie
Was so very nice
In this season
Of hail and ice

So thanks so much
And to rule out a fluke
At some point next week
Can you wear your olive green suit?

All of a sudden it comes to me, and I throw my head back laughing, suddenly embarrassed and clamping my hand over my mouth when the guy making the hoagies looks up mid-squirt with his plastic vinegar bottle. Of *course* J.P.'s going to wear the suit. It was right there in front of Jenna's face. Problem was, in front of Jenna's face, it was red, not olive green.

"And don't forget to change the dummy copy on *this* one, Toby—it's very important," Sarah says slowly, shaking her finger at me like I'm her starbaby and I've gotten into a big jar of custard. "Also, I'm sending you up to Toy Fair next week. I can't go, with the baby and all"—she smiles and grows misty-eyed just thinking about her sweetums—"so I'm counting on you. Isn't that girl you know from preschool going? Kathleen; is that her name?"

"*Caroline*," I say irritably. She and Sarah just worked together last Monday on the try-me packaging design for Bounce 'Em Bears—couldn't she remember a blessed thing?

It's Wednesday and I am aggravated, annoyed, and premenstrual—a winning trio for putting up with Sarah's demented conversation, to be sure. The week is young, but J.P. hasn't worn his olive green suit yet, and I nearly hyperventilated this morning trying to first contain my excitement and then conceal my disappointment in front of Lisa Carlton when he appeared in his royal red tie and gray suit combo, which I hate. My stomach then remained in knots during my ride to work with Rich; the ice and sleet coated the roads like hard frosting on a stale Tastykake and Rich's bald tires were no match for the slick surface. I also made the mistake of mentioning that I heard about a sale on Firestone tires at a local store, only to have Rich rant bitterly about his current financial situation, what with the divorce and the alimony and the child support.

I stomp around the corner of the hallway and nearly faint when I see Rod Winters standing stock-still in front of my cubicle, staring hard at the cheap carpeted walls. I slow down to stall for time and rack my brain to remember what might be pinned up there that would interest him—the final engineering drawing of the Flower Fun playset? No, that went back to Joe weeks ago. The cost sheet for Sweet Treat Babies? No, girls' toys were the domain of the other engineering director, the Korean guy who microwaved his pungent-smelling lunches with such reckless abandon that he could clear out the whole floor in minutes. The packaging layouts for Fuzzy Friends' comb and brush sets? The Rockin' Rhino guitar's sticker sheet plans?

And then just as quickly as I notice him, he is gone. He sees me plodding down the hall, straightens himself up to his full height, and marches off without a word. Before he rounds the corner, he glances back at me for a millisecond and rubs his five o'clock shadow. What the hell could he want? I think as I flop into my cheap chair and let my eyes dart all over the walls of my cubicle.

I've got my "Toby 'Some Assembly Required' Morris" sticker; a tattered Flyers schedule; the packaging layouts for Fuzzy Friends' accoutrements; bits of notes and drawings; banana-colored Post-its from my sister with names of herbs I should be taking; a glossy picture of a BMW 318ti; an old snapshot of Michael, his cousin Sheila, and me caroling while very drunk one Christmas (for some reason we got it in our heads that it would be fun to sing the Peter Gunn theme); and a burgeoning gallery of fantastic finger paintings and drawings from my pint-sized pals at Children's Hospital.

In the mere five weeks that I've been volunteering there, I've formed alliances and made more friends than I ever would have imagined I could have on that shaky first day. Now I can take in scary scars with nary a shudder, help plan elaborate birthday celebrations, command a good-sized group when reading Disney classics, and talk about treatments with lisping five-year-olds who should never have to learn words like radiation. In return they've deluged me with that classic kiddie form of payment, the adorable drawing. Drippy yellow suns and V-shaped birds, dogs with seven legs, people composed of heads, limbs, and not much else. The watercolors bleed and blend into one another and make a purply-brown mess that reminds me a lot of my painting palette in my freshman-year painting course.

The adventurous ones try their hand at printing, with varying degrees of success. Many of the crinkly sheets sport variations on my name, which more often than not reads "YBOT." And of course, those budding Picassos who can sign their names always do so; I've got a KATIE timidly written in a pink scrawl in a corner of a drawing of a psychedelic-looking flower and a DAAVE K., complete with an extra *A* in his first name, painted above a detailed rendering of a robot. My favorite patient, Tracie, was inspired to print her name *vertically* down the side of the paper after seeing me do so at the craft table, but it proved much too challenging for her in the end. Her letters were turned every which way, with her capital *E* sporting more lines than I could count and her *A* a ringer for a geometry lesson in isosceles triangles. There was a letter on the end that I couldn't even make out—it could have been an *M* or a *W* or perhaps a Greek epsilon—no matter, though. I told her it was beautiful, and I believe that it is.

Well, screw Rod, I decide as I get ready to go to lunch. Who cares what he was looking at here? I'm sure he'll be riled up and yelling about whatever it was later on, so I know I'll hear about it then.

Lisa hates when Michael plays the intro from *Rhapsody in Blue,* which I'll never understand as long as I live. It's so tickly and cute and adorable—but then, these are three words that I would never use to describe Lisa Carlton. Michael's not even a big fan of the piece, but his composer friend Anthony told him early on in school that the old Italian guy who owns the music store on the edge of campus adores it. Adores the whole thing, but especially the intro. Adores clarinet students who will come in and play those first notes for him, and when they've got perfect fingering and breath control and they make him break into that huge smile that shows off his dentures, he gives them twenty percent off their reeds and sheet music. I could identify with Renzo: When Michael would play for him, the hair on my arms would stand on end. It amazed me to see his fingers fly like that, although for him it seemed as natural as blinking and he shrugged it off, just happy to see that "–20%" on the cash register receipt.

Tonight he is playing it again, and Lisa is sitting on the sofa, holding the *TV Guide* taut in front of her face. I planned to settle in for the night to watch inning seven of my video series, but when she plopped onto the couch, I knew that my date with the Yankees dynasty was not to be. It was OK; I wasn't in the mood for their smug New York faces anyway.

"Why do you keep playing that?" Lisa whines.

"I told you, remember?" he says. "I'm going downtown tomorrow, and this guy always counts on me to play this part of this piece. It's silly; you wouldn't understand."

"You don't need the discount, Michael. So why do you have to worry about it?"

"Well, as it happens, honey, I do need the discount," he answers patiently, as I nearly gag upon hearing him call her honey. "But that's not the point, anyway," he says, pulling a new spitty reed from his mouth and loosening the screws on the mouthpiece of the clarinet. "This guy *knows* me, and he's going to want to hear it."

"Well, whatever," she says, rolling her eyes from behind an article about a movie of the week. "Just seems like bad retailing to me, you know? What if we gave a discount to every guy who walked in and"—her lack of creativity is so profound that she is futilely searching for some kind of analogy—"did a dance or something? We wouldn't make any money. It just sends a weird message."

"That reminds me," I say to Lisa, clearing my throat. "Speaking of messages, I mean." She puts down the *TV Guide* and ever so slowly tightens her scrunchie. I wonder briefly if this is like animals I've seen on the Discovery Channel getting ready to rumble, puffing up their fur or displaying their plumage or whatever. "Have there been any messages for me? Phone messages?" My voice squeaks a bit like Michael's new sax and clarinet students practicing with their mouthpieces for the first time; this is uncharacteristically confrontational for me and I'm sure I'm going to break out in hives in a moment.

Lisa juts out her lower lip for two seconds and looks at the ceiling. "Nope," she says finally. "Not a one." Michael glances over at me with a quizzical look, then turns back to his clarinet. I fix Lisa with an angry stare but it's too late; she's safely ensconced behind *TV Guide* again, not at all guilty for having lied about Jenna's calls. Thank God Toy Fair is next week, I think as I walk upstairs to look at my picture of J.P. Cody.

Chapter 13

The elevator is doing its damnedest to close, but the two doors try to kiss shut for the fourth time, and *crack*—they hit the moose's antler and immediately propel themselves open once more. A nattily dressed woman who is juggling a day planner, calculator, and cell phone looks up from her conversation and says curtly, "Please, can't you wait for the next one? There's not enough room for you in here."

"No, I can't, I'm sorry," the moose shoots back, raising his fuzzy, brown-mittened hands to the sky in exasperation. "I have to get to one of the sixth-floor showrooms now. I can't wait for another elevator." The woman snorts and turns back to her phone, speaking quietly but urgently about projected international sales. Caroline pokes me in the ribs as she stifles a chuckle, the moose finally contorts his body and bends his neck just so, and the elevator starts up the narrow shaft of the Toy Building with a groan.

We are at Toy Fair, the toy industry's yearly beauty pageant, the fashion show of the year, the stuff that dreams are made of. For one week in February, the International Toy Building in the lower part of Manhattan becomes a dazzling display of glitter and magic and money and power. This is where the major players pitch their wares for the upcoming Christmas season, and decisions are made by hawk-eyed buyers that will influence kiddies worldwide as they sit openmouthed and laboriously write their lists to Santa months from now. There are reporters and camera crews pressing into one another as they try to film their segments on this year's must-have piles of polypropylene. Pop stars and sports heroes breeze through the crowded lobby on their way to get a glimpse of their likenesses in creamy plastic. Tiny knots of businessmen in the hallways discuss in low voices whether or not they should bet the farm on ant farms. The only thing conspicuous in its absence is the focus of all this cash and high-gloss PR: Search high and low and you won't find even one child at Toy Fair. Plenty in the commercials, yes; in the flesh, no.

It's a study in contrasts: the moose and dozens of other similar felt-covered monstrosities hired to walk the halls and promote the hot new toys. The rich, white men who for just one moment need to close their eyes and imagine what it's like to be a four-year-old girl playing with dollies. The bouncy, bubbly actors and actresses hired to demonstrate a toy over and over and over, praying silently that the prototype toy won't break like it did in front of the last group of buyers. The grizzled union electricians, who make sure the thousands of TV monitors will be able to show the products' commercials ad nauseum. Then of course, there is us: the employees packed into tiny rooms *behind* the showrooms, cursing, sweating, and laughing as we try to put the finishing touches on the hundreds of displays before the all-important buyers tour the showroom. The buzz is that Toyland spent a cool three million on our showroom this year, and it certainly doesn't show yet—but it will when we are done with it.

Caroline and I enter the crowded back room, where Joe is sitting on a high stool, hunched over five Awesome Avalanche racers with their electronic guts splayed everywhere. He is nimble, deftly handling an array of tiny screwdrivers and wire cutters, and it reminds me of a segment Michael and I watched on *20/20* in which they did an exposé on assembly-line surgery in Russia. The anaesthetized people came down a conveyor belt, and zip, slash, dash, each doctor did his part and passed them on down the line. I'm mesmerized by Joe's work with the mini wires and hardware when Fiona, a tough marketing woman who hails from Wales, pushes past me.

"Joe, are you done with them yet?" she pleads in her marbles-in-the-mouth accent. "The actresses need to practice."

"No," he says flatly. "I promise I'll let you know when they are done." As he finishes his sentence, loud-mouthed Alyssa from the girls' activities department bustles by with a six-foot cardboard nail-polish-bottle prop, nearly knocking Joe off his stool. Fiona sniffs, turns on her high-gloss, expensive heels, and leaves.

"I told her the work will get done whether she panics or not. The first buyers don't even come through for another day yet. She'll have her toys," he says defiantly, slamming the plastic battery housing onto a racer and grabbing a screwdriver. "Welsh bitch," he adds.

"Hey," Caroline says, saving me from Joe's rant. "Where do they have you working, Toby? I've been put on Pretty Kitty detail," she says, brandishing a giant, industrial staple gun.

"I talked on the phone to The Third Sex before we left New Jersey," I say over the din of the radio that someone's tuned to a New York disco station. The Third Sex is the nickname I gave to Sarah's boss, Bill. A genteel, doe-eyed guy, he doesn't seem gay, but he doesn't seem quite straight, either. He never speaks of a girlfriend or of a "friend" of any type, for that matter, and his office is devoid of any clues. Strangely asexual, The Third Sex is threatening and disquieting in the most passive way possible. I suppose when I really thought about it, he is most likely a "non-practicing homosexual," like the guy in that John Irving book I read on vacation last year. What was the name of that book again? The one that Kerrin read after I finished it and called "the one with that little twit in it." Oh, yes, that's right: *A Prayer for Owen Meany.*

"What?" Caroline says quizzically, shoveling a pile of

Pretty Kitties onto a cart, their silly, googly eyes looking heavenward and their soft tails and ears pointing in every direction.

"Nothing. Bill said if he's not here when I get here, I have to go to one of the little rooms down the hall, that's where they have the graphics people holed up. I'll come visit you later though, OK?" I slip past Joe on his stool and make my way down the hall, stopping to grab a small strawberry off a cart containing a lavish lunch spread that's barely been touched by the upper-management types. I pop it in my mouth and hold it there for a minute, savoring the sweet taste and bumpy texture before biting down.

I spend the rest of the afternoon with giant pieces of red and pink holographic Mylar and my X-Acto knife, carefully cutting out hundreds of tiny stars, hearts, and puckering lip shapes. These shapes will help form the eye-popping backdrop for the Razzle Dazzle Decal area, a section of the showroom that will be promoting none other than the Razzle Dazzle Decal kit, an elaborate craft center that lets the kid design and make her own decals. (Refills sold separately.) When my hand cramps so much that it turns one of the lip shapes into something closely resembling Mick Jagger's mouth, I decide to take a break and tell The Third Sex (who has been popping in and out for the last few hours—but where has he been? But where? If you can't figure out your sexuality in a place like New York City, there's not much hope for you, Bill) that I'm going to visit Caroline. I make my way through the showroom, past the blond, giggly boys' toys presenters who are outfitted in tiny shorts and crop tops that will make them jiggle in all the right places for the male buyers, past the wires snaking all over the floors and walls, past the smell of baby powder that's been puffed liberally into the air in the infant toy section. I'm shuddering, thinking about how much will have to get done in less than forty-eight hours when I happen upon Caroline, who is on her knees and stapling Pretty Kitties to the wall of the Pretty Kitty display area with gusto.

"Try it, it's fun," she says, running one hand over her short, spiky blond hair and sliding the staple gun toward me on the floor. "Get him right through the paw," she adds. I must look aghast because she says flatly, "Trust me, Toby, if you dealt with this product day in and day out every day for almost a year, it wouldn't look so cute to you anymore." She grabs the staple gun and stands up, leaning against the fake white-and-pink trellis that's been built into the display. "How about . . . here," she says, stapling a black-and-white Pretty Kitty to the trellis by its tail. She gives me a satisfied grin. "What time do you think you'll get out of here?"

I shrug. "I don't know—I guess it depends on how far they get with building more of the displays. I'm on Razzle Dazzle now."

"I don't think I've seen that one," she says, sifting through the remaining Pretty Kitties in the cart. "If it's not preschool, I'm totally out of the loop. What about this one for over the archway?" she asks, holding a calico Pretty Kitty high in the air and not waiting for my answer. "Well, he'll do, anyway," she says, sinking a staple into his back paw so he dangles adorably over the entryway to the display. "I'll call Doug in a little bit and tell him we'll be by sometime tonight. I'm sure he'll be smashed anyway by the time we see him, so it almost doesn't matter what time we get in," she says with a hint of bleak laughter in her voice.

At eleven o'clock Caroline and I are settled into Doug's small but cozy East Village loft, with its shower stall in the kitchen and funny little doors that lead to nowhere. Caroline's alcohol-addled older brother is a head writer for one of the major late-night talk shows, and he has offered us a place to stay during Toy Fair. We could have stayed in the hotel that Toyland offered to put us up in, but it seemed to be a fleabag place and had been featured in the news recently as the site of a gangland-style shooting. That was enough for me, and although Caroline and I hadn't really spent all that much time together outside of work to date, I had eagerly accepted her generous invite.

I climb into the pullout sofa bed and grimace as I lay down; my neck and upper back are sore from leaning over and cutting Mylar shapes until well into the evening. I guess I don't have it so bad: Caroline bore the scratches and cuts of having the Pretty Kitty trellis fall on her unexpectedly, and she complained loudly about it in the cab all the way over here. We know one thing is for certain: Tomorrow will be even worse.

I hear Caroline grunt as she hoists herself up into the loft in the adjacent part of the apartment.

"Caroline?" I call into the darkness.

"Yeah, what's up?" she asks, sounding like the trek up to her brother's bed sapped whatever strength she had left.

"Are you sure Doug won't be back? I feel bad taking up this whole sofa bed—you could sleep here and I could sleep on the floor, and he could sleep up there. I don't mind."

"Don't worry about it. He said he would be at his girl-friend's tonight, so he wouldn't be sleeping here any-way. Really, it's OK," she says, her voice fading fast.

"All right," I say dubiously. "Well, good night; try not to dream about Pretty Kitties," I tease.

Caroline doesn't answer and soon the apartment is quiet; except for the occasional car horn and clanking of the radiator, it's just the sound of my breathing and the vast expanse of black space filling the room up to the high ceiling. I'm strangely alert now—after waiting for the cab in the bracing cold and then helping Caroline crack the code to unlock the many locks on Doug's door, I've gotten a second wind, and my mind is starting to race. I turn on my side to try to soothe the sore muscle in my left shoulder and think about last Friday and my conversation with Kerrin.

I was sitting at work that afternoon making a list of all the supplies to bring up to Toy Fair when Kerrin called me, her voice high-pitched and cheery. In fact, she sounded almost as excited as I had been when J.P. Cody had worn his olive green suit that morning. It had been a long, long week, waiting every morning with my heart pounding, and each day he had disappointed me. But then Friday came—magical, wonderful Friday—and this time I hadn't had to conceal my joy, because Lisa Carlton and Michael hadn't even been around. Instead, I had leaped around the living room, shaking up the Apple Jacks in my stomach and giving myself a rosy glow that rivaled the most expensive blush I've ever purchased.

"But why did he wait until the end of the week?" I asked Kerrin. Not to look a gift meteorologist in an olive green suit in the mouth, but I was curious.

"Toby," she answered breathlessly, "he's *flirting* with you!" She drew out the first syllable in *flirting* so it sounded like *"fuh*-lirting."

"Do you think?" I asked, my heart skipping a beat. "Really?"

"Oh, God, what's this?" Kerrin said, and I could hear the sound of an envelope being ripped open. "Holy shit! It's the name of a therapist from this chick in my department. I told her this morning that I was really tense about all my deadlines, and she suggested I 'talk to someone,' " she guffawed.

"Kerrin, please, why do you think he's flirting?" I implored her.

"I can't believe the nerve of these people!" she shouted, fuming. "I'm tense, so I need unsolicited advice about a *therapist*? I told you about the one time I went to a therapist, right? How my mom made me go after my dad left? The guy kept checking out my rack the whole time! I'll never do that again!" she finished angrily.

"Kerrin, I'm sure he wasn't checking out your rack, you were twelve . . . will you focus for a minute?" I sputtered.

"Yes, but I was very developed by then, don't forget! Sorry, OK, where was I? Oh yeah, flirting. He could have worn it any day this week, right? But he was making you wait. Making you watch him, making you wonder when it was coming. You should be quite pleased."

"I am!"

"Well, I'll be sure to get a postmortem on it from Len this weekend—we'll hear the guy's perspective, whatever the hell that's worth," she laughed. "Now don't get lazy, Toby—you've got to think of something really great to do next."

Something great to do next—what could that be? I wonder as an ambulance roars by into the New York night. I'm massaging my neck and racking my brain, but nothing is coming, nothing exciting and J.P. Cody-worthy, anyway. My eyelids start to flutter, and soon I'm deep in dreamland.

Bad kitty karma—I made fun of Caroline less than eight hours ago, teasing her not to dream about Pretty Kitties, and now I am having a scary nightmare about one. It is sitting on my face, a plush lump, with its little limbs splayed in every direction. No matter what I do, I can't get rid of the Pretty Kitty. It's so heavy—it weighs me down, pushes into my cheeks and lips, rises and falls with my every breath. I slowly wake up and realize with a start that it isn't a Pretty Kitty at all, but a man's hand on my face—and I'm guessing it belongs to Doug. His palm smells like a combination of warm hay and illicit substances, and his arm and the rest of him are lying fully clothed next to me on the bed. I'm stuck as I lie here trying to figure out what to do next. Luckily, after an agonizing minute, I hear the clock radio go off next to Caroline's head, and she pops down out of the loft. I can see her walking toward me in her T-shirt and Notre Dame sweats, but she can't see me until she rounds the corner past a pillar. I slowly wave and wordlessly point to my face, and she opens her mouth and lets out a giant scream.

"You idiot! Get your hand off her face!" She runs to my side of the sofa bed and yanks his hand away, letting his arm flop down on the bed like wet spaghetti. "Move it!" she shouts, poking him in the back.

"Hmmmm?" Doug asks, looking from me to Caroline with a bewildered expression. He closes his eyes again and turns over so he is facing me. "Unngggh," he says, trying to pull the covers up around him.

"Stop it, Doug! What have you done to my friend?"

"Nothing," he answers, scratching his face. It's true, although I can't decide if I should be grateful or disappointed. On the one hand, he smells drunk and probably has some kind of hideous social disease. On the other hand, he's got a fantastic cleft chin (remarkably like Caroline's, in fact), and his striped Oxford shirt is unbuttoned just so and his blond hair hugs the nape of his neck and I'm not getting any other offers these days.

Caroline puts her hands on her hips and inhales and exhales deeply through her nose. "Well, Doug, this is Toby. Toby, Doug."

"Heyyy," he says, reaching out his hand and shaking mine. "Sorry about all this," he says, sitting up slowly and smoothing the blanket. Caroline pours him a blue Tupperware tumbler of orange juice, and he takes it from her gratefully.

"What about Gloria?" Caroline asks pensively, sticking her face in his. Their two heads are backlit from the sun streaming in the nearby window, silhouetting them and making a quirky Rorschach blot of cleft chins and close-cropped hair.

"Yeah, well, you know how that can be . . . I thought I could stay, but then plans changed, so I had to come back here." He smiles shyly, like a little boy who's been caught. Doing what, is what I'm trying to determine, and from Caroline's expression, I can tell it's something she is truly disgusted by.

An hour later I'm waiting for Caroline out in the cold, bright sunlight. She's run back inside at Doug's request, and when she reappears she is holding a tiny key on a long string. We walk wordlessly toward the subway, but as we reach the corner, she steers me toward one of those stores that sells stamps and bubble wrap and mails packages at a premium. I follow Caroline inside and she strides over to the post office boxes, brandishing the key. She opens one of the post office boxes, peers inside, and slams it again. When we are back out on the street, she pulls out her cell phone, dials, and barks, "Nothing, OK? Yeah, maybe we'll see you later." She closes the phone with a crisp *click*, turns to me, and says, "Let's get a cab, all right? It's on Toyland anyway."

"Of course," I say, wary of her mood.

We are in the cab, sitting solidly in morning traffic, when Caroline apologizes. "I'm so sorry, Toby," she begins.

"It's fine," I say in what I think is a reassuring tone. "Your brother seems nice."

"He *is* nice," she says, frowning. "He's just so screwed up. He drinks too much. He's at bars until all hours with all these TV weirdos. And do you know why he was in your bed last night?" she asks in a loud voice. I lean forward to hear her answer; even the cabbie is peering in his rearview mirror with a look of anticipation.

"Because Gloria is married. He's having an affair with a married woman! This city is full of single girls, and he has to be with someone who's married. When you were in the bathroom he told me that her husband came back early from a business trip and that's why he had to come home," she finishes angrily. Apparently this story is tame compared to other ones the cabbie must hear in the naked city, because he's stopped listening to us and is now singing softly to the radio.

"And the post office box—that's so they can mail each other things and not be found out. They each have one. Doug said she told him to check his mailbox, that she had sent him something, and he felt too hung over to venture out this morning," she spits, compulsively picking at the stickers on the seatback of the cab. She is able to grab one at its corner and begins to peel it back, exposing all the sticky glue, when we arrive at the Toy Building. As we leave the cab, she guiltily tries to press it back into place but it's too late. The corner of the sticker springs away from the seatback and will now become the project of some other fare with long fingernails and a lot on her mind.

All day long I call upon my muse to help me think of what to do next for J.P. Cody, but I have no luck. I help Alyssa with her giant nail-polish-bottle prop for the Fingernail Frenzy display, but nothing comes to me as I sit on the floor slowly lettering the oversize label with the words "Magnificent Mango." I let my mind go blank and attempt to let some creative ideas flow as I sit wordlessly with The Third Sex, cutting out hundreds of daffodil stickers for the Delightful Daffodils display. I try to clear my head by taking a break with Joe and walking through the area of the showroom where the actresses all sit and preen, so he can ogle the red-haired one with the awesome ass (his words, not mine). I take a late lunch by myself in the overpriced café in the ground floor of the Toy Building, sandwiched between the poor moose from a day earlier and a harried-looking salesman wearing a name tag branding him as one of Toyland's competitors. I close my eyes over my expensive ham and cheese croissant and try to tune out the noise filtering in from the crowded lobby, but it's no use. When I open my eyes, the moose is waving to a girl dressed as a farmhand and the salesman is furiously scribbling in a notebook, but nothing about me has changed. I've got nothing.

When I return to the showroom, it's madness and mayhem and no one will slow down long enough to talk to me. I finally am able to stop Fiona, but her cheeks are ablaze and she's speaking a mile a minute and I can't understand a thing she is saying. I'm walking by the kelly green wall of the Goofy Gator game display when Caroline runs by with an armful of plastic gator heads, throwing them down and dashing toward the back room. I follow her in hot pursuit and she pants, "We don't have until tomorrow morning. The CEO of Toys "R" Us is coming *tonight* at ten o'clock."

"Ten o'clock?" I repeat incredulously, stopping in my tracks. Caroline doesn't even break her stride, so I run to catch up with her. "Who comes to tour a showroom at ten at night, Caroline? Why would he do such a thing?"

"Because he *can*," she says. This was a toy manufacturer's worst nightmare: not enough time to pull together the entire showroom, to make it shiny and slick and beautiful and capable of eliciting dancing dollar signs in the buyers' eyes. Not enough time to make sure the actresses know exactly how to yank the rip cord on the racecar. Not enough time to ensure that the Penny Piñata commercial is properly rewound to the English-speaking version first, then the Spanish-speaking version next. Normally, the first buyers would make their rounds of the showrooms starting at seven in the morning, which would mean people like us would be up until midnight, one o'clock, two o'clock the night before, whatever it took. By that time, we'd be sick to our stomachs from inhaling glue and paint fumes and laughing from the incredible punchiness and crying from whoever dared venture a thought that our products' displays were less than perfect. But it would all get done and done perfectly: the toy cars would shine, the dolls' hair would gleam, the games would all be perfectly poised and ready to be played, and the stuffed animals would all peer out from their areas in adorable poses.

Now, because of the whim of some suits, it's all being threatened, and before The Third Sex can even find me, I swing into action to help Caroline with the Goofy Gator display. She shows me how to assemble the gators' upper and lower jaws, how each gator head fits into the green plastic base, and how the mouth opens and closes. Then she dashes off to help her friend Josh with the Super Spyman display, which at this moment is nothing more than three bare, gunmetal gray walls. I don't like Super Spyman or Josh. He and I butted heads several times over the development of the stickers last fall—he wanted them much too small for children to work with, and he wasn't interested when I tried to explain about kids' fine motor skills or lack thereof. I decide to stay put and spend a lot of time on the gators, with their silly mouths and huge, white teeth.

I'm just putting the finishing touches on the gators when Caroline and Josh run by with a box of Super Spyman Spycams and she shouts, "Batteries, Toby! Don't forget the batteries!" When I walk to the back room to pick up the forty batteries I'll need to give the gators life, I'm shocked to see it's six o'clock already. Joe is sitting back on his stool munching on a piece of pizza.

"You should get some," he says, nodding to a stack of white boxes. "Not everyone knows it's here yet. It's not bad—if you like New York–style pizza."

I wolf down two slices and put a few slices on two paper plates and make my way back out to the show-room, which is now fairly buzzing. The actors and actresses are running their lines, and together they make a funny, disjointed poem, an Ode to Unctuous Advertising, as I walk toward the Super Spyman display: "Every girl wants to be like her mom and now she can with . . ."/"Get the Goofy Gator's mouth open and reach in—if you dare!"/"Fingernail Frenzy's commercial is a thirty-second romp through . . ."/"The try-me packaging for the Awesome Avalanche racer means retailers can expect an avalanche of sales this holiday season!"

When I reach the display, Caroline squeals with delight and gratefully takes a slice of pizza; Josh eats his and says nothing. I sit on the floor, catching my breath before I go to install all the batteries in the gators, calling on my muse again. Still nothing, although from this angle I am afforded an excellent view of Josh's torso as he stands on a ladder and reaches up, and I'm satisfied to see that he's wearing ugly, white Jockey underwear.

Three hours later we are all completely exhausted and cranky, but everything looks wonderful. I even have to hand it to Josh, who, with Caroline's help, was able to pull the Super Spyman display together into a sleek silver, gray, and black homage to gumshoes. The actors manning the display mill around in trench coats, hats, and sunglasses, talking to one another via their Super Spyman walkie-talkies.

"OK, everybody in the back room, unless one of your displays is at the *end* of the showroom," Fiona yells, her eyes wild. "The Toys "R" Us people will be here very soon, and except for the actors and actresses, I don't want to find anyone out here working as they take their tour. Understand? Last third of the showroom only, if you have finishing touches to make."

Caroline and I scramble with the others to the back room, where someone uncorks a bottle of cheap wine and passes it around. We all take thirsty gulps, and Alyssa turns the radio up even louder. We all start to relax a little bit—until Fiona pops her head back in and shouts angrily, "*Who* is Super Spyman?" I wonder briefly if this is some kind of metaphorical question, but then I realize that to Fiona, a person is no more than the sum of his or her product lines.

"That's mine," Josh hollers from the back of the room, where he is trying to unearth his coat from under a huge pile of cardboard boxes.

"Well, it's *falling apart,* and you need to fix it. They're already here, so hurry up! Come on, move it!" Josh snaps his head up and looks quizzically at Caroline, who pleadingly gestures to me to come with her. The three of us race to the Super Spyman display, where the slick, empty packaging has fallen off the silver and gray wall and now lazily litters the floor like it's Christmas Eve at the toy store.

"Fuck—the sample packaging! I knew we shouldn't try to tape it up there, Caroline—the walls were still too wet for it to stick!" Josh whines, taking a sip from a paper coffee cup he's carried out there with him.

"Well, whose fault is that?" she retorts flirtatiously. "Too bad you were out at the used record stores in the Village when you should have been here. We need a hot glue gun now."

Fiona peers around the display and looks disapprovingly at the shiny packages on the floor and then up at the empty spaces on the wall. "They're around the bend, at the Voice Command Real Racers. You've got ten minutes, tops," she hisses. Josh hurries off and returns with a ladder and a glue gun, its tip drippy and warm with melting glue. He plugs it into an outlet hidden in one of the gray walls, and he and Caroline begin trying to reconfigure the packages on the wall. "Toby, how about I throw you a box, you put some hot glue on it, you hand

179

it to us, and we'll put it back up here?" Caroline whispers, wide-eyed.

"Um, OK," I say, realizing I don't have much of a choice—I can now hear the murmurs of the Toys "R" Us buyers around the corner. Caroline, Josh, and I work in silence, save for the syrupy voice of the actress presenting the Voice Command Real Racers and the buyers asking probing questions about units and sales and advertising budgets. Every so often, there is a loud, metallic clink from where Caroline and Josh are working—Doug's post-office-box key on the string is around Caroline's neck, and each time she hands a box to Josh, the key pops out of her T-shirt and makes contact with the ladder. It happens a few times before I realize what it is; Josh looks perplexed until he looks down and catches the key hitting the ladder at exactly the right moment, too.

Now the buyers are at StuntTrix 5000, oohing and aahing over its giant wheels and "extreme turning action" (so the blond, vapid actress says), and we've only got one box to go. I squeeze the trigger on the glue gun and cover the back of the Super Spyman Book 'Em Fingerprint Kit with long trails of goopy glue. The glue is so hot now that it steams and bubbles, and as I hand the last box to Josh, it comes to me. I know what my next move is with J.P. Cody! Yesssss! That's it! Unfortunately, I'm so distracted by my joy that I let the glue gun drip a huge blob of burning-hot glue squarely onto my right palm. I want to yell, cry, curse; the glue is unbearable on my skin, holding in the heat as it dries into a stiff, hard mass in the center of my hand. I scream noiselessly as Caroline grabs Josh's coffee cup and plunges my hand into it without so much as a word. The coffee is warm but not as burning hot as the glue, and my hand shakes as I hold it under the overpriced French roast and tears well up in my eyes. Josh is staring at us while he scoops up the glue gun, hooking the ladder under his arm and finally pressing the packages against the wall once more for good measure. We scurry to the back room as we hear the buyers come around the corner into the boys' activities section, relieved that we've saved the day for Super Spyman. And, more importantly, I'm relieved that I know what's in store for J.P. Cody.

Chapter
14

"Look what she's got! Look, it's Toby, and she's got *toys!*"

"Well, they're not really toys," I say guiltily, spilling all over the playroom floor of the children's oncology unit the dozens of cute promotional pieces I managed to pick up in the lobby of the Toy Building last week. There are adorable rubbery keychains that sport bright-eyed ducks with perfectly round heads, tiny mini glow-in-the-dark Frisbees, and minuscule stuffed animals with party hats and ribbons stamped in silver bearing the line, PARTY PETS: THIS YEAR'S SURE SELLER. Everyone crowds around me like I'm Penny Piñata herself, paying out in tiny trinkets.

After the skirmishes have been broken up over who gets the last Frisbee, Tracie sits down cross-legged next to me on the blue-and-yellow striped carpet, hooks her finger in her mouth, and asks shyly, "Did you miss anyone?"

"Did I *miss* anyone?" I repeat, dumbfounded, my voice dramatic. "I missed everyone!" It is true: Toy Fair was great, the three days following the Toys "R" Us buyers' debacle went without a hitch, and the angry burn on my hand is healing nicely, but I missed more people than I thought possible. I missed Tracie and Ben and a new teenage boy named Kevin whose dream is to beat his brain tumor so he can learn to ride a motorcycle. Before I left, he engaged me in a lively debate about whether or not helmet laws were a good idea (I thought they were; he didn't). When I asked him what the point was of fixing his brain now if he was just going to smash his head up on the Pennsylvania Turnpike later, he fixed me with a cool stare and then a grudging grin. "Yeah, maybe you have a point," he said, nodding slowly and looking at me through narrowed eyes. I also missed seeing J.P. Cody every morning and wondering what he was saying and how delicious he looked while we watched the painfully disingenuous New York weathermen on Doug's TV. I missed hearing about Kerrin's work antics and wondered how she resolved the issue of the unsolicited name of the therapist.

I did not miss Lisa Carlton and only thought of Michael twice. Once was in the back room when Joe's work on the Awesome Avalanche racers reminded me of the *20/20* segment we watched together. And on our last night in New York I thought of him, when Doug convinced us to join him and his staff to sing karaoke. Caroline and I drank too much and ended up onstage lustily singing "S.O.S." by Abba. A long time ago I had been listening to it while getting ready to go out with The Head Wound. As Michael had stood in the bathroom doorway and watched me put on mascara that evening, he had lectured me about how the song's piano intro was stolen from some such classical composer, I can't remember who.

"I like Toy Fair," Tracie says, cuddling her promotional Party Pet. "I went there once."

"Oh, really?" I ask, humoring her.

"Mmm hmmm," she answers, nodding. "We went to New York, and I rode in a taxicab."

Now my interest is piqued and I'm about to respond when I hear someone say my name—it's a guy's voice, but much deeper than the usual pipsqueak sounds from most of the boys here. I turn around and see it's Mark, Len's roommate. He gives off the same air of intensity that he did when we met a few months ago, and I can swear that Tracie shrinks back a tiny bit from his force field.

"Hi, Mark," I say, standing up and straightening my orange pom-pom sweater. "How's it going?"

"I was going to ask you the same thing! Len told me you're volunteering here. That's really good of you," he says, unblinking.

"Oh, I don't know," I say, embarrassed. "It's fun—I like seeing everybody here. It's a cool place."

Mark keeps staring at me, so I keep talking. "I only come here once a week, for a few hours after work. It's good," I babble, shifting my weight from one foot to the other. "I need to ask someone here where Ben is, though," I add, partly because it's true and partly because I'm desperate to fill the space in the air that hangs between us. "Do you know him?"

It occurs to me then that I can't describe Ben beyond his first name and how he looks because I don't know any of the kids' last names. It's not that it's kept a secret from me, although when I once told Len that I only knew them by first name, he ventured that maybe it was to protect the families' confidentiality. "Puh-leeze," Kerrin said, rolling her eyes and stopping mid-strike with her match. "If you saw all the 'confidential' faxes people leave lying around in my department—those papers could reforest Brazil. Confidentiality my butt."

"Ben, yeah, I know him," Mark answers, pausing as Tracie loses interest and walks away. "I think he went to Boston for some experimental treatment," he says, his face impassive.

"Really? Is that unusual? Is he going to be OK?" I whisper.

"I don't know any more about it, sorry. Tell Kerrin I said hello," he says, looking down at his beeper and striding down the hall away from me.

I spend the next few hours engaging in complicated stories focused around the Party Pets, which have seemed to snag the attention of both the boys and the girls, making me wonder if they really will be this year's sure seller. At one point I remember that I want to ask Tracie about her time in the taxicab at Toy Fair, but she and a rail-thin boy named Ethan are engrossed in putting her Party Pet into a toy ambulance and I don't want to disturb them. I also keep an eye out for Janet the entire time so I can find out more about Ben, but I don't see her and none of the nurses seem to know where she is. As I'm leaving, I finally run into her, hearing her before seeing her, thanks to the jangly bells on her Indian-print skirt. I am about to ask about Ben when she throws me a curve ball, informing me that Tracie is going in for some exploratory surgery later this week. They have reason to be concerned that the cancer is in her spinal fluid, she says, as I look at the floor and swallow hard.

I'm stepping off the bus later that evening and walking back home when it occurs to me that not knowing everyone's last name isn't just good for protecting confidentiality. It's also good for protecting my heart.

Will is doing that strange thing with his hands where you make an *L* shape with your thumb and index finger on each hand, then twist your wrists so your thumbs touch the index fingers on the opposite hands and form a box that you can look through. After completing four years of art school, I don't think I saw anyone do that once, not when looking at a painting, a nude model, a photograph, a landscape, nothing. But Kerrin once told me that Will was a political science major, so I have my answer there. A true artist is too busy nursing his hangover to spend time looking at things through a little box, I suppose.

Kerrin and I are at March's First Friday, trolling the galleries for free wine and cheese and laughing over the story that's buzzing around about some poor artist's donut exhibit that got eaten by mistake. Apparently he artfully poised a stack of donuts atop a wooden stool and, not fifteen minutes later, turned to discover the toddler of some gallery goer covered in powdered sugar.

"I would have paid to see that one," Kerrin says enthusiastically. "I mean, you work in the Krispy Kreme medium, you take your chances."

"There's an idea—paying to see it happen. Maybe it would have made a good performance art piece. Are you sure they're Krispy Kremes?" I ask, eyeing the remaining donuts on the stool, suddenly hungry.

"Oh, I'd recognize their chocolate glazed anywhere. Mmmmm."

Will suddenly notices us and drops his finger frame long enough to saunter over with his new girlfriend in tow, a Japanese beauty with impossibly clear skin and delicate, fawnlike legs. I feel a twinge of joy at having once been the object of Will's affection when he introduces us to Delia; perhaps I have fewer pimples and skinnier legs than I previously thought. Luckily, I don't feel anything that even comes close to jealousy, and it makes me heave a sigh of relief. Will is still sweet and cute but still not my type.

"Toby, weren't you at Toy Fair? I saw something on

the news about it a few weeks back," Will beams, un-doubtedly imagining that working at Toy Fair must be like suddenly being transported to the land of the Keebler elves, all happy, singing, assembling toys, throwing fairy dust around.

Oh, yes, I want to ask, the place where I burned my hand and had to work fourteen hours a day and had to clean up the empty ice-cream wrappers left carelessly on the showroom floor by buyers after they toured the Magic Ice Cream Maker area? That Toy Fair? Instead, I just smile and nod.

"Well, that must have been fun," Delia muses, tossing a sheaf of shiny black hair over her shoulder and turning to look at an abstract painting of a carcass. She winces, and Will shuffles her away to the more delicate paintings of blades of grass at the gallery across the street. Kerrin turns to me and says, "So? Got anything to tell me?"

"I suppose you don't want to talk about the Phillies' spring training?" I ask hopefully. I had been scouring the sports section all week, and I finally discovered some news about it in the paper at lunch today. Unfortunately, Joe had gone home from work early, sports talk practi-cally induced vomiting in Michael, and my parents were away for a long weekend.

"No. And shhhh, these artistic types will stone you if they get wind of someone talking about sports. You'll have to wait until we go out with Len again. He likes that kind of thing, but I feel pretty sure he's an Orioles fan."

"Yuck. Wait," I say, tugging my hair as Kerrin pauses to spread a generous goop of Brie on a cracker. "I did have something else to tell you. Not baseball-related. What was it?"

We leave the gallery and walk down the crowded street, away from the temptation of the Krispy Kremes, and as we pass a beat-up mailbox it suddenly comes to me. "I know, Kerrin! I got more cards to send to Lisa Carlton!" I exclaim jubilantly.

"Excellent, way to go," she says, smiling. "You got such good results with the last batch, I can't wait to see what happens to that bitch next," she says as we turn into the Trisomy Gallery.

"Trisomy, this is a repellent name," Kerrin boasts, looking up at the blue-and-black sign over the door. "Len says it refers to some kind of chromosomal mutation or something. I'm glad to have this place in my neighborhood," she finishes proudly, but I'm not listening. I'm thinking about the times I've heard Lisa wailing and whining to Michael about all the mystery items she's been receiving at work. Her Complete Guide to Locksmithing. Her bridal consultant starter kit. Her sample pee-pee pads to combat her nighttime bedwetting problem, which she petulantly threw on the living room floor when Michael dared to laugh out loud at them. No matter if it was an instructional video about McDonald's franchising opportunities or a booklet from the Latter Day Saints, she was stymied each time and it was all he could do to console her, the poor guy. When she came to our place to show Michael the set of fifty tiny religious medallions that I'd sent away for, it was all *I* could do to keep from exploding with laughter. And she looked so downtrodden a few days later when she arrived with a tube of special weight-loss lotion that I toyed pretty seriously with not sending any more postage-paid cards to these unknowing manufacturers.

But then I went to New York, the mecca of all things perverse, and I couldn't resist. Caroline and I had walked to Doug's local supermarket to pick up some first-aid cream for the combat wounds she'd suffered in the name of Pretty Kitty, and on our way out, I couldn't help but scan that board of mail-in offers and coupons. Miracle arthritis creams. Sample numerological readings. Blessed crosses and religious tracts. Information on how to become a prison guard, on how to drive a big rig, on how to make your first million in real estate.

Even the subway there was rife with opportunity: There was information about genital wart removal, conquering addiction through hypnosis, laser hemorrhoid surgery. I dutifully took down the 800 numbers from the garish ads with their poor lighting and ugly models, called up for information, and later mailed in the cards I'd swiped in the supermarket. Pity, though, that I lost my all-time favorite one, a little blue card I was handed on the Manhattan street that could be mailed in for more information about the rights of transgendered individuals. I wasn't even exactly sure what transgendered meant, but it sure sounded suspect, and I hurried to fill in Lisa's particulars. I figure I must have left the card in Doug's apartment the day that Caroline and I had to quickly pack up and catch the overheated van back to Toyland. I even considered asking Caroline if she could phone up Doug a few days after we got back, but she's had her hands full with Josh lately. They spent a torrid afternoon in his fleabag hotel room one day during Toy Fair, and she's been regretting it ever since. Actually, since the moment she returned to the Toy Building later that afternoon, now that I think of it. Perhaps it was the white underwear. Oh, well, I can get by without the transgendered mailing.

"I'll have to let you know what shakes out," I say to Kerrin, who nods eagerly and smacks her lips.

"Let's get outta here and drive to Delaware," she says. "My car's right around the corner. I really want some Krispy Kremes."

Almost three weeks after Toy Fair, I have finally finished putting everything away in the long, flat files in the middle of the packaging department. The holographic Mylar sheets are tucked snugly in the appropriate drawers and won't see the light of day again until next February. The pieces of presentation board in every color of the rainbow have been stacked neatly. All the X-Acto knives and French curves and mechanical pencils and erasers and rulers and T-squares have been returned to the supply closet, undoubtedly lamenting bitterly to one another about the rise of the Macintosh computer and its foxy design programs. I feel completely refreshed, not a lot unlike the way I feel when I finally clean my room—the work is not at all mentally taxing but brings immeasurable satisfaction.

When I return to my cubicle, the voice-mail button on my phone shines ruby red. I listen to the message, and I'm disappointed to learn that it's Rod Winters and that he is coming over at eleven-thirty to discuss Wacky Wallaby. I've been dreading this conversation for weeks; I don't understand the wallaby's hand mechanism and how it's meant to grab the tree trunk (tree sold separately), and I can't illustrate the assembly instructions without understanding it. And woe to the designer who thinks she understands a mechanism and doesn't—there will be weeping kids and anguished parents on the company's customer-service line, all gripping the instructions and screaming about why a toy can't be assembled properly.

Rod comes to my cubicle at exactly eleven-thirty and refuses a seat, preferring to stand in the doorway as he describes the spring hinge in the wallaby's hand and the grooves in the tree trunk. The design quickly becomes clearer, but I would actually understand it a lot better if I weren't so distracted by his incessant staring at the cubicle wall behind me as he speaks. He is looking over my head as he talks to me, avoiding eye contact and instead focusing his attention on something else. I'm racking my brain again trying to think of what might be back there, and I unwittingly keep half-swiveling around in my chair to see what could be so compelling. He reaches a critical point in discussing the wallaby's hand assembly when he says sharply, "Miss Morris, if you would please look at me instead of turning around, it would help."

"I'm turning around because I'm trying to figure out—" I sputter, turning around yet again to scan the wall.

"I'll get Joe to do a simple drawing of the mechanism for you. That will help you," he says, his voice cracking on the word *help*. When I swing my chair back around to face him, I am utterly shocked to see that he is misty-eyed and tugging at his collar uncomfortably.

"OK," I say warily. "Thank you; I'll talk to Joe about that later."

I roll my chair to the edge of my cubicle so I can watch him trudge down the hall to the door of the engineering department. He looks down the entire time, his fists jammed in his pockets, his shoulders hunched. When I roll back, I remember that I am supposed to call Caroline to make lunch plans.

"Caroline," I whisper into the phone, "Rod Winters is cracking up."

Chapter
15

"Owwwww," Michael is moaning from his bedroom, and for the first time in a very long time, I actually sympathize with him, rather than berate him for his hypochondria.

He has come down with chicken pox, a virulent, tenacious case, and he has been hurting and itching all over for several days now. He caught it from one of his students, who had contracted it at school but hadn't broken out in the telltale red spots yet. I could tell that something was up with this kid the day he came for his lesson. A normally sweet and gentle seven-year-old, Todd sniveled uncontrollably when Michael suggested he practice more, and then practically threw a tantrum until he was allowed to play "Crocodile Rock," instead of tunes from Michael's suggested lesson-time playlist. I was sitting in my room sketching the wallaby's hand and listening to Todd's outburst coming from the third-

194

floor studio and suddenly remembered what my mom used to say when one of us became cranky for no apparent reason: "Somebody's getting sick!"

Well, get sick he did, and when Todd's mother called to tell Michael, he blanched on the phone and said that he had never had chicken pox. Lisa told him there was no way she could take care of him if and when he got sick, never having had chicken pox herself and needing to stay healthy for the springtime sale at her store. Which leaves me, two-time champion of chicken pox (the first case was so light it produced just two spots, the next so intense I was out of commission for ages) to help Michael. And he is truly in need of help: He is feverish and exhausted, and the sickness that initially struck me as kind of funny—a kid's disease and all—is quickly becoming less funny as each day passes. His red spots seem to multiply every hour, and he complains of dehydration. When I told Kerrin about his plight, even she recoiled a bit at the prospect of having chicken pox as a grown-up, saying that she'd heard that the disease could leave an adult male sterile. "Not that I'm sure that his type should be procreating, anyway," she added airily.

"All right, I'm coming," I yell, pouring a large glass of Gatorade. I tuck the newspaper under my arm and go upstairs and enter the room, where Michael is propped up on several pillows and looking greasy, pale, and miserable. Sweaty blotches are popping out all over his chest, like there's some kind of fungus eating the trees on his Tanglewood T-shirt.

"Ewww, it smells like the heart in here," I say, referring to the giant heart at the Franklin Institute Science Museum. Everyone who's ever been a schoolchild in Philadelphia has walked through this huge exhibit of a human heart, stopping to pause by the septum and race through its ventricles. The problem now is that the heart is in desperate need of transplantation, or at the very least a bypass, because after decades of runny-nosed kids running through it, it has taken on a funky smell and grimy texture. Michael never experienced the heart firsthand as a child, and when Sheila and I took him there in college, the three of us reeled from the pungent odor.

"It doesn't smell that bad, does it?" he asks weakly.

"Maybe not," I lie. "Do you want this newspaper?" He shakes his head no, and I hand him the glass of Gatorade and turn to go.

"You can stay if you want," he says, almost pleading. I guess he must be very lonely in here all day, so I say, "OK," and sit on the edge of the bed.

"Good Gatorade?" I ask.

"Yeah."

"It's from the new place down the street, which I still think is a front for something, I don't care what you say," I say.

"Toby," Michael says while fighting not to scratch a blister on his wrist, "if you only went down the street, why were you gone so long?"

"I wasn't gone that long," I say defensively. Actually, I was gone for about fifteen minutes; that was how much time it took me to walk to the post office, dig out my key, peer in my post office box, slam the door disappointedly, and come home via the corner store.

"I also had to go to the post office," I add evenly, half-hoping Michael will ask me why and half-hoping he won't.

After I returned from Toy Fair, I promptly visited our local post office, a sad affair with yellowing dingy walls and even dingier postal employees. But sure enough, there were post office boxes lining one short wall, and after pacing the lobby for about fifteen minutes, I worked up the gumption to get one for myself. I decided if it could work for Doug's love life, it could work for mine, and I came home, took out Mr. Clackety Clack, and typed:

I'm so flattered
you've been wearing those clothes
So thank you for doing so
Your attention really shows

But some might say
Our communication is very one way
So if you'd like to get to know me better
Please respond to this letter

At the bottom of the letter, I put my name and PO Box address. I ruminated for ages about whether or not to send the letter; it might seem to start to border on stalking and scare him away, I thought while sitting at work daydreaming about it one day. But eventually I decided to bite the bullet, and I mailed it a week ago. It was a good thing, I decided. Gutsy, nervy, aggressive, full of moxie. Nothing like me, in other words.

"I have stamps if you need them," Michael croaks, pointing weakly to his desk.

"I went to the post office to check on my post office box," I say challengingly.

"Why did you get a post office box?"

"So if J.P. Cody wants to write to me," I say simply, watching Michael's glassy eyes grow wide. "I just thought the relationship was becoming . . . a little one-sided, I guess."

"Toby," he ventures, "you don't *have* a relationship."

"Well, don't rub it in, just 'cause you do."

"No, I mean you don't have a relationship with this weatherguy. You're going to really be lucky if he writes you back. I can't believe I'm even thinking about this logically; it's got to be the fever," he rationalizes, draining his glass of Gatorade.

"Well, I've got *luck*, Michael. There were only about a dozen boxes left and I chose number ninety-nine for luck and in homage."

Michael's face registers nothing. "Number 99? The Great One?" I ask, peering at him intently as his expression remains blank.

"I—I'm sorry, I don't know what that means, Toby."

"Come on! The Great One! Don't you remember that's the Trivial Pursuit question that you picked that killed us last year during that snowstorm? When we played with Sheila?" I ask wistfully. I'm referring to the time when she and her boyfriend and his brother came into town for the weekend and Philadelphia was unexpectedly hit with a foot of snow. We played game after game of Trivial Pursuit those two days, and although Michael kicked the opposing team's ass in virtually every category, his team members would suck in their collective breath every time he rolled, praying that he wouldn't land on a dreaded yellow "Sports and Leisure" square. When he drew the card with the yellow oval asking, "Who is 'The Great One'?" everyone yelped because the question was so easy. Only a minute later, Sheila nearly choked on her Jiffy Pop as she watched me throttle Michael because he had no idea what the answer was.

"Michael, come *on*," I beg. "Don't you remember?"

"I'm sick here! How can I remember?"

"*Wayne Gretzky*, Michael. Number 99. The Great One! It's very important—he's part of our nation's heritage!" I say proudly.

"How can he be part of our nation's heritage?" he asks, finally giving in and scratching his wrist, heaving a sigh of relief. "He's Canadian."

"But," I say, utterly confused, "if you can remember that he's Canadian, why can't you remember who he is?"

He coughs and looks at me pitifully, shaking his head. "Toby, I guessed. He's a hockey player, so chances are pretty good he's Canadian."

"Oh, you!" I say, taking a smack at his clammy arm sticking above the covers. "No fair using powers of deduction on me," I yell, making him jump slightly.

"I have to sleep now," he murmurs, his eyelids looking heavy. "I'm tired, OK? Just *promise* me that you won't get too worked up when he doesn't write back," he says, drawing on the last of his energy reserves to work a snicker into his voice.

My mouth drops open and I leap up from the bed, propelled by profound disappointment. "That's fine, Michael," I say, heading for the door. "Oh, and I was lying before. It *does* smell like the heart in here," I hiss for good measure, but I think he may be asleep already. I suddenly feel exhausted too, and I head across the hall to plop down on my bed. I push my chin hard into the heels of my hands and fret about Michael's comment. Am I truly insane to try and take my crush with J.P. Cody to the next level? Was spending money on a post office box just plain stupid? Will he ever write back? Am I really like a stalker? Should I be expending this much energy on someone I don't even know, when there are plenty of geekily dressed and sweaty but perfectly nice engineers at Toyland who could probably show me a good time?

Some beautiful springtime weather is coming our way. But will it last? Hard to tell—you know what they say about March.

I'm watching J.P. Cody very intensely this morning—

exactly what for, I don't know. Since I've stopped giving him fashion directives and begun asking for a letter, there's no real reason to focus on what he's wearing. Although he does look lovely today in a burnt umber suit and a murky slate blue tie with large geometric shapes.

Look at all the low-pressure systems bunching up right in our part of the country—now this is pretty unusual, even for this time of year.

Why won't he write back? I wonder to myself while fiddling with the buttons on my eye-popping vest. Michael calls this my "Who Shot the Curtains?" vest, because of its quaint gingham pattern and little bunches of cherries splashed liberally around the blue-and-white checked background.

So look for a lot of sun today—but be careful driving, because there might even be some glare during your morning commute.

He's so thoughtful, I'm thinking as I note the look of concern on his face, when Lisa Carlton trots down the stairs and smiles at me with her lips closed. She looks from me to the TV ever so slowly, and she consciously controls a sneer. Then she wordlessly grabs her ugly clutch bag and is out the door.

Well, I'll show her, I decide as I watch J.P. pause introspectively before he launches into a monologue about where the sun glare is worst on the Schuylkill Expressway. Just wait, I say quietly as I get ready for Rich's arrival. I turn off the TV and set the metronome in motion, this time a slow, sleepy cadence that fits my mood today.

"Just wait," I repeat in time with the beat and very loudly, emboldened by the memory of Lisa's nasty expression. "I'm going to get through to that meteorologist yet."

"I'm *so* sorry, Toby, I had no idea that I was expected to go to this thing. Are you sure you're not mad?" Jenna asks piteously.

"No, it's all right," I say, trying to conceal the disappointment in my voice. I made plans with Jenna to hang out at the Twin City Diner tonight and have been eagerly anticipating it for days. We haven't seen each other since our accidental meeting the day of the auto show, and I was elated at the idea of spending the evening someplace other than my house. Since Michael bounced back from his bout with chicken pox, he and Lisa have been making up for lost time, and she is at our place day and night. If I see one more hair-strewn scrunchie lying on the table or on the bathroom counter, I think I might be sick.

"I feel really bad," she laments. "I thought for sure my boss would be the only one going."

"What is it you have to do?" I ask, waving to Joe as he passes by me with an armload of engineering drawings. He mouths the word "Sarah" and jerks his thumb behind him, so I immediately turn my chair toward the corner and lower my voice. I am in trouble again with Sarah today, the infraction a common problem: I forgot to change the dummy quote on a package proof once again. She dramatically pulled me into her office this morning bright and early, lecturing me sternly about paying attention to the package proofs. Toby, she asked seriously, what would happen if the 250,000 packages got printed and they didn't say, "Sand dollars and sunflowers are my favorite barrette shapes—and I made them myself!"? As she pulled her pearly pink lips into a pout, I couldn't help but look away from her, wanting to laugh and cry at the same time.

"It's some vendor who sells the software we use for the news graphics," Jenna answers. "They're taking us to dinner in Center City and they want to treat everyone on the design staff."

"Oh, well, that sounds like it will be tasty, anyway," I say, my voice low. "Sorry I have to whisper; my boss is around the corner and I'm on her shit list today." As if Jenna would ever know what it's like to be on anyone's shit list.

"I know; it'll probably be a good time," she sighs. "But I wanted to spend time with you," she adds earnestly.

"Oh, come on, Jenna, you can't pass up an opportunity like this to eat the greasy special at the Twin City Diner, though." I slowly straighten up and turn around to see if Sarah's still nearby, and when I poke my head out of my cubicle, there is no trace of her. Instead, I see Rod Winters at a center table in an animated conversation with a graphic designer named Matt. Rod is sporting his usual red face, and Matt is standing with his arms folded over his chest and his expression defiant.

"Speaking of Twin City Diner, I saw your friend the other day."

"What friend?" I ask, turning my chair back so I'm facing the corner again.

"J.P. Cody. He was coming out of the men's room. He had toilet paper on his shoe," she giggles. Oh, oh, oh, if I didn't love this man before, do I ever love him now. And I thought I was the only one whose shoes attracted toilet paper at work like magnets. And the only one who was too obtuse to notice a white strip flailing behind me as I made my way down the hall, past my sniggering coworkers.

But then I'm perplexed for a moment. "Why did the Twin City Diner remind you of J.P. Cody?" I ask, trying to sound cool. Did he hang out there? Had she seen him with takeout from there? A Twin City Diner T-shirt? My mind is reeling.

"Twin City—he's from Minneapolis, remember?" she says.

How could I have forgotten? I thought about it every time his words leaked that funny, open, Midwestern accent, with the aggressive *s*s and the soft *o*s that sounded like *a*s. Which was every weekday morning, of course. I just had never connected it to my beloved, greasy diner. The Twin City Diner! Maybe it was there when he was a child, and he would eat a plateful of fries and a shake before going home to do his science experiments.

"So how's it going at the hospital?" Jenna asks, quick

to keep the conversation moving. For her, the Twin City Diner/J.P. Cody connection is nothing more than a casual observation. For me, it is reason to feel as though I am going to barf up my heart, my chest is so tight and full of excitement. "You said you were volunteering there?"

"Oh, yeah," I say, trying to sound chipper about it, but today it is very difficult to work up a lot of enthusiasm. On my last jaunt there I was ecstatic to hear that Ben was benefiting from his experimental treatment in Boston, but then I came crashing down to earth when I learned that Tracie had been felled by a severe, mysterious infection after her exploratory surgery. She was being monitored in a small room at the end of the hall, not a two-minute walk from the playroom, yet she wasn't allowed out, and naturally, none of the other children could see her. I walked by at one point and waved to her through the window; she smiled back weakly from her bed and then quickly looked away from me. I felt like a great weight had been dumped on me as I watched her there, and I probably stayed too long, allowing tears to well up in my eyes.

"What do you do there?" Jenna asks, genuinely curious.

"Um, hang out with the kids, mostly. It's the oncology unit, so it's all kids with cancer. Some of them are really cool, they're amazing. I should probably go, though, OK?" I ask. I suddenly feel like I need a bit of fresh New Jersey air—the ultimate oxymoron.

"Sure. I should, too. But we'll make plans to get together soon, right?" she pleads. I assure her that we'll reschedule our diner outing for another night, hang up my phone, and turn around to see Rod Winters in the doorway to my cubicle. His mouth is open, and he looks like he's just about to say something. But he thinks better of it, because he gruffly mutters something like "hello" under his breath and walks off. This is it, I decide, jumping up angrily and smoothing my green jeans. Enough is enough. I'm going to yell at him until the walls of Toyland shake. What does he want from me? Complain, criticize, rough me up, just be done with it! I'm seeing red as I fling open the door that separates the engineering and packaging departments.

But of course, once there, I veer right past Rod Winters's door and instead end up at Joe's drafting table, near tears and accepting his offer to go outside and keep him company while he smokes.

"I *adore* this place," Kerrin says lovingly, stealing a lone, leftover French fry from Len's plate and liberally shaking salt onto it. "I just don't come here enough, and Len has never been here at all."

We're finishing our dinners in the Twin City Diner, just two nights after I was supposed to meet Jenna here. Since my conversation with Jenna, I've had a hankering to come here, partly driven by hunger and desire for the greasy food and thick shakes, and partly driven by hunger and desire for knowledge about the place itself and when it was moved here from St. Paul. It could be good fodder for something in a future missive to J.P., I think.

"You've never been here?" I ask Len, genuine shock in my voice.

"No, they keep us pretty busy over there on the other end of town," he says, reaching for his battered blue canvas wallet with the Velcro closure. I make a mental note to tell Kerrin that a new wallet would make a splendid birthday gift for Len, until I remember that Kerrin would never buy a boyfriend something as mundane as a wallet.

"Yeah, I see Mark racing around whenever I'm at CHOP, that's for sure," I say.

"He said he's seen you there a couple of times," he says, fishing a bunch of greasy bills out of his wallet. "I guess your schedules have synchronized, huh? Although for him there isn't much of a schedule. He runs around and stays awake even more than I do."

"Here, don't be stupid; put that away," Kerrin says, waving Len's money away and taking out her credit card. "Yeah, these guys, they even take naps in the cafeteria. Isn't that gross? Wouldn't you scream if your doctor showed up smelling like turkey tetrazzini?" She chuckles at the thought of it and hands the bill and her credit card to the painfully thin waitress with the dyed-black hair and dead eyes.

"Such a fine line between looking cool and looking like you're ready for Betty Ford, don't you think?" she asks, following the waitress with her eyes. "No, Toby,

I've got yours," she says, shaking her head when I try to hand her my share of the bill.

"Thanks!" I say enthusiastically. "Why are you in such a good mood?"

"I got the funniest thing at work today, it's had me smiling all afternoon. I brought it to show you—you won't believe it," she says, beaming. Len rolls his eyes and she says, "I know *you've* seen it already; I'm sorry. But I have to show Toby, OK?"

"Don't keep me in suspense! What is it?" I beg.

"Well," she begins, reaching into her bag and unfolding a piece of paper, "first the background. We're finishing up a big project at work, some dumb grant where we're trying to get old men to get their prostates screened for cancer."

"That's a very important screening, Kerrin!" Len says sternly.

"Yeah, OK, Doc," Kerrin teases. "*I* don't have a prostate, remember?"

"Stop, both of you!" I shout over the strains of "Ring of Fire" coming from the jukebox. "Then what?" I ask as the waitress clumsily clears our plates and glasses.

"Oh, so they're having a happy hour at some woman's house to celebrate that the project is over. A party—sounds fun, right? I mean, not to me, but I could endure it for a little bit if I had to, I think. So today I get this in my inbox," she finishes, presenting the paper with a flourish. I look at it closely and it says:

**HAPPY HOUR
FOR THE PROSTATE CANCER PROJECT**

**Rachel's House
After work–???
March 30**

Please check any special dietary requirements:

❑ Vegetarian
❑ Vegan
❑ Low salt
❑ Low-fat
❑ Gluten-free
❑ Lactose-free
❑ Low cholesterol
❑ Other _____

*Please return to Debbie, Rachel's secretary,
no later than March 28*

I grin and hand it back to Kerrin as she throws on her oversized blazer and turns sideways to shimmy out of the narrow booth. "That's pretty good," I say. "They're serious? For a happy hour?"

"Of course they're serious! This is what they do! Obsess about food," she says disgustedly on the way out the door, pausing to put a quarter in a tiny gumball machine that spits out a pile of small, brightly colored gumballs.

"You should write something in that's totally crazy," I say as we walk toward Len's car. "Like, 'I require Hostess Snoballs and heroin,' " I offer in an uncharacteristic display of literary creativity.

This gets smiles from them both. "Ooh, I like it," squeals Kerrin as we climb over the liquor bottles in the gutter and into Len's car. "The alliteration is what's really nice about it," she adds, working her jaws to soften the stale gumballs.

Len lights a cigarette, starts the car, and looks at me in the rearview mirror. "How about 'I require Mallomars and methadone'?" he asks, giving me his gap-toothed grin. Kerrin claps with delight; we're really riffing now. "I know! 'I require Little Debbies and lithium.' Or 'I require gin and Jolly Ranchers,' " she shouts.

"We could do this all night," I giggle. "All we need is a list of drugs, alcohol, and snack foods," I say, recalling how Caroline once filled me in on how most toys are given their names. Apparently the marketing people just sit on their expensively clothed behinds and create list after list of words, combining the lists until they hit on something as inspirational as, say, Funtime Phone or Darlin' Doggie.

"You can't beat that memo, that's for sure," Kerrin laughs, gripping the door handle as Len takes a hard turn near the museum.

"I think I can, Kerrin!" I exclaim excitedly, and Kerrin swivels in her seat with a challenging look on her face.

"How can that be?" she asks. "No one's got pc Nazis like the ones I work with."

"Well, I saw a memo that I think may give yours a run for its money, then," I say quickly, since Len is now turning onto my dimly lit street. "The other day I was in Sarah's office getting reamed out for doing something stupid, and I couldn't even look at her. So I was looking at her desk and there was a memo about 'Equality in packaging photos.' " I pause here for effect as Len pulls up to the house.

"Go on," urges Kerrin. Even Len is waiting eagerly, his eyebrows arched in the rearview mirror.

"So it said something about using pictures with kids with disabilities on our packages. Kids in wheelchairs, kids with other problems, I guess. They want to start with a kid with Down syndrome, from what this thing said."

There's a second of silence as this sinks in, and Len is the first to excitedly speak. "Like your neighborhood gallery, Kerrin. The Trisomy Gallery! Remember, I was telling you about the chromosome problem that causes Down syndrome?"

"They are *so stupid*, Toby!" she explodes, more angry than amused, and ignoring Len's impromptu genetics seminar, which makes him frown. "They think the world's going to be all happy-happy, nicey-nicey because they put some poor, deformed kid on the box? What the hell is wrong with them? It's like some kind of freak show for the new generation!" she says, her eyes fiery. "All they want to do is get a touchy-feely public image so they can make more money. How is making money from someone's misfortune different from freak shows, huh?"

"I dunno," I say, unbuckling my seat belt and stepping out of the backseat of the car. I'm suddenly grateful that the end of my story coincided with the end of my ride; I shudder to think of what might have happened if I'd told my story first, back in the diner. I lean into Kerrin's open window and thank them profusely for dinner and the ride. "I'll let you know if I hear more," I say cheerily, hurrying inside out of the brisk nighttime air. It's only after I'm up in my room that I realize I forgot to investigate the long and illustrious history of the Twin City Diner.

Chapter
16

I'm sleepy this evening—sleepy, sad, and disappointed. As I do every year when it's almost time to change the clocks, I woke at the crack of dawn today, listening to the baby birds singing merrily in the trees outside my window. I thought about sitting up in bed and trying to brainstorm more poetry for J.P. Cody, but a loud laugh erupted from behind Michael's door, propelling me out of bed and into my pink terry robe with the egg-and-flapjack pattern on it. I was dressed and ready for work well before J.P.'s weather segment, hanging around downstairs, when I realized that if I timed it just right, I could get to the post office and back before Rich came. I stealthily slipped out the door—I didn't want Lisa to hear the screen door creaking and have her ask Michael where I was going—and walked quickly to the post office. I took a long, slow breath before putting in my key and turning it ever so slowly. When I looked in the box,

I wanted to cry. I've reached the end of the line, I thought bitterly on the way back while dodging the huge piles of dog doo left by Barney, the neighborhood Labrador retriever. He's not writing back.

Now it's almost twelve hours later and I still don't know what possessed me to do such a thing, I decide. Kevin ambles toward me, plopping down heavily on the Lego-strewn carpet.

"Yo, yo, To-*bey*," he says, adjusting his eye patch. All the radiation to his brain tumor has left him with a milky cataract in his left eye, and the last attempt to remove it with lasers was successful, giving him much-needed hope that he would be right on schedule to take and pass his motorcycle driving test. "This thing is really itchy."

"How's it going?" I ask disinterestedly, reaching across him to pass a juice box to Gisele, a tiny girl in a wheelchair.

"Eh," he shrugs, matching my listless mood as only a teenager can. "I'm OK. It's my mom who's going crazy. You should see how thin she is. I'm like, 'Mom, you can't live on Sanka and bologna sandwiches.' And my doctor, I can't stand him anymore. He's, like, a total faggot."

"That's true," I yawn, deciding to ignore the epithet. "I mean about the Sanka and bologna sandwiches. I was going to bring you in one of my car magazines tonight. It had a motorcycle feature that you would have liked."

"So where is it?" he asks.

"I forgot, sorry." He shakes his head and fiercely scratches around the edge of his eye patch.

"You're looking glum today, Toby. Why the long face?" I look up from my spot on the floor and see Janet, smiling broadly and dressed in a hideous, nubby textured, pea green poncho. She has a dirty canvas tote bag slung over her shoulder, and she fumbles in it for her keys. When she bends over to help Gisele puncture the juice box with the miniature straw, Kevin puts his hand up to the side of his face and uses his other hand to discreetly point to her poncho, sticking out his tongue and screwing his face into a repulsed expression. I laugh out loud, the first laugh I've had all day.

"See, that's more like it!" she says, turning around and beaming. "That's the Toby I know!"

How she could have any idea of the Toby she knows is pretty mystifying, since, like tonight, she is often on her way out of the hospital shortly after I arrive. I'm contemplating this when I remember what I want to ask her, and I scramble to catch her at the elevator doors.

"Janet," I ask breathlessly, "how is Tracie? I don't see her."

"She still has a fever, still not doing that well," she says, toying with one of her dangly earrings. "It's never good when they can't figure out what's causing the problem. Day to day, that's my motto. Wait a minute— this isn't your night, is it, Toby?" she asks, perplexed. "You aren't usually here on a Thursday."

"I couldn't come last night because—um, I had some problems at home." Our refrigerator broke and surprise, surprise, Michael was out with Lisa, leaving me to deal with the scary landlord with the big cigar and the yellow "pizza-pit stains" on his undershirt, as Kerrin calls them.

The elevator arrives with a *ping,* and as she steps on, I have to control the urge to get on with her, away from this place that's making me so sad tonight. The problem is, I don't know where I would go, unless the elevator has magical powers that can transport me to a place where kids don't get sick and meteorologists answer their mail.

When I return, Kevin is lying on his back with his arms in the air, playing with his Game Boy and pausing every few seconds to pick at his eye patch. Another sometime volunteer, a university student named Renée, has arrived and is slowly picking up Legos that were left by a bratty boy with leukemia and a permanent sneer on his face. She is gently chiding him, encouraging him to help with the cleanup, and he sniffs and walks toward the reading area. Once there, he begins flinging books around until he's sure that Renée's seen him. I sigh exasperatedly and decide to check on Tracie, just to see if she's in the same room as before.

I walk down the long hallway, away from Renée's cry about the far-flung books in the reading area, my heart feeling as though it's in a vise-grip. I'm rounding the corner toward Tracie's room when I hear shuffling footsteps, and I instinctively look down. Seeing weepy parents and grandparents with their pained expressions and anxious, glassy-eyed stares is enough to bear when I am feeling rested and perky; in my current sleep-deprived and sad state, I know that I would be moved to tears. I keep my eyes fixed on the floor and watch a man's shoes go by me very slowly. It's only after the shoes are safely past me that I dare to turn around and look at him, and when I do, he is still walking slowly, but he is not looking where he is going. Instead, he is looking right at me, his face a peculiar mixture of surprise and confusion and maybe even a tiny hint of contempt.

It is Rod Winters.

He continues to walk in slow motion, his neck craned around so he can keep an eye on me, as he makes his way down the hallway, past the playroom, and out to the elevators. I am standing in front of Tracie's room, barely breathing, barely moving, nearly jumping out of my skin when a message over the PA system finally pierces the air.

Then I turn on my heels and begin running, running past Renée and the mess of books, running past gurneys and bored-looking nurses sitting at the nurses' station, running down the crumbling stairs, running past the bloodbank with its poster featuring a little character shaped like a plump drop of blood, past the pool with its intense chlorine smell, past the physical therapy department, cast room, emergency room. I'm wearing my blue vinyl sneakers with the four-inch wedges, so I'm forced to run with itty-bitty, mincy baby steps, like the way Babe Ruth runs around the bases in my baseball documentary videos. I'm pushing past two doctors deep in conversation, ploughing past the psychology department, skidding past social work, my head full of the pictures in my cubicle at Toyland, the cubicle that's held Rod's rapt attention for so long now. Tracie. Tracie W. I finally take a right turn at the gift shop and am hit head-on with the putrid smells wafting from the cafeteria. I stride past the salad bar and into the dining area, breathing heavily and sweating around my hairline.

It is here that I find him, asleep at the back in an uncomfortable-looking plastic chair, his head tipped back and his mouth wide open. I walk over slowly, trying in vain to catch my breath.

"Mark," I pant.

Nothing, so I clear my throat and try it a little louder. *"Mark."* He still doesn't move, doesn't respond, so I gently touch him on the shoulder. He wakes with a start.

"Wha?" he asks urgently and looks immediately at his beeper, confused. "What is it?" He quickly pushes away the orange tray that's in front of us on the table and rests his elbows on its swirly, laminated surface.

"Mark, what is Tracie's last name?" I ask, my mouth open.

He holds his head in his left hand and uses his right hand to massage his eyes, relentlessly manipulating the skin under his eyebrows. Eventually he looks squarely at me, blinking hard and finally alert.

"Winters. Why?"

"So, any word from your friend?" Michael asks casually as he zips up his bright blue jacket and tightens his hood against the driving April rain. We are leaving the Super Fresh, a rare shopping trip for the two of us these days. It was quite nice; we even had some genuine laughs when I bet that I would be able to remove ten cherry tomatoes from the salad bar using only a pair of wooden chopsticks, which Michael offered to buy in the spirit of the wager as we rolled our cart past the Asian specialties section. But because the slick little suckers were dead center in the middle of the salad bar, I failed miserably—and I am now sporting lively splashes of Zesty Italian and ranch dressings on my shirt to prove it.

"You look like a Smurf in that thing; loosen it up a little, will you?" I chuckle as an orange rolls from one of the shopping bags and hides in the corner of the Honda's backseat.

"I don't care—at least I'm not getting soaked," he says, pointing to my dripping hair. "Well?"

"Well, what?"

He shoots me a look before peering past me and taking a right turn. "Well, did you ever hear back from your weather friend?"

"His name is J.P., if you don't mind," I say a bit huffily. "Not my *weather friend*. And no, I haven't heard back from him yet."

"Well, remember what I told you about my friend Tom—he's still available, you know," he says, referring to a violinist he knows who supplements his income in the spring and fall by working for the city. He gives schoolchildren tours of Independence Hall while dressed in embarrassingly accurate period costume, complete with knickers, a three-corner hat, and black shoes with over-sized buckles.

"I don't think so, Michael—powdered wigs make me sneeze."

"Well, suit yourself," he says, shrugging and finally loosening his hood three blocks from our house.

"He'll write back to me, you'll see," I say reassuringly, although I'm not quite sure whom I'm trying to reassure at this point. "Don't you worry about a thing."

Caroline licks her lips and puts her face close to the microphone. "Two plus two is four!" She pauses for a beat. "Two plus two is four!" Beat. "Two plus two is four!" Beat. "Good job!" Beat. "Good job!" When she pauses for more than a second, I rap gently on the tiny window, and she beckons me inside.

"I'm going to play these back, Caroline. Some of them sounded like winners," a disembodied voice booms into the small room with the carpeted walls. I jump with a start and look over and see that the voice belongs to Peter, who is hidden in a pile of audio equipment behind a piece of thick glass. He is wearing one of his many Hawaiian shirts, and his dishwater-blond ponytail swings as he bends down to adjust a piece of sound equipment.

"What are you working on today?" I ask as Caroline takes sips from a cup of water. Soon after she arrived at Toyland, she was "discovered" by a member of the preschool marketing team. She had been working at her drafting table and reducing her coworkers to paroxysms of laughter by shouting, "I need to go potty now, Mama!" in that high-pitched, squeaky-clean voice reserved for the mouths of plastic baby dolls. Greg the marketing guy, astounded by her "talent," asked her if she wouldn't mind saying a few more sample lines. Egged on by the other preschool designers, she gushed earnestly, "You're my favorite friend!" and "I hope you come to my birthday party!" The rest, as they say, is history.

"My First Calculator. It's pretty cute. This is the second one I've done this month for preschool, though! They also had me do My First Fax Machine. Do you know how much I would get paid if I were a real voice-over actress?"

I know better than to answer; Caroline has asked me this question many times before, usually after her voice is hoarse from so many takes and she has come dangerously close to missing design deadlines.

"I should go to California—none of this two-bit stuff there. You know they have an off-site sound stage with hired voice-over people?" she asks rhetorically, referring to one of Toyland's major competitors. "Although, I have to say, this is a good place to avoid Josh."

"He's still bugging you?"

"Yeah. He wants me to go see his band this weekend, Soothing Sounds for Sasha."

"That's a great name," I admit.

"Uh-huh," she agrees. "Good name, bad guy. But listen to this: you know that new guy Kyle in Boys' Toys? He told Josh that you have a billion-dollar butt."

"Really?" I ask, arching my back and craning my neck to get a look at my behind. Unfortunately I am wearing my oversized mint green pants with the giant Fortuny pleats today, so there's no real way to determine the monetary value of my rear. Caroline clears her throat dramatically, and I snap my head up to see Peter looking at me inquisitively with his head cocked to one side.

"How about that turnover this morning, huh?" she asks, referring to the process of handing over toys from the creative, colorful product development stage to the dour, soulless engineering and production stage. Turnover meetings are attended by people who work on every aspect of the project, including the packaging and stickers, which is why I was there. I was never given a good reason why the process is called a turnover. We also have a process at Toyland called a key line review, which has been affectionately nicknamed a "key lime review." Between the turnovers and the key lime reviews, I often wonder if what the CEO of Toyland really wants to do is run a bakeshop.

"Yeah, pretty crazy, a fight over a stupid helmet," I scoff, secretly remembering the relief I felt when a loud argument broke out between the engineers about how to mold Sally Skateboard's plastic skateboarding helmet. I was silently praying that we would run out of time before we got to the graphics part of the project, and luckily, we did. The reason was that I thought my drawing of how to assemble Sally's little skateboard was less than stellar. That was Lisa Carlton's fault, the jerk. A few evenings ago, I left the prototype skateboard on the table near the door while I went upstairs to talk to Kerrin on the phone. While on the phone, I could hear Lisa complaining loudly to Michael about the free hemorrhoid cream and informational video she'd received at work. The conversation ended with Lisa slamming the door to Michael's room and leaving in a huff. In her rush to put on her raincoat, she must have carelessly knocked into the prototype. I couldn't put it back together for the life of me and was too embarrassed to appeal to anyone for help, so I truly had to wing the drawing.

"No, I don't mean that, Toby," she says, acknowledging Peter's wave and walking back in front of the microphone. "I mean the way Rod Winters was looking at you. Didn't you see? It was really weird. He kept sneaking peeks at you. Wow, you're going to have your hands full—Kyle and Rod *both* love you!"

She plants herself in front of the mike. "Eight plus eight is sixteen!"

I shiver and shake all the way back to my desk. For the last week, since my unexpected run-in with Rod at the hospital, I've been avoiding him like the plague. I take the long way around the engineering department to go to the ladies' room. I don't visit Joe. I move my projects around so I don't have any engineering questions. I wave off Sarah's suggestion for Rod to come and explain the Use Your Noodle game's spaghetti extruder. I sat far away from him at the turnover, but apparently, not far enough to avoid his stares. Now, having an inkling about why he's so freaky with me is even worse than having *no* inkling about why he's so freaky with me. And I am very afraid of what might happen next.

Chapter

17

"Eek," I whisper to myself from the back of the A4 Apothecary in Rittenhouse Square, as I grab a tissue to rub the Activating Charcoal Scrub from the back of my hand. It smells sweet and looks lavender in the tube, but on my hand it burns and turns a tarry brown. I take a furtive glance around the store as I head toward the sloughing creams; I've been here for thirty minutes already, and I fear that if I don't buy something soon, the snooty salesgirls may throw me out into the street. I take a long, deep whiff of a pineapple-infused facemask and reel from the smell, which practically brings tears to my eyes. After enduring another one of the salesgirl's languid stares, I impulsively decide on a key-lime-pie-scented body wash with matching room spray. Perhaps a room that reminds me of the Florida Keys is all I need. On my way out the door, I sadly remember what Kerrin said so many months ago about my only sensual pleasures coming from beauty products.

Instead of brooding on the bus on my way back home, I decide to focus on one good thing that happened this week: Yesterday Sarah announced excitedly in our Friday design meeting that her starbaby had been "discovered" at the Cherry Hill Mall. She'd been shopping after work with him in tow, and apparently an agent had approached her, gushing and drooling all over his blond ringlets. This was all Sarah had needed to hear—finally, the world recognized how beautiful he is!—and she'd quickly made plans to take him to New York this upcoming week for photo shoots and go-sees.

As she explained how she'd dutifully bought all the required clothing and accessories, I couldn't help but feel bad for starbaby. If it went well for him in New York, he could look forward to a childhood dominated by cameras, hot lights, yelling adults, stints with tutors, and maybe some kind of breakdown by age thirteen. Although I don't ever expect to produce offspring attractive enough for TV commercials, it only took one photo shoot in Vancouver to convince me that under no circumstances would I ever do that to my child. It was chilly those four days, with a cold, brisk wind that swept through Stanley Park, and the little girls in the commercial obviously couldn't wear their coats over their cute dresses while shooting. When I spotted the bright pink, raw skin on the bare legs of the young girls and saw their teeth chattering, it made my heart sink. On the other hand, if it went badly for starbaby, Sarah might never get over it. Either way, it meant a full week without Sarah for me.

I clench my jaw as I walk up the street with my A4 Apothecary bag, trying to decide whether or not I should turn left at the corner and go up to the post office before it closes at its two o'clock Saturday time. I've just about given up on hearing from J.P. Cody; watching him in the morning is even starting to frustrate me now, giving me a sense of panic that rises from my chest and leaves my head in a fuzzy buzz by the time Rich comes for me each day. I round the corner and see Evie and the twins from down the street jumping rope, singing:

Girls go to college
To get more knowledge!
Boys go to Jupiter
To get more stupider!

They sing and swing faster and faster and the ropes make a blur, until Camille finally trips over a rope and crashes to the sidewalk. They all laugh raucously and look up to see me standing awkwardly nearby.

"Toby! Where'ya going?" Evie asks, bending down to tighten the Velcro on her sneaker.

"I don't know," I answer glibly, and they all start laughing again. "Should I go home or should I go to the post office?"

"Post office! Post office!" they all chant in unison.

"OK. Want to come with me?"

We make our way up the street, me and my merry band of giggling, cackling jump-ropers, and I'm wondering how I'm going to keep from tearing up in front of them when I see my empty, black hole of a post office box again. We pass in front of my house just in time to see Michael pushing Ed, a heavy-lidded, dark-haired kid who plays the oboe, out the door in order to welcome Kim, a tiny, blond, flute-playing pixie from six blocks over. Michael's business has begun to boom in the last few months; word of mouth has spread, and now it is all Michael can do to juggle his many students. He left his lesson schedule out on the table one night when he was unexpectedly summoned to meet Lisa at the mall, and I couldn't help but be amazed by how many new students he has picked up. I also overheard him telling a friend that he even expected to have a waiting list soon, and judging by the schedule, that day doesn't seem too far off.

I give Michael a cursory wave as Kim delicately picks her nose with the hand that isn't gripping the flute case, and we continue on our way. We reach the post office, and the girls immediately crowd around the wanted posters, scrunching up their noses at the creepy-looking men and the descriptions of their scars.

"Look, this guy has five names!" Maria shouts, rousing the near-sleeping postal clerks. "Rufus James, Randall Jones, Ray King, Roy Rodner, and Rick Johnson!"

"Yeah, pretty crazy," I say halfheartedly, turning my

key and opening my post office box. I peer inside and am mildly stunned. There is an envelope in there, stark white against the dingy gray. For some reason, I look to my left and then to my right, as if I'm doing something illegal, and I gingerly pull it out. Sure enough, it's got my typed name and PO Box address, and it's postmarked from downtown Philadelphia. I can't decide if I want to jump, scream, throw up, faint, or cheer, but I know I've got to get out of here.

"What did you get? What did you get?" the girls yell, turning away from the wall of posters.

"Nothing," I say too quickly, my voice pinched. "Just a letter from a friend. Come on, we've got to go back now," I say, shoving them toward the door. They drag their feet and move infuriatingly slowly back down the street, chatting about their teacher and knocking into one another. I hurry in front of them and dash up the steps to my door.

"See ya, guys," I shout, sweating through my pink T-shirt with the ladybug pocket detail. I race upstairs to my room, where I flop down on the bed, slimy-palmed, dry-mouthed, and staring at the envelope. I finally reach for my Hello Kitty letter opener and slowly, gently, open it.

Three hours later, I am walking into Kerrin's apartment, weighed down by two thick photo albums and some random photos I've peeled from the refrigerator, a bulletin board on the back of our basement door, and a photo collage on my mirror. Amazingly, Kerrin has managed to unearth an impressive collection of photos as well. They are not in albums but in their original paper envelopes that come from the photo developers at the drugstore.

Kerrin opens the refrigerator and takes out two beers, roots around in a shoebox on the countertop for the bottle opener, unearths it with a flourish, and opens the beers. Kerrin's apartment is unlike any other place I've ever seen. It isn't that it is dirty or even exceptionally cluttered; rather, there is no rhyme or reason to anything. A bracelet in the butter dish. A pile of buttons and Brazilian coins in a plant pot. An empty litter box, unused since Kerrin grudgingly agreed to catsit for her neighbor's kitten last summer, now filled with old magazines and journal articles. Two cassette tapes propped up on either side of a decrepit patchouli candle in a zebra-striped ceramic dish. My mom, who has a natural flair for decorating and even dabbled in interior design courses when I was younger, once pronounced Kerrin's decorating style as Early Chaos. Today I notice a man's wooly sock and a battered spiral-bound notebook in the corner, which I can only guess is Len's contribution to the Early Chaos movement.

"I think this activity calls for something a bit madcap," Kerrin says, messily piling her hair on top of her head and putting a Flaming Lips CD on her stereo. We sit down at the table with the hundreds of photos, and as the singer's nasal wail fills the room, the phone rings, a rich, cheery *brrrrrrinng*. Kerrin would rather be strung up by her thumbs than suffer the shrill pierce of a modern, cordless phone, instead preferring a solid, shiny black Radio Shack model with a heavy handset and a stubborn 7 button.

The phone is on its third ring and I say anxiously, "Aren't you going to answer it?"

"No," she says firmly, trailing her hand across the messy, multilayered collage of photos that cover the tabletop. "We have important work to do. Whoever wants me can leave a message."

The answering machine picks up and she smiles as her brother's sleepy voice comes softly from the speaker. "Hey, K," he begins. "Just calling to say hi, see how you're doing. Also, I broke up with Miss Saigon. Talk to you later."

Kerrin laughs out loud, throwing her head back and ruining her precarious bun, her hair tumbling onto her shoulders.

"Is your brother going out with a Vietnamese girl?" I ask.

"No! That wouldn't be so bad! That's the nickname I gave her. He's been going out with this girl for three months and her birthday comes around last week. He told her he would take her to see or do anything in New York—*anything*, any show, any ballet, any art exhibit—and she said she wanted to see *Les Mis* or *Phantom of the Opera*. Good God! Is there any worse pox on the planet than the musicals of Andrew Lloyd Webber?" she clucks.

"When that happened, he *knew* it was over." She inhales deeply, composing herself. "OK, let's see the letter. I know you read it to me, but maybe it will give us some inspiration."

I pull the letter from the envelope and hand it to her, holding my breath as I watch her scan the single sheet of white paper. J.P.'s letter is as pithy as my letters to him were, typed single space on a computer:

Dear Toby,

Thanks for the letters, your poems are great. I look forward to hearing from you again. Can you send me a photo of yourself?

Best,
J.P. Cody

"This isn't that inspired," Kerrin says critically, "and it's got bad punctuation also—but what can you expect from a guy, right?"

"Hey, come on!" I protest. "Aren't you happy for me?"

"Very," she says earnestly. "Sorry. So what should we look for in a photo?"

"I don't know, Kerrin," I say nervously. "I'm terrified. You know I don't photograph well. I always look like I'm wearing a rubber nose."

We pore over the hundreds of photos during the entire Flaming Lips CD, then through a Rolling Stones double album, and finally Best of Elvis Costello. We're slowly but surely narrowing down the collection, throwing out the photos with red-eye and the ones from my pre-contact-lens days, when I wore glasses with thick black frames. There are even some pictures that feature both the red-eye and the glasses, making me look like Satan's librarian. Because there are so many photos fighting for space, dozens of them overlap, and every so often this makes for a disappointing find, like when we spy one that features my bare legs and rickrack-trimmed miniskirt, only to pull out the rest of the photo and discover that my eyes are closed. In another one, I'm having a stellar hair day, but when I disinter the lower half of the picture, I groan when I see that I'm wearing the bright yellow jumper that Kerrin says makes me look like I won the part of the lemon in the parade of citrus fruits.

Finally Kerrin bores down deep enough into the pile to strike gold. "I love this one!" she crows, pulling out a long shot of me at the zoo, standing next to a monkey and wearing my flowered jersey Betsy Johnson dress. "And this one's not bad, either," she adds, squinting at one where I'm wearing a saucy red halter top and smiling with a come-hither look. "Very sexy, and no monkey."

"Oh, and check this one out," she laughs, pointing to a partially covered photo. "Look at this smile. This must have been from the night you doubled up on your pain pills for your period by mistake—remember how you thought you wouldn't have to clean your room anymore because you saw your clothes jumping onto the hangers?" She reaches into the pile and yanks out the photo, and we both laugh when we see that I've got my arm draped across Michael.

"Pain pills for sure," we say to each other, as Kerrin rolls her eyes and throws it back on the pile. She turns away from the excavation site to light a cigarette. "If you like it, we could crop him right out of it, you know," she says to me as I look at the picture. "But I'm not sure about the vest, to be frank with you," she warns, turning her nose up at my "Who Shot the Curtains?" vest.

"No, that's OK, I don't think that photo is that good, either. How about this one?" I ask, pulling out a favorite of mine. In this one I'm seated and wearing a wooly black sweater with a plunging neckline. Due to some trick of the lighting and the positioning of my arms, I appear to have luscious cleavage. It's shot from a weird, high-up three-quarter view, so you can also see my waist and a bit of my butt.

"Yes!" Kerrin exclaims. "Your face looks good, and you can see your body, too. What did that guy Kyle at work call you? 'Hot Seat'?" she asks, twisting her lips to the side and exhaling a mouthful of smoke. "You should capitalize on that, if guys think you have a nice rear."

"No, not 'Hot Seat.' 'Billion-dollar butt.' "

"Well, either way, it's a good thing. Maybe if this doesn't work out, you should go after him."

"I don't want to go out with Kyle," I say stubbornly. "I want to go out with J.P. Cody."

"I know. But any port in a storm, right?" she asks.

We opt for the shot of me in the black V-neck sweater, and Kerrin tips it in the light to look for fingerprints. I stay for another beer and tell her all I know about Kyle, what's going on with starbaby's plan for superstardom, and how the first package proofs are about to come back with photos of a kid with Down syndrome on the box.

"Crazy," she murmurs. "What the hell are future generations going to think? Oh, well. You want a ride home? I'm going to meet Len at the urology lab. 'House of Wiz 'n' Jiz,' as I like to call it."

Back in my room later that evening, I look at the letter once again and think about how Kerrin said it was uninspired. Who cares? I got a letter from J.P. Cody! Maybe he's shy. Maybe he doesn't do poetry. What the hell does Kerrin know anyway? She's never had a letter-writing tryst with a meteorologist. Perhaps she was high.

I put the letter away, stuff the bag of reject photos under my bed, and pull out a copy of *What Car?*, the oversized, glossy British magazine that sells for nine dollars. I flip to the article on the new Subaru that they swear will be coming to the U.S. any day now with both the four-wheel drive *and* the one hundred thirty horsepower engine, but everyone knows that they lie and that the only way to take a test drive is to hop a plane to Europe or Japan. My eyes start to feel heavy, and I am abruptly woken up an hour later by Michael and Lisa coming into the house, whispering noisily and bumping into each other as they make their way up the skinny staircase.

"You're very happy for a Monday morning," Rich remarks as he merges into traffic at the base of the bridge. "Anything to do with your boss taking a week off unexpectedly?"

"Oh! I forgot all about that!" I exclaim. "Wow, you guys heard about that over there?"

"Everyone's heard about it. I wouldn't be surprised if my ex hears about it," he spits, using his own awkward segue to launch into a monologue about how nosy his ex-wife is. I'm nodding and uh-huh-ing him to death, but I'm really still lost in thought about my letter from J.P. Cody. I spent the weekend in such a happy state that I even joined Michael and Lisa for dinner last night. Lisa was unusually quiet, peering at me out of the corners of her eyes, and neither of them asked why I had a moronic smile pasted on my face all weekend. After she went into Michael's room and closed the door, I whispered *pssst* to Michael when he was on his way back from the bathroom.

"Michael," I said quietly from my bed, waving the letter. "Look what I got."

He took it from me and read it, his eyes growing dramatically wide with surprise. His mouth fell open, and finally he spoke. "My goodness," he said, nodding.

"That's all you're going to say? Aren't you happy?"

"Yeah . . . sure. I'm just—I'm surprised. It's . . . it's hard to believe."

"What, you think I'm some kind of freak?" I asked, clutching my Secret Wish Horse to my chest. "You don't think I deserve a letter?"

He put his hands in the air with the palms facing me and said, "Of course you do. This is good news, right?"

"Shhh, not so loud," I said, pointing to his closed bedroom door. "I don't want her to know about any of this, remember?"

"Yup, I remember," he said, looking at the floor before leaving my room and walking across the hall to his room.

I'm humming tonelessly at my desk and waving to Joe as he smokes under the green awning when the phone rings. It's an inside call, just one ring, my least favorite kind. Caroline is away for a wedding and Joe is outside, so the call could only be work related.

"Miss Morris," Rod Winters says, his voice crackling through the phone. "We are having difficulty figuring out your drawing for the Use Your Noodle game sticker sheet. Can you please come here." He doesn't phrase the last sentence as a question; instead, his voice drops off at the end, implying that I don't really have a choice.

"OK," I say, gulping. Leave it to Rod Winters to kill my J.P. Cody buzz. My heart starts pounding as I wade through my pile of sketches in the Use Your Noodle file drawer. When I walk into Rod's office, he is sitting at his desk, his hands folded in front of him, looking at me intently. I take a seat and compulsively smooth my skirt, like I'm in the fourth grade and facing a scary teacher.

"This is a compound curve," he begins, pointing to the engineering drawing of the Use Your Noodle game base. "Do you know how to design stickers for a compound curve?"

"I do," I answer weakly. "I'm not sure it was a compound curve when I used the old engineering drawing. Luke gave it to me"—I start shuffling through the file for the drawing that the games engineer gave me weeks ago—"back in March. Has it changed?"

"Of course it's changed!" he roars, and I flinch, dropping the entire file to the floor.

"But . . . but no one gave me an updated drawing," I sputter helplessly with my head down, eyes up. "This is the one I had."

"Oh. Well. Let's see, then." He picks up the phone and hits the keypad, staccato punches to Luke's extension. "Luke, when you get back to your desk, please come see me. We've got an issue with the stickers here for Use Your Noodle, and it appears that the designer doesn't have the most up-to-date drawings." He slams down the phone and says, "I'll call you when he gets back to me."

"OK," I whisper, collecting the file from off the floor and cringing like an injured dog. I'm almost out the door when Rod quietly and gruffly says, "Miss Morris."

"Yes?"

"My granddaughter is doing much better."

"Oh?" I ask tensely, turning back around to face him but keeping my eyes firmly planted on the top of his desk.

"Tracie is my granddaughter." When I slowly raise my eyes, I see that he is nervously rubbing his hands together and shifting uncomfortably in his lumpy chair. I awkwardly push my hair behind my ears to stall for time, hoping he'll say something else, but he doesn't.

"I sort of figured that out," I say finally. "She's . . . great," I add.

"Yes, yes . . . she is," he says, getting a faraway look. I silently step back into his office and sit down in the chair opposite him. He sighs heavily and leans back in his chair, choosing his words very slowly and with the same precision he uses with his engineering drawings.

"You know what she's been through . . . I guess that's why I'm sometimes like a . . ." he mutters, his voice trailing off.

"Like a what?" I ask, leaning across the desk, my eyes wide.

"Like a grouchy bear around here. You know, a bear gets upset when something is wrong with one of the cubs," he finishes in his Southern drawl. A grouchy bear! I can't help but giggle out loud at this description; after listening to Joe and Luke and all of the other engineers describe what it's like to work with Rod, not one of them ever used the expression "grouchy bear." Jerk, yes. Jackass, many, many times. Worthy of being choked, of course. But *grouchy bear* sounded almost sweet, so benign, like he could be calmed down from one of his rages with a big sticky pot of honey.

"I'm sorry, I'm not laughing at you," I say apologetically, when he looks at me with a hurt expression. "I'm actually going to see Tracie in just a couple of nights."

"I know. She is looking forward to it," he says, trying desperately to contort his face but finally giving in and smiling at me. I smile back, and it's the first time ever that looking Rod in the face doesn't make me want to run and hide under my desk or throw an engineering drawing over my head to escape his malevolent stare.

When I get back to my cubicle, there is a pile of packaging proofs from China awaiting my review. Sarah bravely decided to delegate the responsibility to me while she was away chasing fame in the name of her starbaby. I clear off the rest of my desk and slowly review each one, my red pen in hand to correct typesetting mistakes or errant printing registration marks. Surfin' Salamanders looks fine, so I OK it and sign off on the pink sheet stapled to the upper right-hand corner. So does My First Blender, the Super Spy Passport Kit, and the blister-card package for Dream Weavers hair refills. I find a weird blotch of ink in the center of the forehead of the girl on the Friendly Ferrets package, so I duly note it and sign off. I finally give everything one more once-over, and, satisfied, I bring the pile to Barb, our fast-talking secretary with the high heels and the thickest Philadelphia accent I've ever heard.

Chapter 18

I am very popular indeed during these sun-dappled May days, but not with Rod and Kyle, as Caroline predicted back in the sound room. Instead, I find that mothers on the gentrified blocks in my neighborhood rush from their homes to meet me and greet me and finger their skinny gold necklaces as they subtly ask how Michael's schedule is looking. Cara's quite bright, one said to me with an intense stare; don't you think he would like a bright bassoon student? Another asked me if Michael had ever considered charging more for lessons. "There's more money to be made, certainly," she hoarsely confided in me while her bubble-gum-blowing son sat oblivious on the sidewalk. One time I was walking with Kerrin, deep in conversation about something stupid Len had said to her, when a petite, wiry mother dashed out with a small tray of six cupcakes. She cornered us, her free hand running through her unkempt hair, as she implored me to bring the sweet treats to Michael and beg him to move her little Ashley to the top of the list. Kerrin and I promptly took the cupcakes home and gorged ourselves, greedily licking the peppermint icing and guffawing about the insanity of baking for a potential music teacher. I ate two and Kerrin eagerly polished off the other four, but not before she remembered that fake peppermint flavoring makes her feel queasy.

I don't feel guilty about having eaten the cupcakes because I seem to be the only one who isn't benefiting from Michael's largesse these days, and I am petty enough to let it irk me. Lisa was parading around showing off her new ring with the moonstone one week, then her buttery leather jacket the next. Evidently they are planning a romantic cruise, because the living room floor is quickly becoming blanketed with thick, oversized white envelopes with logos featuring ocean waves and return addresses like Norwegian Cruise Lines and Carnival Cruises. Michael has even taken to buying nicer candy to ply his students with—they are now making off with a full-sized chocolate bar or fancy bag of jelly beans, instead of a lone, stale Tootsie Roll. Meanwhile, I'm still waiting for him to cough up his half of the bill for the refrigerator repair, and the left sole of my hyacinth mule sandal is developing such a big hole that I'm afraid the ball of my foot might poke through any day now.

But the long walk home past all the aggressive mothers isn't something I can really avoid, since I am now compulsively checking my post office box on most days. When I excitedly mailed the photo of myself to J.P. Cody, I hoped that he would respond instantly. When he didn't, it spawned days' worth of insecure feelings and fears that kept Kerrin's loud phone jangling day and night. What if he thinks I'm ugly, Kerrin? What's the holdup? What is he waiting for? I *knew* it looked like I'm wearing a rubber nose in all my photos; that must be it, right? Right?

"Want to see these head shots?" Sarah asks, her cheeks flushed and her face full of expectation. Do I have a choice? I want to ask.

"Sure," I answer coolly, nodding. She delicately opens a portfolio and holds her breath as she slides the black-and-white glossies of starbaby across the drafting table at me. She blinks hard, one, two, three times, and for a split second I wonder if she's going to cry, such is her emotion at seeing these photos. But she doesn't, and I instead press my lips together and nervously tug at the oversized decorative buttons on the front placket of my orange shirt.

"Nice," I say, bluffing. Actually, it isn't that starbaby is so ugly anymore—he has certainly grown out of his wizened, wrinkly look—but I honestly don't find him that darling. Sarah grows doughy-faced and slowly collects the photos one by one, holding them delicately and tentatively, as if they were a hundred years old. She's almost completed this painstaking exercise when Rod Winters

sails by with a gem-studded My Magic Mirror prototype, glancing over his shoulder at the drafting table.

"Look!" pleads Sarah, grateful for a fresh set of eyes.
"My little starbaby!"

Rod sets down the prototype and indelicately grabs
one of the photos, putting his thumb squarely in the
lower left corner and making Sarah wince. He holds it
up to his face and studies it, slowly nodding his head.
After a long minute that I'm sure is going to cause
Sarah's head to explode with anticipation, he tonelessly
offers his opinion.

"Very nice. Very nice indeed."

He cocks his head and gives his fake, sharp smile to
Sarah, then turns his back to her and faces me. "Very,
very nice," he repeats again, winking a huge wink that
only I am privy to.

"Uh-huh," I agree, biting my lower lip as he scoops
My Magic Mirror under his arm and walks briskly off in
the direction of The Third Sex's office.

"He is just so beautiful," Sarah sighs, tilting her chin
up and holding the photo in her outstretched arms over
her head, like she's giving her two-dimensional baby an
airplane ride. "Aren't you now, my little starbaby," she
coos, pursing her lips and widening her eyes as if the
photo will emote back. "Does this picture lie? I don't
think so! I don't think so!"

She stops mid-coo, suddenly aware that several of the
designers are watching her with barely contained
amusement. "Well, we'll have to see what happens when

we hear from his agent, won't we, then?" she asks no one in particular, closing the portfolio and giving it a little pat with her French-manicured hand. "By the way, Toby, did I thank you for working on those package proofs that came in during that week I was away? I'm *so* grateful," she says, as if checking over the proofs is something as tense and tricky as hostage negotiation. "You might just be able to do my job yet!" she adds, giving me a gummy smile that makes me want to race outside and start running down the highway. Instead, I walk back toward my desk, looking down at the floor, and thanking God that our half-day Fridays are starting in two weeks. Midway down the hall, I am wordlessly joined by Rod, who is leaving The Third Sex's office.

"That wasn't nice," I playfully whisper to him as we walk together. His polyester pants—regulation gear for all the engineers I've ever worked with at Toyland—are making a loud *swish-swoosh* sound with every step he takes, and after a few seconds of silence, I'm not sure whether or not he heard me.

"But funny," he finally says back without looking at me, veering away from me as I enter my cubicle, continuing down the hall toward the door into the engineering department. When he reaches the door, he turns and gives me a smile, a real smile. A real smile from Rod Winters.

"Arrrgh," Kerrin says, her voice muffled by the T-shirt that she's pulling off over her head in the changing room next to mine. "I don't even know why I'm trying this on—I usually go skinny-dipping, anyway."

"Come on now!" I shout to her through the cream-colored wall that separates us. "You know you can't go skinny-dipping at Len's family's beach house. Talk about making a bad impression as a houseguest." I shimmy out of my ice blue culottes and leave them in a heap on the pin-strewn floor, then I reach for the sweet linen skirt with the tiny embroidered flowers and the gigantic price tag. As I pull up the zipper and reel from the sticker shock, I have a flash of anger at Michael—he still hasn't paid me for the refrigerator repair, and now Lisa Carlton is sporting a new watch with a fancy, oversized bezel. The watch isn't my taste—a bit too flashy and shiny—but she has made a big production out of bending her arm dramatically to look at it in front of me several times in the last week. Nauseating.

"Whaddaya mean? You don't think I'd look good swimming in the nude? Don't answer that, Toby," she cautions.

"No!" I begin to apologize. "I mean you can't go skinny—"

"I know what you meant, silly," she yells back. "Oh, man! This bathing suit's got a Wonderbra in it. Did you know this when you saw me pick it off the rack?"

I have to admit that I didn't; on this first half-day Friday shopping trip of the season, I was drooling with lust in the shoe department while Kerrin was sadly moaning across the aisle in Resortwear.

"Wow!" she exclaims. "This is pretty impressive. Too bad it makes you feel terrible once your tits are squished in there. It's like it gives you the seven warning signs of a heart attack! My whole chest hurts, I feel short of breath, and I have a shooting pain in my arm and shoulder from this freakin' thing."

"I think you're spending too much time with Len," I say as I pull off the linen skirt and try on a pinky-red pair of twill shorts with big patchwork pockets. "You don't need a Wonderbra anyway."

"Yeah, I know," she sighs, as if having a big chest is a liability. "I have to get going, I guess—you're so lucky with half the day off. I wish I had that. Not that the people I work with would even take advantage of it, of course—they'd be too busy hiding from the evil, cancer-causing sun to appreciate it."

She slams the door to her changing room, and through the crack in the door I can see her emerge empty-handed and aggravated. She starts fidgeting with the fingers on her right hand, anxiously bending and pushing them together, and I know I've got five, ten minutes, tops, until she will need to go outside and smoke.

"OK, this is the last thing," I say quickly, opening the door and pirouetting for her. I've tried on the last piece in my pile of options, a royal blue knee-length silk sundress with spaghetti straps and a flouncy, bouncy ruffle at the bottom.

"It's . . . *pretty*," Kerrin says, stepping back.

"It is," I agree. "I don't know where I would wear it,

but it sure is sweet." As soon as the words are out of my mouth, I know exactly where I will wear it, though. A big, closed-lipped smile slowly crawls across my flushed face, and I hurry back into the changing room to take it and the dress off.

I pay for the dress, watching in horror as the cashier shoves it into a shopping bag like it's a pile of wet paper towels, and Kerrin and I walk down Market Street trying to guess what her weekend will be like with Len's family. The last time his parents came into town, they took Kerrin out to dinner, where she enthusiastically engaged Len's mother in a debate about vegetarianism. When the discussion was finished, Kerrin calmly returned to her pork chop, but she had the sneaking sensation that Len's mother might have been a bit cross. "I was just debating for the sake of debate," she sputtered to me when I shook my head in amazement at the story.

When I get home, Michael is hunched over the kitchen table with his schedule, and there is a towering stack of colorful music books on the floor. He is so engrossed in his activity, gnawing aggressively on the end of the pencil and squinting at the list of students taped up to the wall, that he doesn't even hear me come in.

"Hey," I say quietly.

"Hi," he says, looking up at me and pushing the chair back from the table. "I can't figure out where to put all these kids. There are so many new ones this spring. One of them is a real brat, too—keeps swearing that her mother made me peppermint cupcakes, or some such nonsense." He turns back to the schedule, drops the pencil on the table, and holds his head in his hands.

"Oh, yeah?" I ask, trying not to sound guilty, even as my mouth waters at the memory of the delicious treats. "Look, Michael," I say, pulling the dress out of the bag and holding it up against my front. "I got a new dress today when I was shopping with Kerrin."

"Nice," he says, without looking up.

"I'm going to wear it on my date with J.P. Cody," I offer.

"Oh, really?" he asks while finally looking at me, perplexed and furrowing his left eyebrow. "When's that?"

"I don't really know yet," I admit, and he laughs.

"Shut up! You're as bad as *her!*" I yell. "It would be helpful if I had some support here, you know," I add quietly. I throw the dress over my arm and trudge up the stairs, the warm springtime air already making me feel like the walls of the house are collapsing in on themselves.

"Hey, this wasn't the Metallica CD I wanted, ya' know. I wanted the *other* one," Kevin whines, walking over and waving the CD case in my face.

"Uh, hello?" I ask him angrily. "How about, 'Thanks for picking up that CD for me,' baldie?"

He immediately looks bashful and drops his head. "Sorry. Thanks for getting it. I guess I didn't write the exact one I wanted on the list."

"Well, that's more like it," I say in a more pleasant tone of voice.

"Why'd you buy Kevin a present?" Tracie asks sweetly, playing with the candy necklace around her neck and giving me a shy smile that makes me melt. "Are you going to buy more presents?"

"No, no," I assure her. "Kevin got a gift certificate to a record store, but he couldn't get there, so he made me a little wish list and I picked up the CDs for him. They're not really presents."

"Do you want a bite of this?" Tracie asks, pulling the elastic away from her neck and exposing hot pink, yellow, and blue blotches all over the skin beneath, a mixture of food dye and saliva, wet and sticky.

"Oh, no thank you," I answer cheerily while trying with all my might not to scrunch up my nose. "I guess if you're eating that, you must be feeling much better."

"Yup," she says, crunching on a tiny yellow piece on the necklace and loudly gnashing it between her back teeth.

"Well, that's good," I say, waving to Mark, who is rushing down the hallway adjacent to the playroom. "What do you want to do tonight? You want me to read you 'Pocahontas'?"

" 'Little Mermaid.' "

"Again? Well, OK. You're the boss, Tracie," I say, walking over to the reading area for the worn copy of the book. It is so well loved that the spine is completely broken, a page is torn in half, bisecting poor Sebastian the crab's head, and there are sticky stains all over the back cover.

"My grandpa's the boss, too," she says proudly as I sit down next to her and flop the book open to the first page. "The toy-making boss."

"Oh, is that so? Well, being the boss must run in the family, then," I say, and she giggles. "Did you know that I know your grandpa?"

"Yeah," she answers disinterestedly. "He told me."

I read about the adventures of Ariel, Eric, and company to Tracie, who, no matter how many times she hears this story, grows misty-eyed at the same parts and gasps when the suspense at the end is just too much for her little heart.

"And they lived happily ever after," she sighs as I close the book. She stretches out on the floor with her head propped in her hands and looks up at me expectantly.

"What's up?" I ask, shimmying quickly out of the way as a loopy little boy named Gabe races toward me on the floor with a fire truck.

"Do you have a boyfriend? Like Ariel and Eric were girlfriend and boyfriend?"

"Not really, Tracie," I say, shaking my head and shrugging. "But soon—maybe really soon, I think." I grin from ear to ear as I remember Jenna's voice-mail message on my machine at work two days ago: "Toby, we *have* to get together. It's been too long! I've been so busy here, I don't know whether I'm coming or going." Then her voice dropped several registers and she finished by saying, "And about your friend here—he seems very happy lately. Every time I see him, he's singing, humming, or smiling. Whatever he's got, I want some of it!"

Well, of course we know what he's got, I thought at the time —the love and adoration of a poem-writing secret admirer with luminous green eyes and who, in her wooly black sweater, looks like she's got impressive cleavage.

"Yes, maybe very soon," I say to Tracie again.

Chapter 19

And then it came—in all of its stark, #10 glory, another crisp envelope from J.P. Cody. I was walking up the front steps of the house, congratulating myself on not compulsively checking my post office box for two days running, and I saw Lisa Carlton's bun and scrunchie sharply outlined in the window. She was sitting on the couch, laughing like a boob at something on TV, and I decided that I just couldn't face her at that moment. Instead, I turned on my newly heeled and soled hyacinth mule sandals and made a beeline for the post office. When I turned the key and spotted the letter, I felt that same euphoric sweatiness that came over me the last time, and my mouth went dry as the place started to spin. I ran home and burst in the door, and Lisa turned away from the TV just long enough to give me an irritating, sidelong glance.

"What do you have there?" she said calmly, fluffing her scrunchie.

"Nothing," I answered as evenly as I could while wiping sweat from my upper lip. Lisa sniffed and went back to laughing at the TV. I dashed up the stairs, flung off my sandals, and flopped down on my bed, forgoing the dainty Hello Kitty letter opener and instead ripping the envelope open with my damp hands. Inside was another one-sheet missive, cleanly typed in that same computer font from before:

Dear Toby,

Sorry it's taken me so long to write back, things have been very busy here at the station! Thanks so much for your photo, I really like it. Can you tell me a little bit about yourself now?

Best,
J.P. Cody

Oh my God, I thought as I pressed the letter to my chest and rolled around on the bed, giggling to myself. He likes the photo *and* he wants to know more about me! I also noted that I got an exclamation point—I'll have to ask Kerrin if expressive punctuation means anything for sure.

Now I'm surrounded by balled-up pieces of paper littering my bedroom floor, just like on sitcoms when they show someone trying to develop an idea, then there's a time lapse and then the person is surrounded by dozens of balled-up pieces of paper. It's late—well past my bedtime on a "school night," as Michael's students earnestly call it—but I can't give up on trying to write this letter describing myself. I've decided to abandon my poems — the photo was actually accompanied by nothing at all— and write a real letter. A normal letter. A regular, normal letter to the most fantastic and charming weatherman in the world.

Unfortunately, like me, my muse must also be hearing Lisa and Michael giggle and laugh from across the hall, and she doesn't alight on the house to help me. All of my attempts to sound cute, sweet, and artsy-smartsy are coming out stilted and forced. I sigh heavily and put on my summer nightgown with the silver stars, then scoop all the aborted attempts at the letter into my garbage can. I slide under the covers and stare wide-eyed at the ceiling, my mind racing. Well, of *course* J.P. Cody was laughing and smiling and singing recently down at the station, I decide. He was getting ready to send me his second letter! Honestly, I think as I roll over on my side, how can things get any better than this?

Ryan walks down the stairs, his eyes glittering as he sinks his teeth into his Snickers bar and clutches his clarinet case under his arm. I like this new kid on the schedule—he's curious and bright and has a mischievous smile and likes to make fun of Michael, which I always enjoy witnessing. I'm sitting at the kitchen table with my Scooby Doo notebook and my pen poised over a fresh sheet of paper; it's the umpteenth time this week I've tried to draft my letter to J.P., and I'm getting aggravated.

"Nice jersey," I say, nodding at his crisp, white Phillies jersey, which he's paired with a pair of red surf shorts.

"You like this side, you should see the back," he answers with such self-assuredness for an eight-year-old that it momentarily takes me aback. He spins around to reveal the neat, sewn-on letters spelling the name DYK-STRA and the number 4.

"Oh, a Dykstra fan, I should have guessed," I say knowingly. Michael comes down the stairs with a piece of sheet music for Ryan, which he politely takes and, much to Michael's chagrin, folds into a small square before shoving in his pocket.

"You like Len Dykstra, right, Michael?" Ryan asks, turning his face up toward Michael and smiling.

"Forget it, Ryan. If you gave this guy a baseball, he'd probably try to spike it like a volleyball," I say before Michael can answer.

"All right, off you go, guy," Michael says, pushing him toward the door. Michael hurriedly says good-bye and heads back up to the studio, taking the steps two at a time. I hear the screen door squeak open as Ryan leaves, and as I turn back to my notebook, I remember a disgusting tidbit of information and shout up the two flights of stairs, "You know the thing about Len Dykstra, though, right?"

"What's that?" Michael yells.

"He gets blow jobs in the dugout before the games!" I bellow as loudly as I can.

"Yeah, right," Michael says as he comes back down the stairs, a look of disbelief on his face.

"What's a blow job?"

Michael and I both snap our heads up in unison at this question coming from the doorway, and we see Ryan standing there looking thoroughly bewildered. For an intense and painful few seconds, Michael and I are both riveted to the spot and mute. Finally, I am able to clear my throat and speak.

"Ryan, didn't you leave? Did you come back?" I ask, my voice shaking.

"Uh, I opened the door but then I decided to take the music out of my pocket and put it in my clarinet case. So I was kinda kneeling on the step . . . right here," he finishes, pointing to the front stoop. "So *what* does Dykstra do?"

"It's not important," Michael answers briskly, looking daggers at me and flushing intensely with something between shame, disgust, and rage. "Forget about it, Ryan. Just forget it."

Dear J.P.,

Thank you so much for your letter. I'm very happy that you liked the photo! It was taken at a birthday

*party for my friend Kerrin last year, right before we
smashed a giant piñata in the shape of a gorilla all
over her floor.*

*I am 25 and I live in Philadelphia, over by the art mu-
seum. (Friends of mine once had plans to race their cars
down the steps of the museum, but this hasn't come to
pass yet—maybe a good thing, I think.) I spend my days
working for a huge toy company across the river in
stinky New Jersey, which can sometimes be a dubious
distinction but is fun most of the time. I like art and fashion and other creative things, but I am a sports fan, as
well. I also volunteer at Children's Hospital, where I get
to meet many great people.*

*You don't sound as though you're from around here—
have you been doing the weather in Philly long? I am excited to learn more about you and hope that you are
having a nice spring.*

> *Looking forward to hearing from you soon,*
> *Toby*

I flip over in bed and look at the clock, bleary-eyed, as
the sunshine pours in the window through my denim-
blue drapes. Ten o'clock already! I stayed up so late finishing my letter to J.P. Cody that I surprised myself by
having the presence of mind to set my tiny toucan alarm
clock before I fell asleep. When it cawed at six this morning, I reached out from under the covers to call Rich and
inform him I wouldn't need a ride, and then fell back

into a delicious sleep, where J.P. kissed me softly on the lips and I fell nymphlike against a fluffy cloud.

An hour later, I'm trilling to myself as I sit on the commuter train into New Jersey, rereading the letter and thinking about how perfect it is. Not too short, not too long, not too cocky, not too mousy. Kind of funny and smart, but not show-offy. I stretch my candy necklace— a gift from Tracie—absently and twirl it around my finger as I wonder about how long it will take J.P. to write back to me this time. I'm lost in thought when the train finally pulls into the station, its brakes squealing and jarring me back to reality. As I step off the platform, I spot Caroline sitting in her maroon Eclipse, bobbing her blond head to the radio and singing. When I reach the car, I give a little rap on the driver's side window, and she snaps her head up, embarrassed.

"Hey," she says as she leans over and opens the door for me. "Late night?"

"Sort of. Thanks for getting me—you know how I hate getting a ride from the guys in Quality Control." Quality Control is the only department that is completely separate from the rest of Toyland, a stone's throw from the train station and the ugly, crumbling suburban shopping plazas. The men who work in this department—and there are only men—are employed to drop-test dolls until their torsos smash, ram radio-controlled cars into walls to see how much force they can withstand, and determine how sharp a piece of plastic would have to be to inflict a wound. It is a frightening place with torturous-looking equipment and quirky, high-strung people who seem a lot like the people in the engineering department had they been locked in attics as children or raised by wolves. When they aren't busy bashing the plastic housing on a jewelry-making kit or yanking on the arms and legs of an action figure, a few of the guys are generous enough to occasionally pick up Toyland employees at the train station and deposit them at the main building three miles down the road. Lucky for me, I caught Caroline at her desk this morning and she cheerfully offered to come get me. Perhaps Josh had been hanging around and breathing down her neck; I didn't think to ask.

"So anyway," Caroline says as we turn into the corporate campus where Toyland sits, "something weird is going on in your department. I went to tell Sarah that I was going to get you, and everyone is all strange."

"Stranger than usual?" I ask, chewing on my candy necklace.

"Yeah. What is that?" Caroline asks, glancing at me as she squeezes her car into a too-small space between a late-model Saab and a canary yellow Mazda. "A candy necklace?"

"Uh-huh. It was a gift from a kid I know. Thanks so much for driving me," I say gratefully as we get out of her car and make our way toward the ugly green awning at the front of the building. When we get closer, I can see Joe standing with his arms folded, clutching a cigarette and scowling in the sun.

"Hey, Toby, what the hell is going on in your department this morning?" he asks, stamping out his cigarette and following us inside to the elevators.

"I don't know," I shrug as we get on the elevator with the worn carpet and the fake-fancy paneling. "Probably something with Sarah's stupid baby. Maybe he was discovered—yuck."

"Well, be sure to let me know, OK?" Caroline yells as the elevator stops suddenly at the engineering and graphics floor.

I walk through the doors into my department, and everything stops—an eerie quiet that only seems to fall when I round corners, walk down hallways, poke my head into cubicles. Don and Dean, twin brothers and designers from the temp agency, follow me with their eyes as they sit open-mouthed and ashen-faced. Barb bustles by me without so much as a hello, her eyes planted firmly on the floor in front of her. Nina, the sweet intern, looks at me with her face pinched before turning back to her cardboard prototype of the Happy Hippo package. I finally reach my desk, my stomach flip-flopping every which way, and I awkwardly sit down, painfully aware of my every move. I'm breathing through my nose to try and avoid hyperventilating, and as I'm turning on my computer the phone rings; one ring, an inside ring, my least favorite kind.

"Hello?" I practically whisper.

"Toby, can you please come see me?" asks The Third Sex tonelessly. "In my office."

I slowly stand up and fluff my hair a little bit, stalling for time. Eventually I make my way down the long hallway toward The Third Sex's office, past the whispers and the anxious stares and the hand-wringing that is going to make me throw up at any second. Tiny beads of sweat are trickling down my armpits now, undoubtedly making a mess of my lavender twin-set with the royal blue piping. I rap on Bill's door, and when he opens it a crack, I immediately crane my neck around him, hoping to see something. Anything. Anything that would explain the tension in the air and the feeling of dread that's threatening to overcome me.

Instead, I see Sarah sitting in one of his chairs at a corner meeting table, with her hands folded neatly on the tabletop. There is also a Chunky Chipmunk stuffed toy, complete in its package, in the center of the table. I knew Chunky Chipmunk was set to come down the pike any day now; the plush brown beast had finally made it into production and was set to hit the toy store shelves, much to everyone's surprise. At Toy Fair, Caroline told me that she distinctly overheard one of the buyers saying, "That thing looks like a rat after wisdom-tooth extraction—what kid's gonna want that?"

"Please sit down, Toby," The Third Sex says, gesturing to the empty seat next to Sarah. He hunches over the table with a pained expression and closes his eyes.

"Perhaps I can ask you what you meant by this, then," he says, trembling as he tries to retain his composure.

"By what?" I ask, squinting and confounded.

It's then that Sarah explodes, springing to life as she jumps from her chair. Her face looks swollen and puffy, not a lot unlike Chunky Chipmunk's, and is hot pink with rage.

"By this!" she screams, angrily reaching for the toy and spinning it ninety degrees on the tabletop so I can see the back of the package in plain view.

And there it is: a little blond girl with Down syndrome, her oversized forehead jutting out under her bright green bow, her misshapen eyes, her smile making a crooked, wet, pink slit across the lower portion of her face. She is wearing a green corduroy jumper with a yellow turtleneck that has a tiny butterfly motif. In her right hand, she clutches a Chunky Chipmunk, and in her left hand, she awkwardly holds one of his special magic acorns. And beneath her, in bold, two-inch high type reads,

DUMMY QUOTE GOES HERE.

"Oh," is all I can whisper, my breath taken away, like when I was hit in the chest by a kickball in the third grade.

"Toby, *how* do you explain this?" Sarah screams, pushing her face into mine. "How could you do this? These toys are shipping to the West Coast. Stores in Oregon and Washington already have this package! How could you do this?"

"It was an accident," I say meekly, bowing my head

and trying my hardest not to cry, every sweat pore on my body now joining in on the action. "I would never—"

"Well, of course we know it wasn't on purpose," The Third Sex interrupts in a voice that he seems to think is soothing but at this moment is exceptionally grating and annoying.

"So what?" Sarah yells. "She was supposed to check those package proofs!" she says dramatically to Bill as if I'm not in the room. "I leave her with one pile of package proofs and look what happens!"

"I—I'm sorry," I plead, now blinking nonstop to try and hold back the tears. "It wasn't on purpose, and I don't think the child model is a dummy. Surely people will understand it's a mistake, right?"

The Third Sex sighs, and he and Sarah exchange a knowing glance, a look so subtle I would never catch it if I weren't in such a heightened state of anxiety.

"Well, Toby, it is going to cost Toyland a pretty penny to get these packages all off the shelves as soon as possible and reprint the rest. We're not really sure what to do, but in the meantime, we're going to"—he breathes deeply here as I dig my fingernails into the corner of my chair—"suspend you with pay. Until further notice."

"What?" I ask incredulously, turning from him to Sarah, who looks away and at the ceiling.

"We need to make a gesture," he says, and I immediately think of a few gestures that I'd like to make to him and Sarah. "Someone from Quality Control will take you to the commuter train. You'll need to wait to hear from us, OK?" he asks, as if I'm the one in control.

I stand on shaky legs, my knees knocking beneath me, as I try to collect my wits. "All right, then," I squeak, my stunned voice not sounding like my own. As I turn to head out the door, the elastic suddenly snaps on my candy necklace, spraying the room with tiny, sugary circles.

I spend the rest of the afternoon walking; walking and walking and walking as if my thousands of footsteps will erase my horrible mistake. I walk all the way from the train station on Market Street back to my house, limping on my purple slides with the chunky heels that were never made for such a long journey. When I arrive home, though, I realize there's no place I'd less rather be, with even more cruise line information stuffed in the mail slot and Michael's boxes of allergy pills all over the place and Lisa's peculiar positioning of her big rig information kit in the center of the kitchen table.

So I change into my sneakers and leave and walk again, this time heading down to the river and walking all the way through Fairmount Park, not even pausing once to ogle the sexy male Rollerbladers with their bare chests and impressive abs. I don't pay any attention to the cute, sniffy dogs or beautiful blooming flowers; all I can think about is that dummy quote and that poor girl with Down syndrome. Why did I miss that package proof? I thought I had been so careful when Sarah was in New York with starbaby, but in my excitement about my strange connection to Rod Winters, did I fail to review that one? But honestly, how could I have missed it? When I've made my mind a complete muddle and finally look up, I realize with a start that I'm most of the way to Manayunk, the once down-and-out town turned arty enclave. Walking down the main street, I can't help but turn my eyes toward the windows of my favorite shoe shop, but then I immediately feel guilty for thinking about footwear at a time like this.

I walk into a coffee shop that has a bored-looking guy at the register wearing a torn T-shirt and several eyebrow and nose rings. He looks up at me sleepy-eyed, and I notice he's also wearing a little bit of eyeliner, sloppily applied. And my mom wonders why it's so hard to meet men.

"Can I use the phone?" I ask, my voice still shaking. These are the first words I've spoken to anyone since leaving Toyland, and my voice still sounds strange to me, like it's coming from outside my body.

"Yeah," he shrugs, pointing to the corner and absently pulling at one of his eyebrow rings.

I take a deep breath and dial. The phone rings three times.

"Adult Oncology. This is Kerrin."

"Hi?" I say timidly.

"Toby?"

"Yes?"

"Where are you?" she asks.

"I'm in Manayunk," I answer. With my free hand I begin twirling my hair, a nervous habit that only manifests itself when I'm under extreme duress. When I was dating The Head Wound, I practically gave myself a home perm with my bare fingers.

"Your voice sounds funny. Are you OK?"

"Not really," I sigh. "I got in trouble at work—but really bad this time." I quickly tell her the whole sordid story, trying to keep my voice low and quiet. I'm almost to the part about being suspended with pay when I realize I'm about to run out of time and I don't have any more change. I hurriedly give Kerrin the number before hanging up. After a few agonizing seconds, the phone rings and I pick it up, my hand shaking.

"So now what?" she asks, skipping anything superfluous, like a greeting.

"So now I'm suspended with pay until they decide what to do with me," I say, a sob catching in my throat. I still haven't let myself cry yet—for some reason, I feel like if I did unleash a torrent of tears, it would be like letting Toyland get the best of me.

"Uggh! What a bunch of *losers!*" she yells in a too-loud voice for her tiny office, her voice echoing against the walls.

"I know," I say sadly, blinking back tears again.

"I don't know what to say. I'm stunned. And pissed off! Those bastards. I wonder if there's any kind of legal precedent for this. I'll ask around, OK?" she says helpfully.

"All right," I say tonelessly, suddenly exhausted. "I'm gonna go now."

I hang up and retrace my steps, back out of the coffee shop, back down the street past the shoe store, all the way back through Fairmount Park. During this leg of the trip, however, I'm more sad and anxious than stunned, and I furiously chew my lower lip to keep from crying. I trudge up the stairs to the house, craving my bed and my Secret Wish Horse. I feel spent, shell-shocked, like my skin is two sizes too small and trying to suffocate my body. When I turn the key in the door, I realize that it's already unlocked, and I groan audibly at the thought of having to talk with anyone else about my day.

I come inside and Michael is in his semi-permanent spot at the kitchen table with his schedule and list of students. He is still very upset with me about sharing Len Dykstra's lecherous habits with Ryan, and he doesn't look up as I slowly walk into the room.

"What are you doing home so early?" he asks coldly, his eyes still fixed on the schedule.

"Ummm, I don't know," I answer dully, grateful that he's not looking at my giant pout, my clouded face, my limp body. "What's up with you?"

"Well, I'll tell you, Toby," he says angrily, tipping his chair back and tapping his pen on the tabletop, eyes still focused downward, "you really got me into hot water with that Lenny Dykstra comment. I can't *believe* you! I had to go down there and straighten it all out with Ryan's mother this morning! It had gotten around already—some of the other parents were really concerned. What is going to happen to my business? Did you ever think about *that?*" He finally looks up at me, his eyes flashing.

And with that, my pout gives way and I come completely unwound. Big, salty tears slide down my face and dampen my neck, my skin turning cold and clammy and the neckline of my sweater adhering to my collarbone. I can't catch my breath because I'm sobbing so hard, snorfing and hiccuping and making other assorted dainty noises. I grab the roll of Bounty from the table and stomp upstairs to my room, slamming the door and throwing myself facedown on the bed crying, now secretly wishing that I took tissues instead of paper towels. A few minutes later Michael raps on the door.

"Toby."

"*Fuck you*, Michael!" I scream as loudly as I can, giving myself an instant sore throat.

"No—your dad's on the phone," he spits. I'm confused, but I suddenly figure out why I didn't hear my Snoopy phone ring; I turned the ringer off this morning after calling Rich. I shudder when I realize that it was only this morning that I did this—today seemed so interminably long that it felt like I had reached under Snoopy's vinyl ear to flip the toggle switch three days ago.

"OK," I say gruffly, turning over. "It's OK—I'll talk to him."

"How come you're home, Toby? I was going to leave

you a message, but Michael said you were here," my dad says when I pick up the phone.

Hearing the concern in his voice makes me dissolve into tears all over again, and I explain my predicament with the eloquence of a three-year-old. "I . . . I did this thing . . . and the girl with Down syndrome . . . I made a mistake with the copy . . . the package is all messed up. Then," I heave, trying to catch my breath, "so they . . . I'm suspended . . . with pay . . . and I hate Sarah, I never saw the package proof, I swear . . . then Lenny Dyk-stra . . . and Ryan . . . and I got Michael in trouble . . . and he yelled at me . . ."

"What? What do Down syndrome and Len Dykstra have to do with each other? No, actually, now that I think of it, maybe that makes some sense," he says thoughtfully. "And *why* was Michael yelling at you?"

"No, no, Dad," I say, blowing my nose loudly into a Krispy Kreme napkin left over from my pilgrimage there with Kerrin. "That's not the important part—the important part is that I totally screwed up at my job."

"Oh, is that all?" he asks. "Don't worry about a thing," he says reassuringly.

"Really?" I snivel.

"Yes. Everything is going to work out fine. You'll see. Do I sound worried?"

"Well . . . no," I say uncertainly.

"So try not to worry, Toby. Enjoy your time off with pay—take some test drives! Where is the closest BMW dealership?" he asks.

"I think it's on Main Line Avenue," I sniff, smiling through my tears.

"Well, there you go. You ask Kerrin to drive you there and drop you off. Maybe she'll even come with you!" he suggests brightly. This finally brings a grin to my face, picturing Kerrin's hair and her cigarette ash flying in the wind as I whip the car around the tight curves of the Schuylkill Expressway. My dad, the eternal optimist.

But the next day, I don't visit the BMW dealership—I don't even get out of bed. When I wake up and realize that I have no place to go, I begin sobbing once more, cursing myself for my stupidity and sloppiness. The house is quiet and I can hear rain softly pinging on my bedroom window; even J.P. Cody has let me down this week. His five-day forecast called for bright sun and breezy warmth, although I'm not sure that I'm disappointed. Being inside feeling sorry for oneself all day is much more depressing when the weather is beautiful, and it somehow feels more natural this way, with the gray, heavy sky matching my gray, heavy mood.

At four o'clock I'm still in torpor when the phone rings. I stubbornly decide not to answer it, but when it reaches its fifth ring, I get annoyed and finally pick it up, baring my teeth at Snoopy's innocent face.

"Hello there. And how are you doing today?" Kerrin asks cautiously.

"Well, OK," I say, my throat thick with tears.

"*Uh-oh*, sounds like you've been crying. Am I right? Now come on, nobody likes a sad-sack slacker," she says cheerfully.

"Yeah, I'll try to pull myself together," I say as stoically as I can, although it's hard to feel stoic when it's four o'clock and you're still sitting in your nightgown with the blinds drawn and your hair is unwashed and the most engaging thing you've done all day is push back your cuticles.

"Hmmm, sounds like somebody could use a little parking therapy," Kerrin muses. "Get yourself together, I'll be there in an hour."

"No, I don't know if I can," I hesitate. "Really."

"Too late. I'm coming. I bring the car, you bring the talent." And with that she hangs up, and I go back to studying my cuticles.

Precisely one hour later I'm sitting on the front stoop studying the cars parked in the street when Kerrin drives up, waving maniacally at me. I hug my knees to my chest and look down to hide my red-rimmed eyes but then snap my head back up when the image registers—Len is with her, sitting in the passenger's seat and calmly eating a Whopper.

"What is he doing here?" I ask angrily as they get out of the car. I notice that Len is wearing scrubs that are the exact color of the beautiful robin's egg blue Estée Lauder face mask that Michael accidentally knocked into the toilet last year. It's a short leap from seeing scrubs to seething anew, and just thinking about Michael makes me even more cross.

"Oh—I'm sorry, Toby," Kerrin says apologetically as Len tugs nervously at the V-neck of his top. "He really wanted to see you do this—he wouldn't believe me. I thought it would be OK."

"Should I go?" Len asks, crumpling the hamburger wrapper into a tiny ball in his hand.

"No," I sigh. "It's all right."

Kerrin pulls her car into the middle of the street so it's aligned just so with our new neighbor's banged-up Volkswagen with the Quebec license plates, and she steps out of the car. She fans herself for a moment in the early June heat and then produces a bandanna from her bag, folding it five times so it's long and skinny. She beckons to me and wraps it tightly around my head; it smells vaguely like pot and Ben's musky, patchouli odor.

"Good? Should the knot be tighter?" she asks.

"A little. I can see a little light," I answer. She gives the fabric another yank and a final pat.

"Oh, and I'm sorry the AC is broken in the car—you'll have to leave the windows open," she says apologetically as she helps steer me into the driver's seat.

"OK," I say, feeling around for the gearshift, stretching out my arms, and wriggling my fingers. Blindfolded parallel parking is one of my favorite activities, and one that Kerrin knew could lift me up out of any kind of depression. It was a skill I cultivated during summers in between semesters of college, a sort of wacky party trick

I developed when sighted parallel parking began to bore me. Most people are surprised to learn that I inherited the perfect parallel parking gene not from my father but from my *mother*, whose deft parallel parking has elicited cheers from groups of total strangers on several occasions. We all suspect that this is one of the reasons my father fell in love with her—how could he not?

Very few people are willing to share in my gift, though; they are either too nervous or scared. Michael can't endure it, and neither can Jenna. Kerrin is the only friend who encourages me to keep up with my special skill and shrieks with delight when watching me perform. Strangely, Michael's mother also enjoyed it, standing out on the sidewalk alone during one of his parents' rare visits and witnessing me parallel park Michael's car while blindfolded. She politely applauded, deeming the activity "infarction-inducing fun" but also warning me that if I ever tried it with her Infiniti, she would kill me.

I take a deep breath and put the car in reverse, and I hear Len say in a terrible French accent, " 'Je me souviens'—that's what that VW's license plate says. Think it's French for 'Bring me a souvenir,' Kerrin?"

"I'm sure it is, Len," Kerrin says sarcastically, laughing.

"Hey, you guys need to keep it down," I shout out the window. "I can hear you through the open windows. I know where you're standing and I don't want any clues."

I back the car up ever so slightly and begin to turn it just a little, gingerly spinning the steering wheel and breathing deeply. I rethink my positioning and pull forward, then backward, then I grab the wheel and give it a good tug to the left. " 'Scuse me while I kiss the curb," I sing to myself in a whisper.

"I can't watch!" Len yells.

"What is wrong with you? Didn't you just hear her tell us to shut the hell up?" I hear Kerrin hiss. Finally I cut the wheel hard and let it spin back just a bit, and I can sense the front end nosing in just so. I give the wheel a tiny turn in the other direction, put on the brake, and yank the key from the ignition. I pull off my blindfold, and Kerrin and Len are both clapping and hooting, so after stepping out I take a little bow before checking my work.

"Pretty good," I say. "Not my best, but it's not bad." Kerrin's car is perfectly equidistant from the VW in front and the Saturn in back, and probably about four inches from the curb.

"What are you saying?" Kerrin says, dropping down to the curb to eyeball the distance. "It looks like four inches; five, tops."

"Yeah, I know," I say, shrugging. "But the front wheel is turned a little bit too much for my liking," I say, pointing to the front end of the car, where the tire is slightly angled toward the curb.

"Oh, come on now, Toby. You're under stress," Len says sympathetically.

"That's right. Thanks for reminding me," I say.

"Seriously," Kerrin says as they get back into her car, "I was thinking about it. You should be regarded as a hero for getting those packages off the shelves. That was the worst marketing ploy ever. That poor girl should be *grateful*. Just wait—I bet one day she comes loping up to you and thanks you."

"*Ker*-rin," Len and I both say in perfect unison.

Chapter
20

The Third Sex doesn't call the next day, or the next, then it's the weekend and I'm left with that strange feeling of knowing I should be relieved it's the weekend, except that I haven't done much of anything to warrant the relief. Which means I don't feel particularly relieved—in fact, I'm not feeling much of anything lately. After Kerrin and Len left the other night, I felt cheery for a little while, but then Lisa Carlton showed up with her crabby face and I was forced to take refuge in my room, crying into my pillow. The only thing I've had to look forward to this week is lunch today with Jenna, and it's a pretty sad scene when you're overly eager to tuck into a tuna melt.

Now Michael and I are home alone, and we've yet to call a truce, which makes mundane acts like making coffee or watching TV very tense and stressful. I'm sitting at the table trying to ignore Michael's banging nearly every kitchen drawer and cabinet open and closed, when the phone rings. It's one of his students—a bratty little thing with braces named Joanne—calling at the last minute to reschedule her lesson. Michael looks as though he might scream, but after hanging up he surprises me by taking a few deep breaths and sitting down next to me at the table.

"Toby," he starts, speaking slowly and somberly, "I want to apologize for yelling at you the other day. I—I was really upset and it wasn't right. If I had any idea you would have taken it this hard I never would have made such a big deal out of it."

"Taken *what* so hard?" I ask, furrowing my eyebrows at him as he anxiously twists the corner of his Mr. Bubble T-shirt. "Oh, Michael," I say as I suddenly realize what he's thinking. "You think I stayed home from work since Wednesday, crying alone in my room, because of the whole thing with Ryan?"

"Y—yes," he says hesitantly, looking at the floor.

"Oh, no, Michael, it wasn't Ryan at all." I begin to grin at the misunderstanding, but Michael is starting to look peeved again, so I make myself think of some of the saddest cases I've seen at the hospital, and this forces a frown back on my face in no time.

"Of course I'm sorry about what happened, too," I say seriously. "I shouldn't talk that way when I think kids might be around. You were right to be pissed. I mean, *angry*—see, I'm already practicing talking less like a sailor."

"Well, maybe," he says, relaxing his shoulders and playing with the spoon in the sugar bowl. "It's just that the music thing is so tenuous, and—wait a minute, Toby. Why were you home this week?"

I sigh loudly and mentally distill the story for him, boiling it down to its most base parts. "I'm in trouble because of a packaging layout I did, believe it or not. Because of this picture of a retarded girl."

"Now, Toby," Michael admonishes, pointing an index finger at me. Michael was raised never to make fun of those less fortunate, or if he was going to, he should at least be accurate in his diagnoses.

"No, Michael; I say this completely without hyperbole!" I exclaim defensively as I fold my arms in front of my chest, lean back in the rickety yellow wooden chair, and accidentally kick a flute case that's under the table. I lean back in toward the table again and start fiddling with the metronome, but Michael gently disentangles my fingers and moves it, putting it out of my reach. "Well, she *is* retarded—she has Down syndrome, and I made a mistake with the copy and now the box basically says she's a dummy," I finish, satisfied to make it through the story without whimpering.

"Really?" he asks, surprised. "So how does this translate into you being home for several days?" He takes off his glasses and studies one of the crooked arms.

"Because I'm suspended with pay until they decide what to do with me. Isn't that a kick in the pants?" I ask, suddenly steamed at Toyland. "I don't know why I don't get into another field altogether—I've really had it with them."

"Yes, it is," he says, tilting his head and looking at me. "A kick in the pants, I mean. It's funny—I've been thinking about some career decisions too, and in some strange way, I suppose I should thank you for that whole Ryan incident. It was one of many recent wake-up calls about what I should be doing. To be honest, I'm not even sure that I still like teaching."

"But business is good," I say, confused.

"I know it's good," he says, nodding. "But is it good for *me*, is the question," he asks, giving the issue the typical Michael twist, spinning it for hidden clues and subtle secrets. "I don't know if I should even stay in Philadelphia—actually, I've been thinking pretty seriously about signing on to work for a cruise line," he finishes while tidying a stack of music books on the tabletop.

So that's what all the thick white envelopes were for, I almost say aloud—not for a romantic sail to Bermuda or the Bahamas with Lisa Carlton but applications and information for making music on the high seas. I try to picture Michael wearing a Hawaiian shirt and multicolored leis, playing "Hot, Hot, Hot" on his clarinet for honeymooning couples and spry senior citizens on the lido deck, but I can't even get past the Hawaiian shirt.

Michael reads my mind and says snootily, "It's not like I'd be in one of those Caribbean bands, with all that stupid music." He pauses as he puts his glasses back on. "I'd be playing in quartets, with other classically trained musicians, for captain's dinners and so forth. It's a really good way to get more experience performing and get your name out there. Plus you get to see the world and meet lots of other people."

"Really?" I ask, shocked. "See the world? Meet lots of people? You?"

As I drag myself up the stairs to the entrance of the Twin City Diner, I hope for a fleeting second Jenna's not there, and I immediately chastise myself for thinking this way. I glance around and spot her, sitting at the counter mindlessly stirring a root-beer float. Her hair is pulled back into a neat chignon, and her nails look newly manicured with a peachy shade that matches her lipstick. Leave it to Jenna to win Best Dressed for Saturday Afternoon Lunch at the Twin City Diner, I think as I approach the counter—although between the hollow-eyed waitstaff and hungover patrons, it's not a hard category to win. She sees me and smiles expectantly; I told her on the phone that I had "weird" news, but I didn't tell her what.

"Hi," she says, grabbing a menu that's sandwiched between two grease-encrusted metal napkin dispensers and handing it to me, her fingers splayed out over the daily specials.

"Nice manicure," I say, taking the menu from her and grabbing her hand. "You did it yourself?"

"Oh, no," she laughs, playing with the straw with her free hand. "You know I'd never trust myself to choose a nice color—much less put it on without making a huge mess." This last part is ridiculous, since Jenna is so neat she could probably perform a splenectomy on herself without making a mess.

"So you got a manicure then?" I ask, impressed.

"Yeah, well . . . I got . . . a little raise at work," she says sheepishly. "So I treated myself."

"Oh," I say, swallowing hard and suddenly studying the menu with the same intensity I used when looking at the control drawings for My First Photocopier early last week. The last time I was at Toyland, I realize with a start. I order my much-anticipated tuna melt and turn on my stool to face Jenna, taking a deep breath to prepare myself. She looks at me wide-eyed as I tell the whole story, beginning with my history of laziness with the package proofs, and ending with the nightmare of thousands of Chunky Chipmunk packages sporting a photo of a little girl with Down syndrome and emblazoned with the word "dummy" in two-inch-high type. The only good part about telling this story, I realize as I'm telling it, is that I've told it so many times now that it no longer upsets me. In fact, it's almost starting to sound funny, out of the confines of work and home, here with Jenna and her shiny, bright nails and the speckly '50s counter of the diner.

"My God, Toby!" she says when I'm finished, cupping her hands to her mouth. "I'm so stupid—talking about my raise at a time like this!"

"No, don't worry about it! You didn't know," I say, but Jenna is already blushing deeply, furious at herself for not having been clairvoyant about my work misadventures.

"Well, what do you think is going to happen?" she asks as I bite into the first triangle of my drippy tuna melt.

"I don't know," I say, swallowing. "My dad seems to think it will blow over. Kerrin is talking to a lawyer, supposedly."

"What about Michael?" she asks, playing with one of the tiny beads on the neckline of her shirt.

"What *about* Michael?" I ask, suddenly perturbed. On my way to meet Jenna, I kept thinking about Michael's pronouncement about taking his clarinet career aboard a shiny cruise ship, and how preposterous it is. "Meeting lots of people" is about as appealing to him as eating our kitchen sponge, and I just know he'd be ill in his cabin every day, racked with seasickness.

"You should see the look on your face, Toby," Jenna laughs. "You can't even talk about him without looking upset. That Lisa must really be getting to you."

"I know it," I say, suddenly eager to change the subject, to not think about Lisa, Michael, Sarah, The Third Sex. "Let's talk about something else."

"Not much to report by me—unless you count the awful news I told you before when you came in," she says, her voice small.

"Jenna, a raise isn't awful news. It's great news."

"J.P. is still very happy these days, I'm glad to report," she says, looking up at the ceiling like there might be some interesting WPHX gossip up there.

"OH!" I shout, bringing my hand to the side of my

mouth and making the waitress behind the counter and Jenna look over in surprise.

"Did you bite into anything funny?" Jenna asks, concerned. The waitress also studies me with as worried a look as she can muster; Twin City Diner has been closed down twice for health code violations, and God only knows what goes on back there in the kitchen. But fortunately for them, this had nothing to do with the quality or cleanliness of my tuna melt. I suddenly remembered that my letter to J.P. Cody was still sitting in my green folder with the Formula One car on the front, which was a gift from Joe last year. In the loopiness of the day I was suspended and the depression of the days that followed, I completely forgot to mail it.

"No," I say, recovering, the waitress heaving a sigh of relief before slamming a set of flatware down in front of a new patron seated on Jenna's other side. "No, I'm fine," I say smiling. "Do you know *why* J.P. is so happy?" I ask, leaning in close to Jenna. I put the stress on the word *why*, but Jenna doesn't hear it that way. Instead of asking, "No, why?" she simply shrugs her shoulders.

And at that moment, just as I'm ready to clue her in on my poem-writing campaign, his letters to me, and how I'm going to be meeting him any day now, I decide not to tell. Not now, not here. I'm not even sure why, but I decide to keep it a secret from her for just a little bit longer. Surely she'll know soon enough.

*   *   *

On Tuesday morning I'm lolling around in my night-gown, flipping the channels on the TV a mile a minute and not paying attention to one thing on the screen. Michael stayed with me as long as he possibly could, even eating a bowl of Apple Jacks with me to show his solidarity, but he had an appointment at the conservatory with one of his old professors, and he didn't want to be late. I have no concept of late, early, on time, morning, noon, or night these days; I'm no longer upset about what I've done, but I'm increasingly anxious about my fate at Toyland and bored to tears.

At eleven o'clock I'm settling in with a horrible talk show whose theme is I Want Out of This Threesome! and marveling how the specimens on the show and I could have the same basic DNA structure, when the phone rings. I answer it disinterestedly, half focused on the heavyset woman with the fuschia miniskirt and bottle-blond hair who wants out of the threesome. To my complete surprise, it's Joe.

"Hello, Toby?" he asks breathlessly. "Is that you?"

"Yeah, what's up?" I ask, turning the sound down on the TV but still feeling compelled to watch another member of the threesome, a young black guy with a pick in his hair, strut across the stage.

"I just wanted to tell you," he says, his voice low, "something is going on. Rod Winters is storming around here this morning like crazy."

"So how is that different from any other day?" I ask, yawning.

"What's different is that he started storming around after asking me when you were coming back from vacation. We were talking about the sticker sheets for the Makit Bakit Microwave Oven—I hate that fuckin' toy. Anyway, I'm like, 'She's not on vacation, she's been suspended.' "

"Ugh—thanks, Joe," I groan. After coming so far with Rod Winters, now I was back to him thinking I was an incompetent twit again.

"So now he's all freaked out—got Sarah in his office, the door's closed but Luke said he swore he heard your name. Then *Bill* came around and went in there, and I've never seen him in Engineering before," he finishes.

"I think it's your imagination, Joe. They're probably just talking about Makit Bakit."

"Yeah, maybe," he answers distractedly, and I can hear him tapping on his keyboard. "I just wanted to tell you what was going on."

"Well, thanks. I appreciate it," I say earnestly, hanging up and turning back to the threesome—by now the third member is on the stage, a painfully thin, raven-haired girl with bad teeth, dirty hands, and combat fatigues. Looking at her makes me realize how sloppy I feel, and I snap off the set and head upstairs to take a shower.

I'm just stepping into the shower with my favorite cinnamon body wash when the phone rings again. I slam down the pink tube and stomp to my room, dripping, naked, and annoyed. This will really have to be good, I think as I pick up the phone.

"Is this Toby Morris?" a voice asks. I can't quite place it, and then I suddenly realize it's the asexual drone of The Third Sex.

"Yes," I say coolly, reaching for my fluffy robe and sitting on the edge of the bed.

"Well. We've been having some . . . discussions this morning, and we've decided it's best if you came back. We'll let bygones be bygones . . . it was an honest mistake."

I told you that last week, I'm thinking, but instead I say, "Thank you very much, Bill. This is great news."

"Well," he answers stiffly, "whenever you get in today, we'll be happy to see you. We're having a Makit Bakit turnover at three." And with that he hangs up, leaving me with my mouth open and staring into the handset of the phone like it's some mystical object.

"Hi, Tracie."

"Hi, Toby. Why didn't you come last week?" she whispers, rolling a tiny blue toy truck back and forth across the legs of a skinny little redhead named Dawn. She is next to Tracie, lying on her stomach and intently coloring in a coloring book.

"Look," she interrupts, holding the coloring book in the air, "isn't it good how I stay in the lines?"

"It's only good to stay in the lines if you want to, Dawn," I say warmly, as I notice that her lush hair has thinned dramatically since I was here last, two weeks ago. Staying in the lines seems less and less important all the time, somehow. "If you color outside of them, that doesn't make it any less beautiful," I add.

"Well?" asks Tracie patiently.

"Oh, sorry. I didn't come last week because I was . . . sick, I guess," I bluff.

"Are you better now?" she asks, rolling the truck up my arm.

"Much," I smile at her. When I returned to Toyland two days ago, I was never so happy to see loopy Eric from Quality Control patiently waiting for me at the commuter train station. Never so happy to see all that glossy processed plastic strewn around the place. Never so happy to see stacks and stacks of crisply folded engineering drawings left in my inbox, starting with the Perfect Tea Party Playset with color-change teacups and ending with the MX-Q all-terrain radio-controlled vehicle with undersea nautical action. Never so happy to visit Caroline in the sound booth and see Peter give me his goofy grin and the thumbs-up sign from behind the glass. Never so happy to hear that tinny *bongggg* of my Mac starting up, of Barb's Philly accent blaring over the loudspeaker, of Don and Dean laughing over some private joke about the stupidity of temping.

And of course, never so happy to attend a turnover, where it became very obvious to me why I was back. Rod sat directly across from me, and our eyes met several times over the course of the meeting, and I knew instantly that Joe and Luke had heard right and that Rod had been rooting for me that morning. Saying what, I'll never find out, because I know I can't ever thank him right out. That just isn't the Rod Winters way—the gruff bear would rather lose a paw in an injection-molding machine or a leg in the oversized blueprint copier than see me groveling with my gratitude. Instead, I let our eyes lock a few times, and I smiled, a tiny grin that said, *Thank you, thank you, thank you. I'm so sorry I ever misjudged you.*

"You know, your grandpa is a very nice man," I say, brushing Tracie's hair out of her eyes.

"Oh, I know," she says, nodding with all the sagacity of a five-year-old.

When I get home from the hospital I just want to drop into bed, but I make some chocolate milk instead and decide to flip through Michael's cruise line catalogs, which he has piled next to the music books on the table. Each one promises glamorous ports of call; unlimited portions of delicious food; a stylish, thumping disco; an alert, uniformed crew available twenty-four hours a day; a luxurious spa; and activities that range from napkin folding to French lessons. Not one of them has chosen to highlight live music, and the few that give even a nod to musicians do so by featuring glossy photos of drunken yahoos doing the limbo, with the musicians in low light and soft focus in the background. Even the smiling bartender with the hot pink tropical drink gets more real estate in the Princess Cruise Line catalog than the pianist in the martini lounge does.

I don't know why Michael's new career direction irritates me so—I had known for some time that things were taking off too slowly for his liking here in Philadelphia, and that his musician friends were telling him to explore new territory. It's just that the territory—literally oceans away—seems so far away that whenever I consider it seriously, I can't imagine it.

Not that I can't picture Michael's life there; granted, it's a stretch, but I could envision him dutifully performing life boat drills, playing at a captain's party and smiling graciously at the polite applause from all the guests in their sequined gowns and tuxedos, and studying the vast expanse of empty sea in his off hours. It's just that I'm realizing right now that I can't picture my life here without him.

I jump up with my heart pounding, leaving Celebrity and Carnival overlapping on the tabletop, and race upstairs. I yank out the bag of loose photos I hastily shoved under my bed after choosing my glamour shot for J.P. Cody that afternoon with Kerrin, and burrow through it until I find the picture of me and Michael. Flopping onto my bed with my Secret Wish Horse, I take a deep breath and hold it as I study the snapshot for a long minute. And then it slowly dawns on me, causing me to exhale so deeply that it makes part of the horse's flimsy yarn mane flutter. Kerrin hates it when she's wrong, but she was wrong that day about this photo, when she pronounced my grin the result of being all hopped up on pain pills for my period, the kind that made me think my room was cleaning itself. I used to take the little white capsules religiously; they prevented me from ending up curled in the fetal position, sweating and sobbing from menstrual pain each month. But I wasn't loopy from codeine the night that this picture of me and Michael was taken. I'm quite sure of it, in fact—and coming from a girl who doesn't even feel sure that she's wearing the correct size bra or that she's always capable of successfully retrieving her voice mail at work, this sureness is most disarming.

I'm quite sure because I am wearing my "Who Shot the Curtains?" vest, and I didn't get that florid garment until well after I stopped having "feminine troubles," as my dad likes to call them. I'm quite sure because that medicine generally made me sullen and crabby and not prone to spontaneous grinning, even as I watched my skirts leap enthusiastically onto hangers and my panties fall into crisp formation in my underwear drawer. But mostly, I'm quite sure because this is a genuine smile, the type that you can see in the eyes and not just the lips or cheekbones; the kind where everything is all right with the world and the girl in the middle of the picture doesn't look like there's anyplace she'd rather be or anyone else she'd rather be standing with. I'm quite sure because I've cringed at countless photos of myself wearing a fake and frozen smile, and this one is so warm and real that it could melt the ice at the Spectrum on a winter day, the way it's melting my insides right now.

And for the first time in my career at Toyland, I am amazed and more than slightly alarmed to think of

Sarah as someone I could learn something from—rather than just a shimmery-lipsticked goofball who exists solely to give me a migraine—when I remember the sentiment she had the day she arrived moist-eyed with starbaby's portfolio. "Does this picture lie?" she asked rhetorically while studying the glossy photograph. She felt sure that it didn't. As I turn over on my back and trace the image of me and Michael on Kodak paper, the f-stop and film speed and flash bulb all conspiring to expose a simple and uncomplicated joy, I smile and wonder if this one doesn't, either.

Chapter 21

"What's that?" I ask Kerrin, who is eating a cheesesteak with gusto and flipping through the pages of a three-ring binder.

"Mmmmph," she answers, wiping at the corner of her mouth with the back of her hand and glaring at a woman who just knocked into her tiny plastic chair. Reading Terminal is not for the faint of heart at lunchtime in July; the combination of the thick crowd, smothering heat, and strong smells is a formidable one, to say the least.

"It's Len's—something he forgot at my place that he needs. Look at this," she says, pausing to rifle through the notebook and running her index finger down one of its inky pages. " 'Maple Syrup Urine Disease.' That must be a good disease to have if you like pancakes."

"Gross!" I say, laughing. "Hold on, I'm going to get a slice. I'll be right back."

"Yeah, well hurry up, I'm dying to hear this story. Also, I'm really hot and crabby, so don't leave me alone here too long, Toby, " she says irritably.

"You're probably hot because you're wearing long sleeves. Why are you wearing a shirt with long sleeves in summer?" I ask, but her attention is already turned back to the notebook with all the medical mysteries and she ignores me, gnawing on her cheesesteak with a vexed expression. I head off, dodging the perspiring business-men on their lunch break, and treat myself to a pepper-oni slice.

"OK, here I am," I say cheerily, setting down my pizza and soda on the wobbly plastic table. "Listen good, be-cause I'm only going to tell it once."

Kerrin props her head in her hands as I spend the next twenty minutes telling her everything, starting with Rod's mysterious fascination with my cubicle walls and ending with him pulling out all the stops to help me get my job back. When I finally finish and my pizza's gone cold, I feel like there's something I've forgotten— something is amiss, not quite right about the situation, but I just can't put my finger on it. Kerrin looks at me ex-pectantly and lays both hands flat on the dirty tabletop. Suddenly, I know what it is.

"Kerrin," I venture carefully, "we've been here quite a while, and you've not smoked. You're not even doing that finger thing," I add, wiggling my fingers and clenching my fists to show her what I mean.

"I know," she says weakly, looking around and then

closing her eyes, breathing in slowly through her nose. "I'm . . . trying . . . to . . . quit."

"Really?" I ask, dumbfounded. "I can't believe it! Why? I mean, not why, but how come now?"

"I dunno," she shrugs, nervously twisting my straw wrapper into a tiny paper worm. "No, I do know. I guess I was getting a little sick of it for awhile, but then when we went to that Christmas party with Len and Mark . . ." she says, with a far-off look. "It was really hard to look around at all those kids there, thinking they didn't do anything to deserve what happened to them, and here I am doing something really dumb. So check it out," she finishes defiantly, pushing up her sleeve to expose a small square of flesh-colored fabric on the inside of her arm.

"Wow . . . my friend Kerrin on the patch," I say, stunned.

"Yeah, but shut up about it, OK?" she snaps, making me think that maybe she could use more than one patch for the time being. She reads my mind or perhaps my hurt expression and says sheepishly, "Sorry—I didn't mean shut up, exactly. I'm real paranoid about the weirdos I work with finding out I'm trying to quit. They'll be all, 'Oh, good for you!' and fucking sending me flowers and other really stupid stuff. That's why I'm wearing long sleeves, see?"

"I get it. I promise I won't bother you with a balloon bouquet at work. But I do have to tell you that I am impressed. Really, Kerrin."

She smiles, a tiny little Kerrin smile, where the lips go up but the teeth don't show. Then she catches herself, shaking her head quickly.

"I'm going to get fat, you realize. I mean, fatter than I am now, even! Hope you don't mind."

"Of course I don't mind. Not that you're going to get fat anyway. I'm just really amazed," I say, as we toss our paper plates and make our way out into the crowded street. A man with three small, ice-cream-covered gooey children pushes into us, jostling Kerrin and making her look as though she'd like to sink her teeth into him and draw blood.

"Keep cool," I warn her as I fan myself with my hand. "This is great news," I call to her from the corner as she steps into the intersection and studies a cigarette butt in the gutter with glazed, hungry eyes. "It really makes you believe that anything can happen, Kerrin."

I'm whistling to myself as I head up the street, bobbing my head to the meandering tune I'm creating and trying to ignore the yelling coming from one of the houses near mine. A few of our neighbors have been known to duke it out at high decibels, especially when the weather gets warm and tensions run high in the stifling heat. But as I get closer, I realize that this argument is not in fact coming from a house on either side of Michael's and mine. It is coming from mine, and I immediately feel my chest tightening and my breath becoming shallower with every step. When I reach my door, I peer inside and see

Michael with an expression on his face that I've never witnessed before; he is scarlet and sweaty and red-eyed and looks ready to pounce. And standing opposite him, with her face defiant, her mouth set in that hard, unforgiving line, is Lisa Carlton. Their bodies are turned in such a way that they can't see me peering in through the screen door, and I stand stock-still, trying to make myself small, even though I'm wearing my new sandals with the three-inch stacked heels.

"What are you telling me?" Michael yells. "How could you have done this and not told me?"

"I don't know what the big deal is," she says, smirking, tilting her head and putting her hands on her hips.

"The *big deal?*" he asks incredulously, shaking his head. "I don't know how you could be so . . . cold! It's so *thoughtless* of you, Lisa."

I'm thinking that as far as I'm concerned, Lisa has never really been any other way, but then she crosses the room and notices me standing on the stoop.

"Oh, well, look who's here," she says sarcastically, nodding her head in my direction. I try to look as though I just wandered up the steps two seconds earlier, and I casually fling open the screen door. Now that I'm inside I can clearly see Michael's mouth turned down in anger; he's breathing heavily and putting his hands under his armpits as Lisa calmly walks over and sits on the couch.

"Toby," he says quietly while looking at the floor, "can we be alone for a minute?"

I silently nod my head yes and run up the stairs,

stopping three stairs short of the landing but giving an extra three clomps while standing still, so it sounds like I'm all the way upstairs. I crouch down into a tight little ball and listen hard, trying to keep my breathing quiet and ignore the sound of blood pounding in my ears.

"It's just like . . . all this planning and deception behind my back," Michael says angrily. "So . . . calculating. And cruel."

"Oh! Like it wasn't des—" She stops abruptly and I can't see what she's doing, but it soon becomes apparent when Michael shouts, "Toby, we can see your *feet* on the step. Do you *mind*?"

Busted! I leap up and race into my room, where I crouch behind the door with a pint glass that Kerrin stole for me from a pub in England when she was visiting relatives last year in the hilariously named village of Sheepy Parva. After a few agonizing minutes during which I can't hear a blessed thing, even with the pint glass pressing against my ear, jabbing my dragonfly earring into my head, I hear the screen door open and slam shut.

"Yeah, well, maybe you'll have a lot of time to think about it, then!" Michael screams, his voice full of venom. "And it's still no *fucking* excuse!" he adds, clearly in too much distress to remember the tongue-lashing he gave me about swearing and discussing blow jobs and the like in front of the youngsters in the neighborhood. In fact, it is so unusual for Michael to swear at all that this last sentence tells me that whatever Lisa did, it must have been a doozy.

He runs up the stairs and gives his door a slam that makes the walls shake. After a few seconds I hear what I think is Debussy's *Martyrdom of St. Sebastian* blaring from behind the door, the oboes and clarinets and bassoons drowning out whatever Michael might be muttering to himself. After a few minutes, I cross the hall during a quiet flute solo and pound on his door.

"Michael?"

"Please, Toby, leave me alone," he begs, his voice ragged and strained.

I go back to my room and sit down on the edge of my bed, rocking back and forth, twirling my hair, and trying to reconstruct the snippets of conversation that I heard. Were Michael and Lisa going to have a love child? Just the thought of it made me shiver, an icy cold running through my veins. Had she cheated on him with one of her coworkers? I could picture him now, nattily dressed from head to toe in color-coordinated clothing from their store, complete with matching accessories like argyle socks and a faux-leather key fob. What had she done to incur Michael's wrath? The only other time I could re-member him looking quite so distraught was when Rod-ney, a fat kid with glasses and what Michael was convinced was an undiagnosed case of ADHD, stuffed a tube of Chap Stick into the neck of Michael's sax. But even Rodney didn't make Michael sputter with rage like he did today; Rodney didn't bring angry tears to his blue eyes.

I spend the next week tiptoeing around the house, hoping Michael will spill his story, but he doesn't. I try to act cheery, then disinterested, then empathic, then aloof, until I exhaust all my possible affects and realize it doesn't make one whit of difference. Michael isn't talking, and when, on my way back from the post office, I catch a glimpse of him coming out of the All-In-One, he hurries home and seeks refuge in his room before I get there. Lisa hasn't called, and her scrunchies look very strangely out of place around the house—no ugly bun awaits them, and so they sit, puffy clumps of cotton and elastic, awaiting the nasty hairdo that never comes. When Sophie, the thirteen-year-old oboe student with the big boobs that she tries so desperately to hide behind excruciatingly poor posture, finished her lesson this afternoon, I even tried pumping her for news on Michael's problem. "Soooo," I said to her casually as she waited for her mom to pick her up, "how's Michael today? Did he talk about anything besides music?" She eyed me cautiously before answering with a resounding no and slumping down in her seat, rounding her shoulders and folding her arms in front of her chest.

Oh well, I think as I try to decide whether or not to take a jaunt to the post office today, I'm sure whatever it is will blow over. Just like my dad said about my job, and that turned out fine. I take a look at Michael's calendar on the kitchen wall and realize with a frown that it's been a little while since I ran out of the Twin City Diner to mail my latest love letter to J.P. Cody. So what is he waiting for? I ask myself aloud as I peer in the mirror by the door and color-coordinate my lip gloss—the pink one with the iridescent sparkles that I stole from the I Made It Myself Make-Up Kit at work—with my glittery, hot pink They Might Be Giants T-shirt with the ripped-off sleeves.

"What's that?" Joe teases, leaning over me so closely that I can smell the cologne on his clothes and the cigarette smoke in his hair.

"Go 'way!" I squeak, hurriedly folding up the piece of paper.

"OK, OK," he laughs, backing off and cracking his knuckles. "I don't want to know about any of your girlie secrets anyway," he says, flashing a smile at Sarah, who is barreling toward us with a glossy newspaper insert featuring a picture of none other than the starbaby. Starbaby is quickly being catapulted toward fame, and his most recent gig was modeling a terry-cloth onesie for the Kmart circular. He sat brightly lit, wide-eyed, and slightly drooly in a yellow-and-orange giraffe-patterned bit of fabric, beaming for the camera and stretching his arms heavenward. Sarah scarcely seemed able to look at the photo without needing to breathe into a paper bag, and she showed it to so many people that I wondered if there was anyone left at Toyland who hadn't seen the Kmart smile of the starbaby.

"Toby, did you see?" she asks sweetly.

"I saw, I saw," I answer, rolling my eyes at Joe.

"Saw what?" asks Rod Winters, who's shown up at the door of my cubicle with a tight, simplified drawing of the Dancing Duck mechanism, the one that's been causing me grief for weeks. I cock my head to take a sideways peek at the tracing paper he's clutching, and in a split second, I understand it completely. Those dumb webbed feet and that stupid living hinge. Of course!

"My *starbaby*," Sarah says exasperatedly, shoving the circular under Rod's nose. He nods and wordlessly shows me the sketch as Caroline and Peter run past, the electric blue and acid yellow flowers on his Hawaiian shirt whizzing by in a riot of color.

"Wait!" hollers Sarah, waving her arms. "Don't you want to see? . . ."

"Ooh, heck yeah," answers Peter while skidding to a stop, even though he has no idea what it is that he wants to see. He and Caroline swing back and take the circular from her, looking from it to each other and back again.

"Very nice," Peter says politely, looking over my cubicle wall and spying Matt working at a drafting table, cutting out a prototype blister-card package for the Super Stampin' Farm Animal Fun refills—the ones with the rubber stamps that are so minuscule that the images make them look like creatures from Chernobyl, with three legs or half a head. "Hey man," he shouts, and Matt clumsily drops his X-Acto knife and ambles over.

"You going to see Josh's band?" Matt asks him. Rod leans over, drops the bit of tracing paper on my desk, glances at Tracie's paintings behind my head, and gives me a conspiratorial smile. I look away from him and suddenly realize that there are now six people huddled in the doorway to my cubicle, a cubicle that feels like a pen at best when there is only one person in it.

"Hey! Excuse me! I have some stuff to do, kids," I say as forcefully as I can.

Everybody slowly scatters, and as Caroline and Peter walk away, she shouts over her shoulder, "It's just that everybody loves you, Toby!"

"Yeah, that's right," I answer without a trace of sarcasm, giggling to myself as I gingerly open the piece of paper that I hurriedly folded when Joe was eavesdropping. I'd picked it up at my post office box this morning, and I am still reeling, almost six hours later:

Dear Toby,

Thanks for your letter! I think it would be great if we could meet sometime. I am usually free most weeknights, Tuesdays and Wednesdays are best. I'll pick the time: 8:00. You pick the night and place.

Looking forward to meeting you,
J.P. Cody

Just reading it again is making me go all dizzy and nauseated with excitement; it's a sensation that is almost identical to the one I get when using the super-bondo glue we apply liberally to the displays at Toy Fair, except without the screaming headache and intense need for fresh air afterward. My ears rang and buzzed when driving in with Rich—so much so that I have no recollection of his latest tale of woe—and they haven't really stopped all day. When I called Kerrin bright and early this morning to tell her of my good postal fortune, she was cranky and very close to lighting a cigarette, barking into the phone that I'd have to call her later on. Well, now it's later on, and after peering around the walls of my cubicle, I flatten the letter on the desk, pick up the phone, and dial, my heart pounding.

"Adult Oncology. This is Kerrin."

"Hi! Are you better?" I ask quietly.

"Mostly, I guess. It still sucks," she whimpers. "Not that I can talk about it too much here, remember. I don't want any help from the freak show parading around here."

"Listen, Kerrin," I begin, ignoring her nicotine itch, " 'Thanks for your letter! I think it would be great if we could meet sometime. I am usually free most weeknights, Tuesdays and Wednesdays are best. I'll pick the time: eight o'clock. You pick the night and place.' " I pause and inhale deeply, cradling the phone between my neck and ear while nervously screwing and unscrewing lids of the jars of puffy paint that come with My Pretty Pillowcase Kit.

"My God!" she yells. "You're really going to meet this guy, Toby! I can't believe I ever doubted you. Where are you going to meet him?"

And so I tell her. There is a place I have in mind, the one place; really, the only place. And I tell J.P. Cody next, in a quick letter banged out on Mr. Clackety Clack that evening, before dancing in my room all by myself, singing and chirping and thanking my lucky stars, sun, moon, clouds, dewpoint, humidity, storm trajectory, precipitation, low-pressure system, generalized thunderstorms, gusty winds, and airstreams for this great chance at love.

Chapter 22

The next few days go by in a blur, with people and things floating in and out of my peripheral vision, like when my sister and I used to practice swimming underwater with our eyes open. I'm in a haze, reading the July issue of *Car and Driver* with the fantastic feature on the new convertibles, trying to coax Kerrin to ditch her Dunhills, leaving funny messages on Caroline's voice mail about Peter, her surprising new love interest—but it's all happening with J.P. Cody in the forefront of my mind. He is the last thing I think about before I fall asleep and the first thing I think of when I wake up, and I've got just four days to go until our big meeting.

The only troubling thing is Michael, Michael with his sad face and staunch refusals to tell me why he and Lisa have broken up or what their angry argument was about in the first place. He's as downtrodden as I've ever seen him, wandering through the house like a man who is looking all over for something but is not quite sure what it is. Between his gigantic argument with Lisa and my rapidly approaching date with J.P., I haven't had too much time or impetus to consider the feelings I had about the photo of us, and now I'm starting to question just how unloved I must have been feeling that evening to be thinking that way. On Kerrin's refrigerator, shoved under a cheesy magnet from Cancun, is a yellowing memo that warns, "Kerrin, your conclusions *exceed your data!*" It had been hastily scrawled by a doctor at her workplace, a man who hadn't taken the time to read the cover letter that said that she was simply the editor of the document that contained the findings, not the researcher on the study. She loved the sentiment, though: a thoroughly clinical way of warning about jumping to conclusions.

I think of the memo now as I reflect on the photo— perhaps, like the misguided researcher on that ill-conceived study, my conclusions exceeded my data, too. I had my *arm* draped across Michael in the photo, not any other limb. And surely if Michael wanted to drape other limbs across me, he had many opportunities over the years. I remember the night that Len, with his cool med student detachment, instructed me to prove my hypothesis about J.P. Cody as he sat surrounded by margaritas and tiki lights. Now I force myself to think with my head for once, and I study my data with the unfeeling gaze of a vivisectionist, the steely calm of a microbiologist. I have sweet, romantic letters from J.P. Cody, now limp and creased from being folded and unfolded so many times, and I have nothing from Michael but hypochondria and clarinet reeds stuck in the sofa cushions and cheap poly-cotton tuxedo shirts forever tumbling in the dryer.

I wasn't going to even fill him in about my upcoming date with J.P. Cody—as I learned from my many years of friendship with the oversexed Kerrin, there is nothing worse than hearing about someone else's good love fortune when your own love life is a complete shambles—but a FedEx came from Kerrin that forced the issue. The envelope contained a fancy pair of lacy thong underwear wrapped in scented tissue paper, along with a note that read:

Good luck on Wednesday night . . . you'll need these in case he mistakes you for a bottle of ketchup at the Twin City Diner and tries to turn you over and smack you on the bottom!

Love,
Kerrin

And written on the back in her tiny chicken-scratch, undoubtedly made even wobblier than usual from nicotine withdrawal:

P.S.—I know you haven't worn this kind of underwear before. Try them out ahead of time, or you'll be feeling like someone is trying to crack your ass with an ice pick during your date!

Michael's eyes widened when I took the scrap of fabric out of the envelope and held it up in the air, embarrassed. And when I explained to him what the thong underwear was for, he blanched visibly and dropped his head, complaining of a headache.

Well, too bad, I thought. It wasn't my fault that things between him and Lisa Carlton didn't work out—I was sick of wondering and asking, and he obviously wasn't going to tell me.

I've got my thong underwear and my weatherman. What else could I need?

I've taken the entire day off from work and I don't feel the slightest bit guilty, since Barb produced a fax from China the other day that had slipped behind the filing cabinet. The fax had been sitting there for over a month, alone and curling up against the wall, and it said:

TO NJ PACKAGING DEPT: HAD NO RECEIVE PROOF FOR CHUNKY CHIPMUNK. PLEASE ADVISE, OTHERWISE WILL GO INTO PRODUCTION. IF NO GO INTO PRODUCTION WILL MISS SHIP DATES

MIN XING
TOYLAND, HONG KONG OFFICE

In other words, I never saw the package proof for Chunky Chipmunk with its hapless child model, just as I suspected from the outset. I felt so vindicated by this 8½x11-inch clumsily worded piece of evidence that I practically gloated when Sarah and Bill came to apologize to me, but then I thought better of it. Caroline told me that Peter is very much into karma and that gloating will most certainly assure me of bad karma coming my way. Tempting though it was, I managed to gnash my teeth and hold back, because I don't need bad karma tonight.

What I do fear is that Michael's bad karma will somehow rub off on me like cheap foundation. While I've been up here singing and counting the hours until I meet J.P. Cody, he's been snapping at his music students with a peevish tone that makes them jump and frightens me, as well. High-pitched squeaks and squeals from the mouthpieces of new students have never seemed to bother him as they do today, and when Brett tripped up the stairs, Michael just shook his head, rather than laughing it off or making a joke as he normally would.

I get into the tub for a long soak with my ginger scrub and loofah, trying to clear my mind and relax, when I hear Michael's studio door slam and Brett walk down the stairs.

"Sorry, Brett, you did real well," he says apologetically. "Today's not such a good day, I'm sorry."

"S'OK, Michael," he answers helpfully, running down the stairs the rest of the way.

"What's the problem?" I shout through the closed door, pausing mid-squirt with the exfoliating crème for my rough hooves. " 'Hey, bulldog!' " I say, quoting his favorite Beatles song, " 'if you're lonely, you can talk to me.' " After a long silence, I shrug and begin massaging my heels, singing quietly to myself. I don't have to do therapy while in the tub; I mean, really—I should be keeping my stress level low in anticipation of my date, my life-changing date, the best night of my life. Then finally, I hear a tiny voice on the other side of the door.

"I can't explain it, Toby. You wouldn't understand."

"Try me," I say gently, switching from my heels to my elbows and rubbing them aggressively. But then I don't hear anything, so I turn on our shower radio and spin the dial away from *Fresh Air* in search of something more fun and flirty. I'm satisfied when I find Blondie and entertain myself by belting out "One Way or Another" for the next few minutes.

Six o'clock! Just ninety minutes to turn from plain, frizz-haired Toby into glam goddess Toby, and I'd feel more up to the task if Michael would leave me alone. Usually I don't mind—he was sort of a permanent pre-date fixture whenever I was primping for The Head Wound—but his presence in my doorway is draining my good love vibes tonight.

In honor of my big night, I use every beauty product in my bathroom, from the creamy lemony-lime lotion with the tiny bits of lemon zest in it to the walnut face mask to the raspberry foot bath to the sesame body oil that I rub into my freckly skin until it gleams. Michael silently studies me as I fiercely pat foundation onto my cheeks and blend it with precision. I'm putting on a sweet, cherry-pink blush that Kerrin said made me look like I'd just had the best orgasm of my life when I tried it in the store. I'm brushing on smooth strokes of deep gray eyeshadow, just enough to bring out the green in my eyes without looking too gothic and weird. I'm starting to sweep on soft curves of rich red lipstick before I remember that I still have to pull my silk sundress over my head, and when I cross the room to grab a tissue, I catch Michael's eye. He looks immediately from me to the floor, frowning.

"Toby, are you sure this is a good idea?" he asks quietly. "I mean, you don't even know this guy. What if it's not safe?"

"Michael, I'm meeting him in a very public place. What, is he going to take advantage of me behind the rotating glass display case of cakes and pies?" I try to ask the question seriously, but my mind starts looping on the idea of J.P. putting his hands up my dress as a Boston cream pie and a devils' food cake slowly spin by us, and this makes me snort with laughter.

"I'm just saying, is all," he answers defensively.

"Well, out with you, then," I say briskly. "I have to get dressed," I explain, blushing and shaking the FedEx envelope at him, suddenly remembering that I didn't take Kerrin's advice about breaking in the thong and wondering if I'll be picking at my behind when I'm supposed to be charming J.P. Cody. Well, it's too late now. Michael leaves, and I slam the door and pull on the underwear and silk polka-dotted sundress. I turn to look at myself in the mirror and laugh out loud at my near–Minnie Pearl moment; the tags are still on the dress, dangling from the left armpit. I grab a plastic pair of safety scissors left over from one of our activity kits from the preschool line and give them a quick clip, apply my lipstick in earnest, slide into my sandals, and spin in front of the mirror.

Not so bad, I think, giving myself a short spritz of perfume and twirling again. I make my way down the stairs, strangely aware of my underwear but trying not to think about it. When I reach the bottom, I see Michael slumping on the couch, nearly horizontal as he slides off the front, and he turns his face up toward me and smiles ruefully. He's sucking on a clarinet reed, and I hear it click against his molars as he starts to speak.

"You look great, Toby."

"Yeah, maybe," I say, smiling shyly. "Well, wish me luck."

"Are you going right now?" he asks, fiddling with a scrunchie he's found in between the couch cushions.

"Well, yeah, I guess. I'm going to walk up to Girard Avenue and get a cab over there, and I want to leave enough time," I say, my words coming out in a rush.

"OK," he says, looking at the floor. "Just—um, I'm concerned for you. Because I don't want you to be too disappointed. If he doesn't turn out the way you expect."

"Michael, which is it?" I ask bluntly, putting my hands on my hips. This is the question I hear him pose to his music students when they lie to him about why they didn't practice, then dig themselves in deeper with a second lie. They first say that they lost the sheet music, then they claim that they didn't understand the assignment. Or they swear that they left their instrument at their friend's house by mistake, and then they change tack and sputter that they just plain forgot how to count in 4/4 time.

"So which is it?" I ask again, feeling the heat start to boil up in my face under my expensive blush. "Are you trying to keep me from going because I won't be safe, or because I'll be disappointed in the kind of guy he is? Because you should get your story straight."

"Forget it, Toby. Just go ahead. You're going to be late."

A minute later I'm out in the street about two houses down from ours, practicing my greeting ("Hi, J.P.!" "Hello, it's so nice to meet you, J.P." "I just love your weather reports, you know!" "It's so great to meet you, finally"), when I hear the unmistakable sound of the screen door squeaking open. I stop walking but don't turn around, gritting my teeth as I await Michael's next disparaging comment about my date.

"Toby."

"Michael, *please*. Can't it wait?" I shout, annoyed,

stamping my foot on the hot pavement as I clench my fists.

"No, I'm afraid it can't."

I heave a dramatically loud sigh, drop my arms to my sides defeatedly, and whirl around, ready to scream at him to stay the hell out of my J.P. Cody–related business. But as I spin around, I bang into something that nearly knocks me off my feet both literally and figuratively—it's Michael, who has quietly stridden up behind me and is now grabbing me hard by both shoulders, pressing his thumbs into my flesh. Stunned, I manage to squeak out a little "Ow!" while looking down at one of his hands; he glances down and looks momentarily surprised to see how tight his grip is, and he loosens it enough to keep from hurting me but not enough to let me walk away from him. My heartbeat immediately starts to quicken, a *thunk-thunk-thunk* resonating deep in my chest like Michael's metronome, and something out of my control is ever so surely sliding the weight down, down, down.

"Michael, what is it?" I whisper, suddenly realizing that I've never been physically close enough to him to say anything in a whisper unless I was speaking right into his ear. *Thunk-thunk-thunk*, my heart is pounding faster, the closeness of Michael's breath hurrying the pace even more. Surely my tired, twenty-five-year-old heart can't escalate to 208 beats a minute, can it? The tiny words hang between us as I look up and study his face, his mouth parted slightly and his eyes a mixture of genuine concern but also warmth and hope, a look that reminds me of the ones parents give their ailing children at the hospital. "What's going on?" I beg as I start to truly panic, my heart palpitating as though the weight's been hastily plunged to the bottom, the pendulum now flailing wildly and without regard for my measured, carefully crafted, even-tempo plans for love. "Come on! You saw how long it took me to put on all that eye makeup! If I cry, it'll all be wrecked, Michael. I can't look my life's love in the face if I've got mascara all over my cheeks," I sputter. A torrent of tears suddenly bursts from my eyes and slides down my face, the muddy gray-black rivulets streaking through my foundation, and I start to sob, all my pent-up emotion giving way in a single explosive second.

"Sure you can," he says quietly, looking from me to the ground and back again.

"I can?" I ask, gulping.

Chapter 23

I slide into the booth at the Twin City Diner, grinning, as he slides in next to me and grabs my hand, all in one smooth motion. I open my mouth but no words come out—very unusual for me, as I'm almost always able to talk about *something*. So I just keep grinning, arranging the flatware on my napkin into geometric shapes.

"Look, Jenna's here," I say brightly, pointing out the window. "I see her parking her car. So I can tell her the whole story now."

"I don't know, Toby," he says, smiling. "There is something to be said for the sort of"—he pauses, searching for the right word as he taps the boomerang-patterned tabletop—"mystique or romance of how couples get together, you know."

"Oh, I know. I know plenty about mystique and romance, don't you worry," I say confidently as he jokingly rolls his eyes at me. Then I laugh to myself as I remember that day in the street, when he pulled me back to him and tipped my mouth up to kiss his. My whole body went weak and soft then, like the squishy Robot Putty prototype Caroline had left on my desk earlier that week, and I kissed back harder, not knowing why this was happening but absolutely sure that it was the right thing to do. It was remarkable because it was the second time I'd been so sure about something in such a short span of time—the first being that evening when I'd lain on my bed, breathlessly studying the photo of us—and two sure feelings so close together *had* to be a lifetime record for me. Then with my eyes closed I murmured, "Mmm. Woody."

"What?" he asked loudly enough to wake a forlorn stray dog that was dozing on a nearby stoop. "You are some kind of crazy pervert, Toby Morris!" he cried, a bit wild-eyed and stepping back from me.

"Oh. Sorry," I apologized, coming out of my daze, opening my eyes, and watching him begin to blush. "Not your crotch. Your mouth—it tastes woody. Like wood. Like a clarinet reed. Makes sense," I reasoned, running my tongue over my lips, taking in the flavor. "I guess that's one thing you should probably know about me," I added sheepishly as he tentatively stepped closer to me. "I always sort of have a way of wrecking a romantic moment. It's a problem of mine, ever since I was young," I continued, remembering how Frankie Cagnoli asked me to dance at the sixth-grade Christmas Enchantment Ball, only to have me barf about five cups of half-digested eggnog down the back of his new suit because I was so nervous.

"Well, here she is," Michael says as he accidentally knocks his spoon on the floor, the metallic *clink* rousing me from my thoughts. We watch together as Jenna swings open the door and immediately spies us, widens her eyes, and looks around the diner as if she's making sure that she's in the right place. She slowly makes her way to the table and arrives just as our orders of blueberry pancakes and eggs over-easy do, her eyes darting back and forth between the two of us and our locked hands on the tabletop as the waitress sets the oozing maple syrup dispenser dangerously close to my arm.

"What's going on?" she asks in a shocked voice, slowly lowering herself into the booth and carefully putting her beaded bag a safe distance away from the maple syrup. "This is . . . different," she adds diplomatically.

"Different it is," I say happily. Things have been very different around our tiny trinity indeed, since that night three weeks back when I was supposed to meet J.P. Cody—or so I thought—and Michael told me everything, after collecting me in the street and taking me inside. How he felt so guilty for telling Lisa Carlton about my PO Box, complete with Gretzky's number 99 for good luck, and trying so hard to confess to me that he'd told her. He valiantly attempted it several times, but he always seemed to have either the right words at the wrong time or the wrong words at the right time. He told me about the jealousy he felt when I began receiving letters back from J.P. Cody—or so he thought—and how those jealous feelings truly shocked him. About the huge fight he and Lisa had when she admitted that it was *she* in fact who was writing to me, not J.P. Cody. Apparently she'd known that I had been the one behind the aggressive direct-mail campaign to her from the moment she'd found the Rights for Transgendered Individuals postcard in our front hallway. It must have fluttered to the floor on my way back into the house from Toy Fair, and she felt that posing as J.P. Cody, writing to my PO Box, was appropriate punishment. An eye for an eye, she'd told Michael.

Michael felt it was unconscionable, felt the disgust and disdain toward her I had experienced all along, felt protective of me, and finally, felt incredibly confused—the showering of attention from the meteorologist that was giving him so much grief was really from his own *girlfriend*. It took me a long time to get it, and I sat on our sofa rocking with my head in my hands, like the mildly autistic but very cute kid Sarah stupidly tried to use for the Plop the Penguin game commercial shoot, until I finally understood. There was no J.P. Cody at the diner, nor would there ever be. But as luck would have it, there was someone waiting for me right at home.

"Well, I'm not surprised," Jenna says, with an uncharacteristically smug tone that makes us both look at her with our eyebrows arched. "Well, I'm not!" she repeats with a little laugh as the waitress hands her an overfilled coffee cup, the coffee sloshing over the sides and collecting in the saucer below. She gingerly places it on the table in front of her and leans forward in the booth. "But you'd better be careful," she teases, pointing to Michael. "She's got a thing for weathermen."

"I know, I know," he says, resting his elbows on the tabletop. "I know *all* about it," he murmurs conspiratorially, slowly looking over at me out of the corners of his eyes and smiling. "I'm only hoping now that I get some poetry. Something music-related, perhaps. Although I don't like being told what to wear, so I'm not sure that will work," he finishes cheerily. Jenna and I both gasp at the same time, she abruptly choking on her coffee and me stopping midsip with my orange juice, the pulp sticking to my upper lip as I slam the glass down.

"Th—that was you?" Jenna sputters. Some coffee sprays delicately from her left nostril, and a droplet hits Michael's watch, which she quickly wipes off with her fingertip.

"What do you mean?" I squeak, slightly hysterical and putting my fork down.

"Well . . . a *lot* of people down at the station knew that he was getting those letters. He—he was flattered but . . ."

"But what, Jenna?" I say, biting my lip and looking at Michael, who has unfolded a napkin and is dabbing the sweat on his forehead and grimacing.

"But he said people didn't do this kind of thing back in Minnesota. I guess he didn't know what to make of it, really. I didn't tell you because I thought you would be jealous, with your crush on him and everything," she finishes, cringing.

"So everyone knew he had a secret admirer?" I whisper anxiously, starting to twirl my hair and disrupting a butterfly barrette from the new MagiClay preteen activity line.

She waits a few condemning seconds before answering. "Not *everyone* at the station. I—I just didn't think for a minute that it could be anyone I knew." She stops as she lets the elements of the story sink in, and her brain fully completes the circuit. "So you really wrote those, Toby? All of them? Because a few of them were really creative."

"I think I'm going to be sick," I say, shoving my plate out of the way and dropping my head on the table, picturing the entire staff at WPHX cackling over my ridiculous rhyme and idiotic pentameter. "They were just for J.P. Cody. I was hoping he'd be more discreet, but hey, that's what I get for being such a dork," I mutter angrily to myself, my voice muffled. "I'm so embarrassed I could scream."

Jenna lets out a whimper and leans in close so I can hear her. "I'm sorry, Toby. I didn't mean to embarrass you, really. For whatever it's worth, things have worked out OK, right?" she asks hopefully. "Excuse me a minute; I've got to freshen up in the ladies' room. I've never had a drink come out my nose before," she says to Michael as she slides across the vinyl seat.

"First time for everything, Jenna," Michael says as I listen to her hurriedly clicking away from our table in her little heeled sandals. Then I hear something plunk down next to me on the tabletop and feel a little tap on my shoulder.

"What?" I ask dully, turning my head ninety degrees to face Michael, who has dropped his head down to my level and is facing me, his cheek pressing against the pink-and-green patterned Formica.

"Am I in trouble? For spilling the beans about your correspondence with J.P. Cody?" he asks with profound remorse in his voice. "I thought Jenna knew, but . . ." He trails off.

"Nah, it's all right," I sigh. "I probably would have told her eventually. Don't worry your pretty little head about it."

"Speaking of pretty little head, you should pick yours up. You've got egg in your hair, Toby," he says while righting himself and leaning back in the booth.

"And on my face," I groan as I sit up and feel the pooled blood drain from my brain. "Michael, do you think I was the laughingstock of WPHX? Does it matter?" I ask.

"Probably. No."

"Probably not?" I ask, confused.

"Probably you were the laughingstock of WPHX. And no, it doesn't matter," he says, reaching over and sliding his thumb and forefinger down a lock of my hair and showing me the yolk on his hand. "Or does it?" he asks, cocking his head.

Does it? I ask myself. I'll never know if J.P.'s chipper

moods were meant for me, whether or not he was really wearing the suits and ties for me, or if we would have ever had the torrid evening in the weather station that I always liked to envision. But Michael is right: It doesn't matter, and I tell him so.

And Jenna is right too, I realize as I watch her emerge from the bathroom to find herself face-to-face with a girl with a perfectly shaved head and a cropped T-shirt that proclaims, "I ♥ Geeks." Everything did turn out OK. Better than OK, in fact. Just as his wood-flavored kisses surprised me but shouldn't have, I shouldn't have been shocked to learn that Michael is a good roommate but an even better boyfriend. Because we've been in such close quarters together for so long, the hard part is already behind us, and there is never any reason to act coy or distant or jealous or unsure or display any of the unattractive emotions and hideous behaviors that are the hallmark of a new relationship. I'm having lots of fun and am deliriously happy, and I don't have to change a single thing about how I act around him. I'm on the surest footing I've ever been on in my life, even when wearing my new four-inch rainbow sandals that Michael brought home for me like they were a multicolored bunch of posies, such was his pride at picking out these shoes himself.

"So is anyone else meeting us here?" Jenna asks as she sits back down, eager to change the subject and sidestep any more questions about Toby the Meteorologist Stalker as comic relief at WPHX. "This is a big booth for just the three of us," she says by way of explaining her segue. "Kerrin, maybe?"

"No, I don't think so," I say, as Michael and I laugh. This new development in my love life sent Kerrin reeling and naturally, the stress caused her to "slip" (as it's called in her line of work) and promptly fall face-first into a carton of cigarettes. Ironically, her quit-smoking plan had been leaked by a nosy coworker only two days before my "date" with J.P. Cody, and she had been deluged with the kudos and support she had so desperately sought to avoid. Now she was smoking again and determined to let them all know it; she told me she had even taken to taking her smoke breaks while crouching directly beneath the red enamel sign on the building that reads, NO SMOKING PLEASE. THIS IS A CANCER FACILITY. But in the next raspy breath, she also admitted that her heart wasn't in upsetting the establishment the way it had once been, and that she would probably try to quit again soon. She had grown to like the feeling of walking up the two flights of stairs to Len's lab without getting winded, of laughing at Monty Python videos with her brother without experiencing a coughing fit, of waking up with her hair strewn across her face and smelling shampoo, not smoke.

And in her own inimitable way, she is being supportive. In between greedy puffs, she has been enjoying embarrassing me with suggestive observations about the fact that Michael is a clarinetist, with lots of disgusting references to fingerings and mouth exercises, so mellifluously delivered that it sounds like she's been practicing them for years. For all I know, she may have been.

"Kinda looks like rain," Michael says languidly, drumming his fingers on the tabletop and looking from the window to me and Jenna. "I hope it clears up; we have a . . . game to go to," he finishes, smiling slowly at me, as I suddenly remember that I forgot my novelty foam "We're #1!" hand at home.

"A game!" Jenna cries, careful to swallow fully before responding. "Now I've heard it all." Me too, I think to myself. If someone had asked me even a month ago if Michael and I would be sharing some Cracker Jack at a baseball game this summer, I'd have convulsed with laughter. I wouldn't have dared to dream that I might actually enjoy listening to classical pieces, but when you have someone who cares enough to explain their nuances in a tone so hushed and tender that it makes you shiver, it's the most beautiful music in the world. I never thought I'd be debating with him about which was the better bedroom for us to share, and it's become quite an impassioned debate, as each has its merits and drawbacks. Mine has much better light and is unquestionably neater than his, but it features very loose floorboards that bounce when you walk on them, which makes Michael jittery. And while his bed is bigger and puffier and much more inviting on a balmy summer night, there is the matter of the spindly music stand that always seems to have fallen on the floor, and the boob-smacking I got after I accidentally stepped on the base and the rest of it swung up and hit me squarely in the front was not to be forgotten. But the Phillies game today will be the real test, to be sure. Ever since he heard about how the Philly Phanatic—the team's plush green mascot with the out-sized googly eyes and the nose like a toilet plunger—copped a feel from my mom at a game two summers ago, he's been terrified. I promised him that if the Phanatic comes anywhere near us today I will sit on him to pro-tect him, which he says is OK because that's one of the places he likes me anyway.

It's blisteringly hot outside, and as we get up to leave, the sky opens up and gives way to a terrific thun-derstorm. I don't know that I'll ever be able to think about storms, or any kind of weather for that matter, the same way again. But it's OK, because I have a strong feeling that the forecast from here on out is very promising indeed.